Mr. Dream Merchant

MR.
DREAM
MERCHANT

a novel

erroll j. bailey

ELEMENT

Boston, Massachusetts • Shaftesbury, Dorset
Melbourne, Victoria

© Element Books, Inc., 1998
Text © Erroll J. Bailey, M.D., 1998

First published in hardback in the USA in 1998 by
Element Books, Inc.
160 North Washington Street
Boston, MA 02114

Published in Great Britain in 1998 by
Element Books, Ltd.
Shaftesbury, Dorset SP7 8BT

Published in Australia in 1998 by
By Element Books, Ltd. for
Penguin Books Australia, Ltd.
487 Maroondah Highway
Ringwood, Victoria 3134

Library of Congress Cataloging-in-Publication Data

Bailey, Erroll J.
Mr. Dream Merchant : a novel / Erroll J. Bailey.
p.   cm. (alk. paper)
I. Title.   PS3552.A3655M7   1998
813'.54--dc21   97-45795
CIP
British Library Cataloguing in Publication Data is available.

Text and Cover design by Kathryn Sky-Peck
Typeset in 10.5 Berkeley

PRINTED AND BOUND IN THE USA BY COURIER WESTFORD

ISBN 1-86204-192-X

First Edition
10 9 8 7 6 5 4 3 2 1

Dedicated to my brother,

Augusta Bailey, Jr.

*For what is it to die but to stand naked in the wind
and melt into the sun? And what is it to cease
breathing, but to free the breath from its
restless tides that it may rise and
seek God unencumbered?*

—KAHLIL GIBRAN

Acknowledgments

THIS BOOK'S COMING INTO BEING would not have taken place without the efforts and attention of many wonderful people. I would like to express my sincere thanks in particular to:

My mother and father for the gift of life and their undying support of every endeavor I have ever attempted.

My wife Alise, and my children, Hamilton and Alexis. You are the foundation of the spirit of my existence.

My sister Kathy, and her husband Sherman, for the joy and laughter you brought throughout this long process.

My spirituality group: Kellie, Charles, Pam, Ed and Julia for instilling within me the courage to go forward with this project.

Cecil Murphey and Kathryn Sky-Peck, newfound friends and teachers. Without both of your technical guidance, literary expertise and vision, the manuscript could never have developed into the book it is today. Thank you both so much for your help.

Monica, my legal counsel, for your advice and direction. You are an inspiration to me. I am grateful for your support.

Susan Smith, whose transcription and technical help greatly assisted this project.

My many friends whose names I don't mention out of fear of forgetting one. You know who you are. I am forever indebted. Thanks.

And Element Books, particularly Roberta Scimone, who was with me every step of the way and always kept my concerns at heart, and Darren Kelly, whose quiet presence and sense of humor added a spark to the joy of completing this project.

one

Father's Day

"ALL RISE." IT WAS THE DARK, heavy-set bailiff. All struggled to rise against the heat that had set down hard in the Atlanta court-room. "The Honorable Walter Dunn presiding." In the stillness, the bailiff's voice echoed loudly against the walls.

The judge entered the juvenile courtroom from a rear door. With a slow, deliberate pace, as if he were inspecting everyone, the judge approached the bench and faced the people in the court-room. He was tall, distinguished-looking, African-American. Everyone stood in silence as he positioned his gown to accommo-date the chair.

Then three sharp blows from his gavel, and he said, "Please be seated. The court will come to order." He paused to look around. He looked disappointed.

"Ladies and gentlemen, I now call forth the juvenile criminal misdemeanor calendar for today. When your name is called, please stand. Only your legal counsel may accompany you to the bench."

He meticulously organized the stacks of paper on his desk.

The bailiff called Chase's name.

Chase's lawyer stood and nudged his fifteen-year-old defendant. An obviously shaken, fearful black boy stood.

"Come on, let's go," his lawyer whispered as he urged the boy on. "The judge is waiting."

Together they walked to the judge's bench. The lawyer cleared his throat. "Your Honor, I am—"

"I know who you are, counsel, but more important, I know this boy personally."

Chase dropped his head.

"Look up at me, boy," the judge said.

Chase looked up and then immediately dropped his gaze. Tears were building in his eyes now, but he was determined not to show any weakness. Something small was stuck to his shoe, and he tried to focus on it.

"Well, what do you have to say for yourself?" asked the judge.

Chase shook his head. If he tried to speak, he knew he would cry and that was unacceptable. Everyone was watching.

"I've known you since the day you were born, and even changed your diapers," the judge said. "I've watched you grow up. I never thought that I would see this day. I can't begin to say how disappointed I am with you. Furthermore, I can't believe you would let yourself get caught up in another situation like this, particularly after what happened to you and Ernie."

Chase felt weak at the knees. He could no longer fight the tears. "Sorry."

"Sorry? Is that all you have to say? I don't want to hear any more 'sorrys' out of you, young man." The judge leaned forward. His tone of voice dropped dangerously low. "Now, you look into my eyes, Chase. I want to make sure you hear me."

Chase obeyed. The tears streamed down his dark-brown cheeks. Chase looked at the judge.

The judge scooted his chair forward. Their eyes locked momentarily. The judge had tears in his eyes, too. He cleared his throat. "Yes, this is a very sad day for me." He removed his glasses and pulled out a handkerchief. He took a long time wiping the lenses.

Chase, unable to look at him, focused on the wall behind the judge. His eyes fell on the state flag of Georgia. With nowhere else to stare, Chase continued to look at it, even though its resemblance to the Confederate flag annoyed him. In front of him was Judge Dunn, a friend of the family, the father of the boy who had been his best friend.

For as far back as Chase could remember, he and Ernie had been inseparable. And then it ended six months ago with a drive-by shooting in a part of town they shouldn't have been in. Ernie had simply been in the wrong place at the wrong time. Chase had been on the street corner that night as well. A bullet only grazed his arm as he fell to the ground. He had lived; Ernie hadn't. Chase had lost his best friend, and Judge Dunn, his only son.

The judge finished wiping his glasses and gently put them on his desk. "What would Ernie say?" he asked in a voice so low that no one except Chase and his lawyer could hear.

Chase opened his mouth to speak, but he had no words.

Suddenly, the door of the courtroom slammed open. A panic-stricken man entered and paused long enough for his eyes to locate his son. "Chase!" he yelled, as he moved toward the bench.

"Stop right there," said the bailiff. "You can't go up there." He reached out to grab the man.

"It's all right," said Judge Dunn. "It's the boy's father."

Chase peeked at his mother. At that moment he felt anger toward his father. How could he be late for a thing like this? Chase wondered. If he cared, he would have been here.

Chase's father came forward and stood between the lawyer and his son. He started to say, "Thank you," to the judge, but the judge was already speaking.

"Chase, you have been accused of drinking under age, public drunkenness, theft and loitering. There is a question of possession of an illegal substance. How do you plead?"

"Sir, I had only one sip of a friend's beer. I'm telling you the truth. Besides, I hadn't been in that place more than three minutes. You can ask them—"

"I am not asking them. I am asking you."

"I didn't know they had stolen the beer. I swear I didn't. I didn't even know they were drunk. I mean, I thought it was just a bunch of the guys, you know, just hanging. I don't drink, Judge, and you know that."

The judge just looked at him. For a moment there was a softness in his eyes, as though he were remembering something very far away. Chase shifted uncomfortably on his feet.

"I mean, well, it seemed harmless, so I tried it. I guess I just wanted to be one of the guys." Chase waited, but could no longer stand the stare. He went back to looking at his feet. Then quickly, softly, he added, "And as for the drugs, you know I don't do drugs either."

The spell seemed to have been broken. "Is that all you have to say?"

"Yes sir."

"I want to say something," said Chase's father. "For the most part, he's a good boy, as you know—"

"No, you may not speak." The judge pounded his gavel. "I've heard enough. Chase, I sentence you to the first offender's program and one hundred hours of community service. You will have a 10:00 p.m. curfew as well as random urine tests for one year. You are to be monitored by the juvenile probation board. Any violation of their rules will result in ninety days in a boot camp detention center. Is that clear?"

"With all due respect, your Honor, that is outrageous," protested the lawyer. "That is far too stiff a —"

4

"Quiet, counsel. This is my courtroom and that is my ruling!" The judge nodded to the bailiff. "Call the next case."

"Please, Walt," said Chase's father.

"In this courtroom, it's Judge Dunn to you."

Chase's father froze as though his face had been slapped. He let out a breath, and started again.

"Judge Dunn, perhaps you're being a little tough on the kid. I think I understand why with what happened to Ernie and all, but—"

"Don't 'but' me. My ruling is final." He told Chase and his attorney to sit down. He stood and motioned for the bailiff to come forward.

The bailiff listened to the judge, and then he announced, "The court will take a fifteen minute recess."

Judge Dunn pointed to Chase's father. "You! Come with me."

Chase stood awkwardly for a moment, then realized he was free to sit down. He turned around and saw his mother standing in the aisle, her arms held open for him. He began the endless walk toward her. If he ever got there, he would tell her again, "I'm sorry Mom. I really am."

Chase's father followed the judge out of the courtroom and down a long hallway. Several people greeted the judge as he walked by, but he only nodded and walked on.

Judge Dunn opened the door. "In here," he said and slammed it behind them. "Sit down."

"Walt, just what the hell is going on with you?"

"What's going on with me? You have the audacity to ask what is going on with me?" The judge removed his gown and threw it across the back of a chair. It slipped and fell to the floor. In his anger, he didn't notice. "Listen my friend, it's time."

"Time for what?"

"Time for you to be confronted, that's what."

"What are you talking about?"

"Listen people do talk, you know! Rumors are circulating all over town about you. I don't know exactly what you're doing, but it ain't good. I do know that much."

"Walt, please—"

"Look J.C. Don't try to fool me. I know you too well." Walt stared at his former college roommate and fraternity brother. "I'm fully aware of what you're capable of when you get stressed."

"Okay, you're right, I have been a bit stressed lately, and working pretty hard, that's all. "

"I don't want to hear your excuses. Just forget them. You know, there's a principle that says you reap what you sow. If you can't change for yourself, then do it for Chase."

"What do you mean by that? This case here today ain't about me. Okay, the kid made a stupid mistake, and—"

"A stupid mistake. Is that your assessment?" Judge Dunn felt his blood pressure mounting. He couldn't remember the last time he had been so enraged at his friend. "My son is dead because of a stupid mistake! Your son, despite all that has happened, is still hanging out with the same crew of boys. Can't you get that straight? He doesn't have many more chances. And unless you do something—"

"I've failed as a father, okay? Is that what you want to hear? Okay, I've failed. But this isn't a case about Ernie or me or even you—"

"You're wrong, totally wrong, and you can't see it. Chase took only one sip of beer. You know why it was only one sip? He got caught. What if he hadn't gotten caught? Would it have been a whole bottle? What about next time?"

"There won't be a next time—"

"Unless you do something, there will be a next time and a time after that. This is your wake up call. It's Father's Day for you, man. Time for you to step up and learn how to be a father—a real father."

"Just who do you think you are to talk to me like that?"

"I'm your best friend."

"Yeah, maybe, but you're still out of line."

Walt stared at Chase's father and realized his words had alienated his friend. "Okay, let me try it again. First, you work too hard. Second, you're never home. Third, you're never at the boy's basketball games. Fourth, you don't attend important events such as PTA meetings. Now am I getting through?"

"Okay, so I'm not a perfect father. But I go to his activities when I can. And like I said, I've been—"

"No excuses. Let me finish. When you are around, it's only in body and not in spirit. Remember, I've been there and watched you. You look awful. Are you working too hard? Is that the real problem?" He leaned forward and put his arms on his friend's shoulders. "Or are there other reasons? I've heard—"

"I'm trying, Walt. I'll try harder—"

"People talk to me. They tell me things—things about you I don't want to hear."

"Then don't listen."

"I listen because I care about you and about Chase."

The judge awkwardly removed his arms from the man's shoulders. From his filing cabinet, the judge removed a file.

"I have something important I'd like you to read that our department has put together. It's a list of what we call 'Father Facts.' But it's more than just a list of factual information." Judge Dunn handed him two sheets of paper stapled together.

As Chase's father took the copy, their eyes met. He looked away quickly.

"These facts are something you need to read—you and every father in this country," the judge said. "That's why it's called Father Facts. And when you get home, I want you to read the list aloud to Chase. Both of you may think you know all this, but I want you to hear it anyway. Got that?"

"You're the judge, right?"

"That's right, I am. Now look at your copy." He began to read: "It is a fact that:

- one in four black males is dead or in jail before the age of 25.
- 72 percent of adolescent murderers grew up without fathers.
- young black men raised in single-parent families on welfare and living in public housing are twice as likely to engage in criminal activities compared to black men raised in two-parent families also on welfare and living in public housing.
- three out of four teenage suicides occur in households where a parent has been absent.
- compared with children from intact families, children from disrupted families are at a much higher risk for physical and sexual abuse."

"Yes, I am familiar with some of these statistics. I read the papers and listen to the news. Give me some credit, Walt. But these facts really don't apply here."

"Don't be ridiculous, and don't act stupid. These boys—and I'm including Chase—are either going to get killed or kill themselves if we don't step up and change things."

"Don't you think you're being just a little dramatic?"

"Oh yeah, dramatic, huh? If I'm so dramatic, why was your son standing before me in my courtroom today? Huh? Why?"

Chase's father clenched his fists. Silence engulfed the room.

"Look J.C. Your son is looking for some man to shine for him, someone to look up to. Be that man—don't let it be some big talker standing on some corner. He needs you. Your son needs a father. He needs one now."

It took everything Chase's father had to stay cool. He was exploding inside; he knew his friend didn't understand. Couldn't understand. And preaching was not the answer.

"Why don't you just mind your damn business?" He stormed toward the door.

"This is my business," Judge Dunn called after him.

"Yeah? Well, he's my son, and I do the best I can. And we're doing just fine." He turned and left the room, slamming the door behind him.

The glass trophy case in the far corner of the judge's room continued to rattle long after he had left. Inside it, Judge Dunn could see that a picture had fallen. He went over to reposition it. Suddenly, his heart fell in his chest. It was a picture of the four of them: Chase, Ernie, J.C. and himself, two years ago at the Junior Basketball Championship. Chase and Ernie had led their team to victory.

Then his body let go of the anger, and his hands shook as he held the picture over his heart. He could no longer hold back the tears. His voice cracked as he spoke to himself.

"I know that you're watching from up there, Ernie. I just want you to know that we love you son, and your mother and I miss you terribly. Right now, your good friend is in trouble. Do something if you can. Put in a good word for his father, too. Okay?"

Chase and his mother were waiting at the back of the courtroom with the bailiff. When the boy's father reentered the room, the bailiff motioned for him to meet them at the exit. To Chase he said, "You're free to go now." He put his right hand on the boy's shoulder. "Kid, let's not see you in here again. All right?"

Chase nodded.

The three of them left together. The walk to the car was quiet. The sun was going down, low on the horizon, and it stretched their shadows strangely away from them. As they got near their car,

Chase's mother looked at her husband. "What went on back there with Walt?"

"Nothing important." He unlocked the doors to their car with his electric key chain.

"Then what took so long?" she asked. "Did you ask Walt to reduce the sentence?"

"It's not important," he said. He motioned for Chase to get into the front seat.

"What do you mean? If it affects our son, it is important—"

"If you don't mind, we'll discuss that later. We need to deal with Chase right now."

Chase got into the car and stared out of his window. He never liked it when his father talked to his mother that way. He sounded harsh and mean, almost as if he thought his mother was stupid. As usual, when his dad used that tone of voice, his mother didn't answer. That bothered him even more.

His father started the car and they entered traffic. No one spoke as they started to drive back to their home in the suburbs.

Chase reached over to turn on the radio, but his father caught his hand and threw it back in his lap.

"No music son. This is no time for music!"

"Sorry—"

"Sorry? Is that all you have to say for yourself?"

Chase knew that no matter what he said, he wouldn't have the right answer. He gazed silently out the window.

"Baby, you're daddy is talking to you. Answer him."

"I don't feel like talking right now!"

His father slammed on his brakes in the center lane of traffic. "Don't you ever, ever use that tone of voice with your mother! Do you hear me?"

Pedestrians looked on as cars started honking their horns.

"Hey, buddy, are you crazy?" a cab driver yelled as he swerved around their Buick.

Angrily, his father stepped on the accelerator. No one spoke again while his father navigated through Atlanta's heavy downtown traffic. They faced less congestion when he turned onto Interstate 20 and headed for southwest Atlanta.

"Well, boy, I am glad you don't feel like talking, because I got plenty to say!"

"We only want what's best for you," his mother said.

Chase remained silent, but his right foot tapped nervously against the floorboard.

"Your mother and I don't understand what is going on with you. Everything points to trouble, son; your attitude, your grades going down, the company you keep, and the choices you make. We're concerned."

Yeah, right, Chase thought, concerned enough to get to the court on time—. But instead, "Okay, I said I'm sorry." He continued to tap his foot.

His father's right hand reached over and grabbed Chase's leg. "Your shaking like that makes me nervous. So stop it."

Chase stopped but he didn't look at his father.

"Whatever happened to those goals you had?"

Chase shrugged. "My life ain't over, you know."

"Yeah, right, but you're playing with fire!" answered his father. "What about those dreams of becoming a Morehouse man? those plans to play college basketball? the aspirations of going to law school and returning home to clean up these streets? You know you can't do all of these things with a criminal record, don't you?"

"I can still do all—"

"Not the way you're going!" His father was beginning to get to him. He was becoming unglued. "First Ernie and now this with you."

Chase finally lost it and screamed, "Stop it, Dad, stop it!" Tears ran down his cheeks. "It's not the same thing."

"It is the same thing. You've started a pattern—"

11

"Whatever you say." Chase turned and looked at his father. "You always have to be right, don't you?"

"Don't you talk to me like that."

Chase gazed sightlessly at the floorboard. Despite what he had said, he knew his father was right. Where had those dreams gone? They seemed so distant now. He knew he needed help—guidance of some kind or someone to talk to—but he didn't know how to ask for it or where to get it. "Okay, I'll pull it together somehow," he said. "I promise I will."

His mother's arm gently fell on his shoulder. "I know you will, baby."

His father pulled into the driveway and left the engine running. "You and your mother go on in. I'll be back shortly. I need to run by the office—"

"The office?" asked Chase's mother. "At a time like this? What on earth do you—?"

"I said I'd be right back." He pulled the two stapled sheets out of his pocket and handed them to Chase. "This is something the judge wants you to read."

Chase took the papers, lowered his head and got out of the car.

"It's going to be okay, son," his mother said.

"Yeah, sure it is," he said as he turned and watched his father drive away. He kept watching until the little red lights disappeared in the growing darkness.

His mother pulled his arm. "You must be tired. Go on up and I'll bring you something to eat in a little while."

Glad for the chance to be alone, Chase said, "Okay," and went on in and upstairs to his room.

An hour later, she brought him dinner. He wasn't hungry but ate a few bites anyway. Mostly he stared at the walls. Life sucks, he thought. Why did it have to be like this? It had been a good life when Ernie was around. Now he had nothing and no one seemed to care.

As the night moved on, so did his thoughts. Everyone expected so much of him, but he no longer knew what to expect of himself. On one evening, on one corner, his life had changed abruptly for the worst. What would it take to turn it around? .

As he began to prepare for bed, his father still had not come home. He flipped on the television, and then remembered the sheets of paper that his father had given him. He skimmed a few of the facts listed on the sheet.

It is a fact that:

- Teens from single parent or stepparent homes are most likely to commit a school crime.
- 70% of juveniles in state reform institutions grew up in single or no-parent homes.
- 80% of adolescents in psychiatric hospitals come from broken homes.
- Fatherless children are twice as likely to drop out of school.
- Suicide is now the third leading cause of death in black children under the age of 25.

Chase couldn't figure how this applied to him—he had a good home, two parents. But his eyes locked on the last fact. He was startled to see that so many black kids were taking their lives. He dropped the sheets of paper on the side of his bed and lay back and wondered why all this had happened to him.

"Why me?" he said aloud. "Why is everything so awful?"

No answers came.

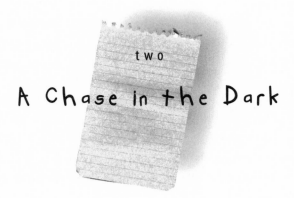

two

A Chase in the Dark

IT WAS HAPPENING AGAIN.

The scream rose up from his dream, deep in his chest and struggled to clear his throat—*Ernie-e-e-e*! In the dream, Chase tries to cry out, but can't, and the pain of the effort strangles him inside.

In the dream it is also night. He turns around and hears the old model Caddy approach, a dark car, smudged against the darkness, its punctured muffler making little sounds of explosion, letting the neighborhood know of its presence. The car slows down, seems to float toward him. Chase knows there is something wrong about this car, but he is stunned still as he watches it hover, huge, toward him.

Then the driver kills the lights, and Chase knows he has to run.

The Cadillac approaches. Chase sees the windows begin to lower, smooth, like ice melting on a black lake. The loud pounding bass of gangsta rap suddenly breaks the silence of the neighborhood. Chase's feet are heavy with fear, and it takes everything he has to move them.

The Cadillac moves steadily closer.

"Run! Ernie, run!"

When Ernie hears his name, he looks up from where he stands in his baggy clothes, posed against the dark storefront window. His eyes widen in surprise and then he, too, tries to run, but he's stuck in slow motion.

Three sets of arms come out of the Cadillac's windows but the hands aren't hands, they are pieces of metal, glinting hard in the streetlight as the car comes closer to the two boys, popping, sputtering, pounding toward them.

Then Chase see sparks and almost instantly there is a deafening barrage of explosions. The hands are spraying the sidewalk and store windows with handgun fire.

"Ernie! Run!" In the dream now, Chase hovers over the sidewalk as he watches the car coming closer, watches his friend.

He sees himself, too, diving into the air, over the dirty sidewalk to tackle Ernie's feet. They both go down hard.

Something burning and sharp hits Chase's left arm. He turns to watch the blood ooze from the wound. I'm shot, he thinks, and I'm going to die.

The bullets start again, and the dark car returns, like a bad movie rewinding.

"Ohhh-h." Ernie groans. The car engine revs up, but this time peels away; the smell of burnt rubber hangs in the air.

And then deep silence.

Chase lifts his head and stares at his friend, who lies on the ground in front of him. Blood pumps endlessly from Ernie's chest, staining the sidewalk. In the dream Chase absently wonders if this is where they will draw the chalk outline that will be all that is left of them. Chase crawls forward, grabs Ernie and pulls him close. "Someone call 911!" he yells. Two people huddle in a doorway. Their faces float in and out of the darkness. "Please! He's been shot!"

And now everything fades away. This is the part of the dream that Chase fears most—the silence, the complete and utter abyss in which Ernie and Chase are alone, embracing. With his right hand, Chase cradles his friend's head. "Come on. Stick with me. Don't die on me, man. Don't die."

Chase feels Ernie's heart beat irregularly against him, and his breathing become shallow.

Tears are flowing down Chase's cheeks as he holds him even tighter. "Ernie, talk to me, man, talk." He is rocking him back and forth. "Please, *please*—"

"Look up," whispers Ernie.

"What?"

"Look up." Ernie takes a final breath. His heart stops beating.

Then the scream that has been trying so hard break free punches a hole in the night. "Ernie!" Chase screams. "*Ernie-e-e-e-e!*"

....

Chase sat up, fully awake, as if he had been struck on the face. His body was covered with sweat and his heart pounded. He was painfully aware of being still alive. Outside, a car passed by on the midnight street, the headlights slicing the curtains, bouncing across the ceiling, splashing in the mirror above his bureau. He stood up and studied his face. He hadn't had a restful night's sleep in six months. Sleep was becoming a torture in which he was forced to endure the nightmare again and again.

The television was on, sound off. Late night characters flashed across the screen, their faces contorted in conversation and laughter. After several minutes of staring blankly, weariness came over him, but the sleep wouldn't come. Chase sat back down on the bed, and rocked himself with his hands across his chest, just as he had rocked Ernie that night, but now it was only himself he was trying to save.

"Please, somebody, take this pain away! I just can't take it anymore!"

Sounds of thunder and flashes of lightning erupted outside of his bedroom window. Raindrops landed forcefully against the roof. A gust of wind blew through his window, knocking one of his basketball trophies off the dresser. Startled, but too tired to move from his bed, Chase lay back on his pillow and pulled the covers over his head. His eyelids were heavy and when he closed them, little flashes of light continued to explode behind them. Somewhere in the no-man's-land between wakefulness and sleep, he dozed off.

Chase began to dream again, only this time, the dream had changed.

....

Behind him, soft R&B plays faintly. He looks around and realizes he's in the courtyard of Gloria's, a popular soul food restaurant in midtown. He's seated far away from the other patrons, his table facing a softly lit street where cars swish by. He stares at the street, and can't take his eyes away. It looks like a hand-painted photograph, the colors soft and pastel, as if they'd been washed out by too much sun. The sun is there too, on the horizon, just starting to set.

The brightness becomes a car, pearl-white, expensive, gleaming nearly a block away. Chase is entranced by its warmth, the soft pumping of the brakes, the shutting off of the engine, the doors opening and closing like heavy wings. He smiles as he realizes he can see and hear everything clearly. He's here, and not here. There, yet not there.

A man gets out of the car. "They need a bigger parking lot," the man says to his wife. "Who wants to park a block away?"

"Even for Gloria's," the woman says. It's a black couple and something about them seems familiar, but Chase's vision, out of his control, now floats down the street. At first, he sees a five-foot-high cement wall in the distance, and then suddenly he has telephoto vision: he sees every detail of the wall, the cracked paint, the rough surface. And he sees a peculiar man sitting on the wall. The man has smooth cocoa-brown skin, long, braided hair, a dirty-looking tee shirt.

Now the man and his wife come into view. Chase recognizes them as Taylor Ewing, the mayor of Atlanta, and his wife Courtney. The man on the wall beckons them toward him, a grand sweeping of his arm through the evening air.

"That man gives me the creeps," Courtney says to her husband.

"What man?" asks the mayor. He is still at the car, locking the bright, white door. This seems to take forever. "Ignore him," he says, and then takes his wife's arm and crosses the street.

"Taylor! Courtney!" the man calls after them. "Wait! I have a message—"

They quicken their pace.

Now the moon begins to rise, and becomes entangled in the branches of a magnolia tree. The rumble of thunder fills the air and the threat of impending rain urges them onward.

....

In his sleep, Chase furled his brow, turned over and curled himself into a fetal position. His heart began to beat harder as the curtains blew into his room and the storm picked up outside. There was the hack, hack, hack of a branch against the black window. The television had gone to static.

....

The mayor and his wife rush into the wind and cross the street, their feet barely touching the pavement. The man leaps off the wall and starts gliding rapidly toward them. "Wait! It's important!" he yells.

"Don't let him catch us," Courtney says. "He's probably a street person."

"Might be one of those crazy types," the mayor replies.

Forks of lightning stab through the sky. Chase thinks it will be hours before the rain actually reaches the city. He wants to hear what the man has to say.

In the restaurant now. The mayor and his wife have a lovely view of the courtyard at the back of the restaurant. Multicolored lights shroud the fountain, giving the water soft tones as it cascades downward. They forget about the man outside.

Soup appears from nowhere and they begin to eat.

"Taylor, look." Courtney taps her husband's hand and shudders.

Outside the window is the face of the man from the wall, now huge against the glass. His eyes are dark and flashing, his large hands clutching his throat as if choking himself. To Chase he seems framed in the window like some old religious painting.

"Some kind of nut case," the mayor says, and looks away.

"He's doing it again. Look, he's doing it again!"

Both of them deliberately turn their backs to him and look across the spacious room.

Chase wants to turn them and make them look, but he can't. He is spellbound by the gesticulating man, held in stasis by this dream unfolding around him.

The waiter brings more food to the table.

"A strange-looking black man with braided hair followed us from our car," the mayor says. "He's still out there!" His gestures are wild.

The waiter looks, but no one is there. Then he, too, disappears.

Suddenly, the mayor's wife pushes her chair away and stands. She grabs her neck with both hands. Her eyes are as wide as saucers. She is gasping desperately for air. Her arms begin to flail.

"Help! Somebody help!" the mayor yells. Chase looks on in shock.

A door slams open and the man with the braided hair pushes past and hurries toward them. He pulls Courtney out of the mayor's arms. "Delay does not matter in eternity, but it's tragic in time. Her time is now!" he says.

Chase runs this phrase through his head, turning it over and over like a polished stone. He wants to understand it but the under-standing doesn't come.

Now the man pulls Courtney to her feet, grabs her from behind, and squeezes hard around her chest. Something flies from her mouth and then "ahhh-h-h-," comes the rush of breath.

Time is frozen again. In the soft light of the restaurant Chase sees the mayor, his wife, this strange man with the braids. It's as if they have all forgotten their lines. No one moves. The music has stopped playing; everyone's face is turned toward this drama . . . . and then, "Please, eat with us——" says the mayor's wife, her smile returning easily.

The restaurant starts up again. Everyone goes back to their lives.

The stranger tucks in his ragged tee shirt. "Thirty minutes ago, you would not stop to speak to me. In fact, you ran from me. Now, you would like to have dinner with me. Anyway, thank you for your kindness and generosity, but I would rather not."

The maître d' approaches, a look of disgust and disdain on his face as he stares at the stranger's dirty clothes. Chase can actually hear the manager's thoughts: "This is one of those street people. They keep coming by here, begging for food, bothering our cus-tomers. I'm so tired of all these street people."

Then he grabs the stranger's arm roughly. "This way, sir," he says without trying to hide his disgust. The stranger smiles sadly and shakes his head. "Such a shame." He looks at the mayor's wife and says, "I must talk with you . . . alone!" Chase can see the inten-sity in the man's honey-brown eyes.

And then he's gone.

And then everything's gone. Chase floats in the middle of nothing, and in the dream fear fills him again, this familiar sensation of weightlessness, the hovering in the dark, not knowing, not understanding. He hovers there in the familiar abyss, as if waiting for permission to leave.

The mayor and his wife walk back to their car.

"Don't turn around!" a hard voice suddenly barks from behind them. "Or you're history. Just hand over your money!"

Chase, frozen in place, swells with panic. He knows this is a robbery.

Courtney stifles a scream. The mayor freezes in surprise.

"The money. Hurry up—I ain't got all night."

Before they can react, they hear scuffling behind them. The braided-haired stranger flips the assailant around and strikes him on the chest.

The thug cries out in pain and then turns and races down the street, holding his arm. The mayor and his wife are staring in disbelief.

"Twice in the same night you have come to our aid—Why us? Why did you come to us?"

The stranger looks at them both for a long time. "Because you needed me." Then he turns to Courtney. "Please, there is something you need to know."

"Well, go ahead," Courtney says.

"No! We must be alone. It's personal."

"What do you mean? Who are you?" she asks. "What do you want?"

"It is clear you are not ready. In time, more will be revealed." The mysterious man then takes their hands in his and squeezes them tightly. "Can we pray?"

Before they can answer, he begins. "Dear Lord, protect this man and this woman. Fulfill their vision of peace and racial harmony in this city. Thank you for allowing me to serve you. Let my life be your will."

The street begins to shake. They all ignore it.

"Give thanks to the Father, who has made us fit to be partakers of the inheritance of the saints in the light. Give thanks to him for delivering us from the power of darkness and translating us into the kingdom of his dear son. Give thanks to him for giving us redemption through his blood and forgiving us for our sins. For by him, all things are created, those in heaven and those on earth. Amen." The mayor and his wife keep their heads bowed, but the stranger looks up. His eyes lock with Chase's own. He nods and smiles.

Like a magnet, Chase is drawn toward him.

The stranger reaches into his pants pocket, takes out a small notepad, and rips off the top sheet. "Here, take this." He lays it in the mayor's hands.

"What is—?"

But he is already gone.

Chase feels himself break into a run. He picks up speed and hurries past the mayor and his wife in pursuit of the mysterious man in the dark. "Faster, faster, I've got to run faster," he whispers to himself, desperately gulping for air.

"Be careful what you seek," a deep voice slices through the night. "You may get lucky and catch it." Thunder-like laughter fills the air. "What will you do then?"

Chase lunges forward and his fingertips graze the arm of the elusive one. As if his touch has triggered it, roaring thunder claps and bright lightning fills the sky.

In those seconds, Chase sees the stranger as if caught in the flash of a photograph. His silver buckle glistens as if it draws energy from the lightning itself. His faded jeans, four inches too short for his tall frame, expose sockless ankles above his worn shoes.

The stranger continues to run, but now Chase is at his side.

"The best dreams occur when we are awake," the man whispers and then smiles, his bright teeth glistening. Effortlessly, he picks up speed as he approaches a stone wall. As if set-up for a Hollywood stunt, he leaps onto a trash can and hurls himself over the wall.

Tired from the effort and ten yards behind him, Chase hesitates a second before he leaps for the trash can. Once again he is following—compelled to do so. As his feet touch the can, the empty, bulky metal container topples over and he falls to the ground. He picks himself up, unhurt, and wonders whether to try again.

Then the ear-piercing scream of an animal rivets him to the spot.

A second later, a black cat dashes out of the trash can. Facing the boy, the cat arches his back and hisses. Then, as if a giant hand had stopped it, the animal pauses. Its blue-green eyes stare at Chase.

Frightened and now in shock, the boy stumbles backward and a feeling of weakness fills his body. He is exhausted and his hands are shaking. His mouth is sandpaper dry.

The cat turns abruptly and, in a single bound, leaps over the wall.

....

Chase lay in bed, awake, with covers twisted over his head. He breathed heavily for a long time. A chill worked its way up his spine and curled at the base of his neck. Although now awake, his eyes remained shut and his lips trembled. His heart pounded faster than it had in the dream.

In all his fifteen years, Chase had never had such a dream before. Goose bumps covered his arms and he felt too scared to move. It took several seconds of deep breathing to relieve his anxiety.

Certain that the dream was over, he now felt safe in his room. The reassuring presence of the television broke through his consciousness. For as long as he could remember, Chase had turned on the television when he went to bed. Although he didn't listen to the voices or watch the pictures, it provided companionship. It soothed him and let him drift off to sleep without thinking too much.

Chase wished he could make light of his problems, that he could act like some of the kids in his school who never seemed troubled or confused. "Yeah, I tried that, but it's hard to be somebody else," he said to himself.

As he lay in bed, he thought of his parents, particularly his father, who didn't seem to care very much. Man, he missed Ernie. The best friend he had ever had. As he lay in bed, his problems continued to hang heavy in his heart. "It ain't easy being me," he said out loud.

He realized that his frustrations didn't revolve completely around Ernie's death. There was more and it had started before that. Although he was intelligent and motivated, he was also angry—mostly because he felt misjudged by a world that didn't understand him. He was sick and tired of the negative perceptions placed on him by society. He felt society feared him as a young black man. Women on the streets moved their purses to the opposite arm when he walked by. Store managers seemed to watch him more closely than others when he shopped. People always acted uneasy when they were on elevators alone with him. And the cab drivers—they would under no circumstances stop for him as he attempted to wave them down in the streets. On and on he pondered over such injustices.

Out of anger and frustration, he knew that he sometimes overreacted to situations. When that happened, he would fit those stereotypes that had been unjustly placed on him. He felt trapped and confused. There seemed nowhere to turn. As he stared with unfocused eyes at the television screen, he desperately longed for help. Surviving as a black teenager these days was becoming increasingly more difficult, day by day. Where would he turn?

Home was definitely not the place to find the answers, he thought. His father wasn't around—had never been around much—but even less these days. He didn't know why he stayed away. He just knew that he didn't like it. He also sensed his mother was covering for Dad. Chase couldn't put his finger on it, but something was wrong in their house.

To do something to pull himself out of his miserable feelings, Chase changed the television with the remote control, flipping from station to station.

His thoughts turned to school. That wasn't a safe place either. Inner city gangs were slowly infiltrating suburban areas. None of the adults he talked to believed it, but he and the other kids at school knew differently. Chase knew the gangs existed because he saw them every day. He was popular and a star on the junior varsity basketball team, and gang members approached him regularly.

"We like your style, man," they would say.

Each time his answer was the same. "No way man, I ain't interested." They often laughed at him and sometimes threatened him. For now, they left him alone, but he knew they'd be back. They always came back.

He had grown taller and his ball-handling skills had become more polished. At the end of last season everyone knew that he would be the new starting point guard on the team. But now, things had changed. The bullet to the arm had left him with a partial nerve palsy that resulted in diminished grip strength in his hand. Although he had been reassured by doctors and therapists that this was only temporary, his progress had been slow. He realized that he was going to have to sit out the year. He was even beginning to question whether he would ever play again.

Chase was beginning to have doubts about his close friends, too, particularly after his last experience on the street corner. Kids he had known all of his life were starting to experiment with drugs. No one forced anything on him, but it was becoming increasingly difficult to "just say no." He didn't want to do drugs, and at the same time he wanted to be one of the boys, just to fit in, to belong. But what a price to pay, he thought.

Then, Ernie was on his mind again. Too painful, he thought. It is just too painful.

He felt responsible for Ernie's death. Almost every night when he dreamed about that terrible night, he awakened, wishing he had gotten the hit and not Ernie. Life without his best friend was lonely.

Chase stared blankly at the television. Now, like some strange, substitute window, it let him know that dawn had arrived. He saw the news anchors' lips moving, but he remained lost in his own thoughts.

Problems! No matter what part of his life he looked at, there they were. They were private, but they existed, and there was no one to talk to about them. Secretly, he wished he had someone— someone who would listen, someone who could understand.

Then in horror he stared at the screen.

The camera showed the mayor and Mrs. Ewing standing in front of Gloria's restaurant. He sat up in bed and turned up the sound.

"—and so we want to thank the stranger who saved our lives twice tonight," the mayor said.

"No-o-o-o-o! It can't be!" Chase's jaw went slack.

"He vanished before we could show our gratitude," Courtney Ewing added.

"My wife and I are forever indebted."

The reporter asked several other questions and then the mayor said, "Before the man disappeared, he left us a written message. If it's okay, I'd like to share it with you. These brief words come as a gift to us all." He held up a sheet of creased notebook paper and cleared his throat.

The camera zoomed in on his face as he read, "Strive to know the thoughts of God. The rest are details." He pointed to the signature. "It is signed Junior D.M." The mayor smiled at the camera, shook his head, and said, "A remarkable thing happened here tonight. We are simply grateful."

"Hey, I saw them! I saw the man, too! I was there!" Chase yelled as if the people on the television screen could hear him. "They were in my dream!"

Yes, it was a dream, but the details were as vivid as they had been when he first awakened. "How could this be?" he asked himself. "How could I be asleep and see that happening?"

Just then a gush of cool wind blew through the room. The curtains over the bedroom window swayed in harmony.

"The best dreams occur when we are awake," Chase thought he heard the wind whisper in his ear.

Chase lay in his bed. The mayor was right: Something remarkable had happened that night, not only to them but to him as well.

three

Close Encounters

THE RINGING OF THE PHONE jarred Chase awake. With his eyes closed and the covers over his head, his arm ventured out toward the phone, like an emissary from a strange land. He said hello.

"I have got some good news for you."

When he recognized the voice of his lawyer, he sat up in bed, eager. "Yeah? What's that?"

"Judge Dunn had a change of heart. He reduced your sentence. No community service, no random urine tests, and no threats of boot camp."

"Really, man? Great!"

"That's right. All you have to do is successfully complete the Troubled Youth Awareness program."

"Youth Awareness program?" asked Chase. "What's that?"

"This is a new thing they're trying. It's a long series of classes. The county juvenile correction board is trying to teach life skills. They teach everything from safe sex to coping skills, but mostly they educate kids about the evils of substance abuse."

"That's all I have to do, go to class?"

"Yeah, but you miss one class and everything else comes back into effect—the whole sentence you heard yesterday. And that means boot camp, hard labor and curfew—the whole shebang. You got that?"

"Yeah, I got it."

"Good," said the lawyer. "They'll be on Saturdays, and you'll start with the next new series. They'll send you a notice in the mail with the exact time and location—"

Just then, the call-waiting signal interrupted them, and the lawyer ended with, "I'll be in touch."

When Chase answered the new call, it was Dr. Nelson and he wanted to speak to Chase's mother. "Mom!" Chase yelled. "Phone."

"I've got it," she answered.

Chase wondered why the doctor was calling for his mother. Curious, even though he knew it was wrong, he continued to hold on the phone after his mother had started her conversation.

". . . a follow-up call to see if you're having any adverse effects from increasing the dosage of your medication. How are you feeling?"

"Well, it makes me a bit anxious," his mother said. "At first I had some nausea and vomiting, but that has subsided."

"Good. Sounds as if everything is going to be okay," said Dr. Nelson.

"Maybe, but I have to tell you that I'm not very comfortable about taking medication. Can't I just work through this on my own?"

Dr. Nelson hesitated, then said, "You need to understand that you don't have a simple case of the blues. You are suffering from what we call 'clinical depression.' That's a problem of brain chemistry, and we need to treat it with medication . . ."

Depression? His mother was depressed? Chase had heard too

much. He quietly hung up the phone and wished that he hadn't been so invasive. Was he the reason for her depression? Not just the court stuff yesterday, but other things, the things that had gone on since Ernie's death. Was he the reason she was taking medicine?

Chase sat on the corner of his bed and tried to think what he could do to help her. Just then, his eyes focused on the television set. It was Mayor Ewing. He turned up the volume on the set.

"Help us find the stranger named Junior D.M.," said the mayor. "He saved our lives twice." He told the entire story once again. He described the stranger simply as "a black male, probably in his forties with long, braided hair, who spoke in a deep, resonant voice."

The mayor's plea ran daily on local television stations and in the local papers. In an interview with the local ABC affiliate, he said, "We assume he's homeless, and we want to help him in any way we can."

One reporter asked Courtney Ewing why they persisted in locating him. "He saved our lives, " she said. "Isn't that enough reason? There is something very special about this man."

To the surprise of many, the *Atlanta Journal and Constitution* as well as local radio and television stations regularly reported on the progress. Not a day passed in which someone didn't make public reference to the event.

The plea to find the good Samaritan caught the attention of Duwayne Portman, a top Atlanta businessman who had been severely wounded in a holdup attempt a year earlier. Only the intervention of "some homeless man yelling for help saved my life," he said. Portman, along with others, took up the plea to find the mysterious stranger.

Atlanta's midtown coalition of businesses soon advertised $5,000 and a variety of job offers if the man would step forward. A volunteer from the mayor's office screened those who claimed to be "the helpful stranger." Over 500 people claimed to be "Junior"—

four of them were women, two of them were white, and more than a dozen of them were over sixty years old.

The elusive one never appeared.

For awhile, Chase slept without nightmares. He also went without dreams about Junior, but the man seldom left his thoughts. His heightened interest began to blot out some of the pain over his loss of Ernie. Several times he thought of telling someone about his strange dream. But who would believe him? Would anyone really care? The more he thought about it, the more he realized there wasn't anyone—not a single person now that Ernie was gone—that he wanted to tell about the dream.

The dream had felt so real, as if he were really there. But it was still a dream. Or maybe I was sleepwalking? he thought. It was driving Chase crazy, so he decided not to think about whether it really happened to him or not.

But he couldn't stop thinking about Junior, couldn't stop wondering where he was, when he would show himself. He knew his name was Junior, but what did the "D.M." stand for?

Speculation arose around metro Atlanta. One woman insisted, "Oh, it's got to mean the Dean of Mystery."

"Nah! It means Destroyer of Madness," said her neighbor.

Still others suggested that the "D" and the "M" referred to his middle and last names. "Dr. Magic" was Chase's favorite.

Each day Chase watched the news, but no new leads developed. Although he didn't want anyone to know, when he was alone in his room Chase prayed for Junior to reappear in some form.

Chase kept busy after school and weekends. He liked keeping busy. It seemed to keep his mind off things. For money, he did odd jobs for relatives and also worked at a local movie theater. When his mother complained about his long hours, he would smile and say, "Least it keeps me out of trouble. Isn't that what you want?"

"It's just that I worry about you," she said.

He suddenly realized that his mom didn't trust him, maybe didn't believe he was working at all, but just hanging out. The lack of faith hurt, made him feel more alone. "You mean you don't trust me. Isn't that more like it?" He knew his words hurt her, but she just didn't understand him.

He tried to not think so much about Junior, but the more he tried not to, the more the stranger filled his mind. At night when he went to sleep, he stayed tuned to Channel 2 because he knew they would report any new development. Every morning, Chase listened to the morning news show. When he went downstairs for breakfast, he grabbed the newspaper and skimmed the box at the bottom of page one called "The Junior Update."

The reward for the stranger had risen close to $7,000. On the radio, he heard one DJ say, "We need more heroes like Junior. His modesty makes him even that much more of one. Let's find the man."

The total rose to $10,000, with small contributions coming from people all over Atlanta. Chase could not figure why the stranger wouldn't come forward. Could modesty keep you from $10,000? Perhaps this guy had a police record, or maybe he had left town and won't ever come forth. Chase tried not to dwell on the reason for Junior's silence, yet he knew—in a way he couldn't explain even to himself—that the stranger would reappear.

The day before the end of school break was a cold, dry morning. Chase got up early. His mother had a bad cold and had been sleeping in, her body entrenched under layers of covers. He felt her getting farther away from him, and didn't really know what was going on. As usual, his father was already gone. He assumed that Dad had gone to the office, but he wondered if that was where he really was. He knew something just wasn't right about his dad, either. His days away from home lasted longer and were more frequent. Sure his father was a doctor, a general practitioner in partnership with three others, but for the last couple of years he seemed to stay away more and more. Chase tried to imagine it was just more work, but lately he wondered if his dad was just staying away from him.

His loneliness compounded. Junior—the mystery—loomed ahead of him like a distant hope.

Chase took a carton of milk out of the refrigerator for his cereal. He was turning back toward the table when a noise—a loud thump—made him start. It sounded as if someone had thrown a ball against the back door.

Another loud noise—just as loud but different. This time it sounded like claws scratching against the metal storm door. Curious, he walked to the back door and opened it. A freezing wind slapped him as he stuck his head outside. He looked around, saw nothing unusual, and started to close the door.

He jumped back as something brushed against his bare feet. He looked down, and a cat stared up at him. It was the deepest, tarriest black cat that he had ever seen. Its piercing eyes focused on him. He felt as if the cat could look inside him.

"Go away!" Chase said as he started to close the door. "I just hate cats."

The cat brushed past him and walked into the kitchen. It stopped near the table and its body pointed toward the milk carton. It sat quietly and stared at the carton.

"Hey, you're one smart cat," Chase said and shut the door carefully so as not to awaken his mother. "But you can't stay in this house."

As he bent over to pick up the animal, their eyes locked again. Those penetrating, blue-green eyes—he had seen them before—and then he knew with an absolute certainty that he wasn't supposed to put the cat back outside.

"Whoa—you're the cat who was in my dreams, aren't you?"

Chase was caught between laughter and shock. "But this just ain't possible, is it?"

The animal's blue-green eyes simply stared back at him.

Half an hour later, it was time for Chase to go to Uncle Cleve's house. His latest job was to rake and bag the leaves that had been sitting on the ground since fall. But what to do with the cat?

"You want to stay here where it is nice and warm? There's a strong wind outside, see? And it's kinda chilly. Real chilly!" He laughed as he said, "chilly."

"Yeah. That's it! I'll call you Chilly!"

As if he agreed with his new name, Chilly brushed against Chase's legs and walked toward the back door. He stopped, turned his head back toward the boy, and purred.

"You need to go out, huh?" Chase said and opened the door. "I've fed you. So maybe you don't want to stay after all. Okay."

Chilly slinked through the open door, but then he stopped and turned around to stare at Chase.

"What's the matter, don't you want out?"

Chilly's blue-green eyes stared back at him.

"Stay inside then." Chase pulled Chilly back inside, closed the door, and put Chilly on a chair across the room. The cat jumped down and walked to the door again. Its paws gently scraped the wood.

"What's wrong with you? You're lonely. Is that it? You want to go out, but you want me to go with you?"

Chilly meowed softly and pawed again.

"Man, you're really some cat!" Chase laughed and put on his heavy navy pea-coat, fastened the buttons and flipped up the collar. He opened the door and walked out. Before he could close the door behind him, Chilly had pushed past him and stopped. As soon as Chase started to walk down the back steps, Chilly raced around the house and stopped at the curb. The wind picked up, making the cold day feel even colder.

Chase pulled up his collar tight. "Come here, Chilly. I'll carry you and protect you from the cold." Just as he reached down, Chilly turned right, ran about a dozen steps, and stopped. It looked up as if waiting for Chase; its piercing eyes focused again on the boy.

"Okay, I get it! You're gonna walk me instead of me walking you? Okay, cool."

Chilly went forward another fifty feet and paused as if to say, "Hurry up."

As soon as Chase got close, Chilly leaped forward. The pattern continued until they reached the corner and Chilly turned left and led Chase for two more blocks. When he got to Kroger's supermarket, the cat raced ahead to the newspaper kiosks and jumped on top of one. As if on command, the wind stopped. The temperature seemed to have risen several degrees. Chilly rested on top of the metal container and licked his paw as if it had nothing else to do.

Chase looked first at the cat and then at the newspapers. "Yeah, now what? You need a rest or something?"

Chilly stopped licking his paws and stared at the boy's deep brown eyes.

As if hypnotized by the animal's blue-green eyes, Chase dropped his gaze and stared into the newspaper stand. There was a new issue of *Street Smart*, an alternative newspaper. Hardly aware of what he was doing, Chase fished a quarter from his pocket and inserted it into the paper box. He pulled out a copy. *Street Smart* was a weekly paper that ran stories on issues about the homeless in Atlanta as well as positive news about reconstructive efforts in disadvantaged communities. He had heard that the proceeds went to homeless shelters and to feed other needy people. He liked to read it because it never had anything about crime, scandal, and injustice.

He paused to read the article on page one.

Chilly hissed and Chase looked up.

Just then, the cat leaped forward and knocked the paper from his hands. A burst of wind separated the sheets of paper. Chase scurried to retrieve all eight pages. Again, the wind stopped and the day turned calm.

Chase looked around, but Chilly had disappeared. He shook his head and mumbled to himself, "What a strange cat." He picked up the final sheet and as he started to put it back inside with the other pages, he noticed that it was open to the section called "Words from the Wise."

Chase read several quotations from James Baldwin and Langston Hughes, excerpts from Dr. Martin Luther King, Jr.'s speeches, and a new poem by Maya Angelou.

Then he gasped. In the lower right-hand corner, he saw a message in bold letters:

> Life is a journey, not a destination.
> The wisdom is in the CHASE not the capture.
> Dream, but don't make dreams your master.
> May this quest reveal your best. See you tonight.

He read all four lines again. "Hey! That's me. That's my name!" Somehow he knew it was a message from Junior. "He's trying to contact me!" His hope grew.

Chimes from the large Methodist Church rang through his thoughts. It was too late to go to uncle Cleve's because he was now supposed to start his shift at the theater complex. Even though it was his last day of work, he didn't want to be late. Except for the page with the message, he wadded the newspaper and threw it into a trash container. He carefully folded the single page and placed it inside his back pocket.

Chase hurried to the theater, and smiled as he realized he had made it a full two minutes before he was supposed to start work. Without waiting for anyone to tell him, Chase fell to his duties.

He went to work immediately and prepared all the products for the concession stands. He made sure the soda dispensers were filled. He checked the cups and brought out more. Then he concentrated on the popcorn machine. For the next few hours, Chase worked methodically through his job. During his fifteen-minute break, he went into theater five to watch the beginning of *The Negro Baseball League Documentary*. When his break time was over, he returned to work.

The theater was especially busy, and Chase seemed to be running back and forth to the storeroom for supplies every few minutes. The night seemed to pass quickly. By the time he got home, he was too tired to take off his clothes. By habit, he snapped on the television. In exhaustion, he stretched across his bed and fell asleep.

....

The dream starts almost the way it did before.

Heavily laden clouds cover the sky, leaving little trace of daylight. This time, a fragment of the moon hangs low in the sky, but its light can't penetrate the increasing dark clouds that snake across the horizon.

Chase is running in pursuit of the elusive Junior. Despite his heavy breathing, this time he feels stronger. He is running fast and soon closes a gap between them.

"You're not getting away this time."

And as that shout comes out of his mouth, he suddenly catches up with Junior.

The clouds open and he sees the beginning of a smile on Junior's face. Then the man chuckles and sprints ahead once more. This time there is no leaving the boy. Chase pushes forward and stays only a pace behind.

Chase sees the same wall ahead, and this time he is prepared to go over the top. Junior charges forward, leaps on top of the trash can, and effortlessly hurdles the wall as he has done before.

Chase jumps without hesitation. His feet land on the trash can, which feels like a trampoline, and he is catapulted over the top. He lands on his feet and feels no jarring from the impact of a ten-foot drop.

He starts to run again, but his surroundings have changed. The darkness has vanished and the brightness of a midsummer day fills his eyes. The sun is intense but feels soft against his bare arms. He can't see Junior anywhere.

Chase looks down at his right hand, suddenly aware that he is holding a piece of paper. He reads the words aloud.

"Being on the right track is not enough. Life can still leave you behind if you're uncertain!"

....

Chase lay in bed, his body drenched in sweat. He could still vividly recall every detail of the dream.

"Who are you, man?" he asked into the darkness. "What do you want from me?" Nothing but the silent darkness.

He wished he could talk to someone about this. His mind clicked down the list of friends and people he knew, but he discarded each of them. "They wouldn't believe me." Chase knew that none of this would make sense to anyone, even if he could explain what had happened. The nightmares about Ernie were gone—and he had an inner sense that they wouldn't come back. But these new dreams had replaced the nightmares, and he was more puzzled than ever.

When Chase was small, his dad used to put him on his lap and answer all his questions. Maybe the reason they didn't talk anymore was Chase's fault. Maybe he was just too big now for his daddy's lap. Maybe his questions had just gotten too hard. "Maybe if I'd go to him, things would be different."

He stared at the clock. It was 1:15 a.m. The night wasn't over. He stripped down to his boxers. He fell on the bed again, feeling as tired as if he'd run a five-mile race, not knowing anymore whether he had or hadn't. He fell into a deep sleep.

In the morning, Chase decided to go to Dad. As doubt crept in, he reminded himself that Dad used to listen.

Chase went downstairs. His father was buttoning his overcoat, his fingers shaking slightly as he fumbled with the holes.

"Dad, can I ask you something?"

"Sure. What is it?"

"Can dreams be true?" His father didn't look up. He sighed audibly as a button slipped out of its hole. Chase hesitated, took a breath, and continued. "I mean, that man Junior, you know, even before he helped the mayor—"

Now his father looked up, furrowed his brow. "Yeah?"

"Well I've seen him in my dreams and—"

"I'm tired of hearing about Junior! Stories are spreading all over town about him. Wild tales about others that he supposedly helped. People are obsessed with that man, and I'm fed up with the Junior stories."

Chase didn't understand the passion in his father's reaction. "But maybe there is something to it."

"Oh, there's something all right. They're all crazy! Listen, son, a patient has been calling my office of late, telling me about this— this Junior guy. Every day he calls and tells me about other people's stories. Even though I don't want to hear and I keep telling him, he still calls. Yesterday, he had a story of his own. Now he claims that he encountered Junior himself. A bunch of nonsense!"

"If it is nonsense, why does he keep calling you?"

"Wants somebody to listen, I guess. Listen to this. Yesterday, he said he wasn't feeling well, and the next thing he knew he was lying on the sidewalk. Someone tried to give him CPR, and Junior—or so he insists—appeared suddenly and pushed the helper away. 'No, not CPR,' Junior supposedly said. 'He needs glucose. Call 911!' My patient said that this Junior guy had a carton of orange juice in his hand and gave it to him while they waited for the ambulance."

"What about the man on the ground? Did he need sugar?"

"Well, yeah, it's true, the orange juice brought him out of the blackout. But why does he have to insist that it was Junior that showed up? It could have been anyone who knew anything about diabetes."

"But that's pretty awesome. I mean—that's great!"

"That's not great! It makes everything good that happens in Atlanta the work of some homeless man that nobody knows."

Chase waited a few heartbeats. "I know him."

"What are you talking about?" His father furrowed his brow.

"Well, I mean, I dreamed about him, and—"

"Oh, yeah, sure. Well, son, I have to go now—can't stay." He patted Chase on his shoulder. As he did so, Chase noticed a slight tremor in his dad's hand. Then his father was gone.

For the next few days, Chase could hardly concentrate in school. He had to figure out some way to meet Junior outside of dreams.

On Sunday Chase woke to discover his father had already left the house. "Your dad had to go out of town," his mom said flatly as she turned away. Sunday meant church. His mother was up early and getting breakfast ready. Chase saw tears in her eyes.

"What's wrong?"

"Nothing, nothing, I'm just not feeling like myself," she said, "Just don't . . . don't ask me anything more."

Chase sat down and ate his scrambled eggs and grits as he always did on Sunday morning. While he ate, his mother went in the other room and sat in her favorite chair. She opened her Bible and began to read the lesson her Bible class was studying that day.

Chase smiled because he often saw her sitting in that chair reading. Sometimes her eyes closed and her lips moved silently. She didn't normally do that when Dad was around, he realized. But then, Dad didn't have much use for anything that involved God.

He went upstairs to finish dressing.

As usual, they were running late. Mom dried her nails as she drove. They came to a red light and that gave her time to put on her lipstick. Chase paid little attention to the traffic or his mother. He was changing the CD in his Walkman when the light turned green. Mom started to pull off and then slammed on her brakes. "What are you doing?" his mother screamed in shock.

Startled, Chase looked up and saw a man washing the windshield.

"I don't need that done," she said. "Please, just get—"

"Yes ma'am, but you will see a lot better after this." He continued, unhurried, even though the light was still green.

Behind them, a car honked.

"You're holding up traffic!" Mom said. "Please, we're late!"

"You are not too late," he said. The man began to sing as he unhurriedly continued to clean the windshield. Chase could catch snatches of the song he was singing. "...was blind but now can see..."

"Just get out of the way!" She pressed on the horn, but he didn't move any faster.

Chase realized that if Mom pulled out, she'd knock the man down. His eyes went from his mother's thumping of her fingers against the steering wheel to the man who worked rhythmically and methodically. Something about the way he moved—a kind of gracefulness about it that didn't seem like the work of a street person.

The man looked vaguely familiar, but Chase couldn't get a steady look at him. He was black, with a full mouth of even, white teeth, but that was all he could see. He smiled between phrases as he sang louder. This time, Chase heard the words clearly: "Amazing grace, how sweet the sound. That saved a wretch like me!"

Chase recognized it as a song from church.

The strange man continued to sing. "...I once was lost, but now I'm found, was blind but now I see..."

The man paused and surveyed his work before he leaned inside the car and smiled. "Now you can both see, ma'am." He spoke to Chase's mother, but his eyes were on the boy.

Mom snatched her purse, pulled out a dollar bill, and held it out to him. "Please, please just get out of my way!"

"Ma'am, no charge for this. I just want the boy to be able to see a little better. There is a big world out there, and I do not want him to miss any of it."

"What're you talking about? Please, just get out of the way."

"Here's your receipt, ma'am." He handed Chase's mother a piece of paper.

"I'm late for church!"

The stranger backed up and waved as the car lurched forward. His honey-brown eyes stared at Chase. He winked.

The boy stared back. Then he knew.

"Mom, Mom! Stop! That's him! That's Junior—"

"We're already late for church." She tromped on the gas pedal and sped down the street—something Chase had never seen her do before.

"But, Mom—"

"Here, get rid of this thing." She tossed the receipt to Chase.

"Mom, I'm telling you—"

"I've got a bad headache, we are running late, and now that man has slowed us down even more. Just this once, don't talk until we get to church, okay?"

Chase turned his head and stared out the back window. The man ran down the street in the same direction they were going.

Although beginning to lag behind, he waved and pointed down-ward. Chase became aware of the paper in his hand. He looked down at it and then back at the now distant features of Junior. He could see Junior nodding.

Silently, he read the message to himself: "*God always answers your prayers. Sometimes he just takes his time. Patience is the window of opportunity through which God must enter. Look not where you have fallen, but instead where you slipped. There you will find the answers.*" It was signed, Junior D.M.

"P.S. Meet me where darkness turns to light."

Both excited and comforted, Chase smiled secretly to himself. He didn't understand the phrase about "where darkness turns to light," but he did know they would meet.

four

The Gift in the Struggle

THE DREAMS ABOUT JUNIOR CONTINUED, BUT NOW HE KNEW Junior was real. He knew each new day held the promise that he might actually find the man.

Chase started his required sentence: the Troubled Youth Awareness Program. The class was in a basement meeting room at the southwest Atlanta community center, where he had spent many happy hours playing basketball. It was early on Saturday morning, and the emptiness and the lack of any activity made the building feel oddly abandoned. It was like coming back to a once familiar building after being away a long time—he didn't know what to expect, what survivors he would meet, or what they would do next.

Chase scanned the room looking to see if there was anyone he knew. He counted nine others: six boys—two white, one Hispanic, and three black; and three girls—two were black and the other was white and pregnant. He didn't know any of them, and could not even imagine why he was there.

"Today's class will be short," the instructor said. "I just wanted to meet all of you and have you fill out a personal questionnaire. My name is Mr. Freeman." Mr. Freeman walked down the rows of chairs and distributed the questionnaire. He was short with broad shoulders and had large muscles that shifted under his dark coat as he passed out the papers. Chase figured he dealt with kids like these day in and day out; he probably wouldn't even realize that Chase wasn't one of them, didn't belong here.

"You will be spending your next twelve Saturday mornings in this room. Your attendance is mandatory."

All ten of the students squirmed in their chairs. One boy's fist pounded his chair in disgust.

"Saturdays? Man, I ain't coming here on no Saturdays."

"Me neither," said another. "That ruins my weekends." A few kids laughed at his swagger, and he looked around at them proudly, as if taking a bow.

Mr. Freeman approached the first kid who had spoken, knelt beside him, his face close, and said in a low, firm voice, "Look young man, it's either here or boot camp. It's on you, you got that? The choice is yours." His stare was hard and unflinching. He stood up and walked back to the front of the class.

The kid remained silent.

"Now, I need each of you to stand and tell me your name."

The instructor's no tolerance attitude seemed to have gotten all of the kids' attention. All but two of the kids stood and said their names loudly and sat down.

Mr. Freeman then stared at the two others. "We need to hear from you two," he said.

Seconds passed before the girl stood. She was white, thin, and frail with strawberry-colored hair. She wore an oversized tee shirt, but it failed to hide the fact that she was pregnant. Reluctantly, she spoke.

"Hey everybody." She was shy and had a rural southern

accent—the words dripped out of her mouth slowly, like spilt milk. "Mah name's Patricia, uh, but mah friends call me 'Trish.'" She began to get flustered and quickly raised her hand to cover her mouth. She was obviously uncomfortable talking in front of people and seemed to be ashamed of a front tooth that was missing in her upper row of teeth. She was so skinny that Chase couldn't imagine her as anyone's lady; certainly couldn't imagine her as anyone's mom.

"And why are you here Patricia?" asked Mr. Freeman.

"Well," she said, as her southern drawl grew stronger, "Ah got some problems. Ah smoke too much and get a little high some-times—the doctors say it ain't good for mah baby. So, the clinic, they sent me here."

"Thank you. You may sit down," Mr. Freeman said. "And you, young man?" He looked at the well-groomed white boy who sat in the back. His hair, wet looking, was neatly combed to the back of his head. He had on one of those "Duckhead" short sleeved shirts, which was perfectly tucked into his Levi jeans. He wore soft Italian leather shoes without socks. He had a gold earring in the center of his left ear. Chase noticed there was a diamond in it.

The two other girls high-fived each other as they looked him over from head to toe. "Girl, that is one fine man," one said. The entire class laughed.

Mr. Freeman opened his mouth as if to bring them to order again, and then let it go. He looked at the boy.

"I'm Brad," the boy said. "I'm from Dunwoody—I go to Peachtree." Dunwoody and Peachtree Academy meant "money" to the other kids in the class.

"Man, what you doin' here," yelled one of the black kids. "You got it made."

"Quiet!" shouted Mr. Freeman. "Why are you here Brad?"

"What difference does it make? I just got caught, okay?" His response was a mix of sarcasm and genuine cluelessness.

"Yeah, ain't that the truth," one of the kids blurted and broke into laughter.

"All right! Enough noise. Brad, you may be seated. It's nice to meet all of you," Mr. Freeman said. "Finish filling out your questionnaires. When you're done, place them in this box to my right. And pick up the reading packet over there before you leave."

Chase heard the boys around him grumble.

"Reading packet?" asked one kid as he walked forward. "Come on, man."

"You're joking, right?" said another kid.

"No joke. Just pick it up," the man said. Chase knew the kids were working hard to resist their urges to talk back or start something. Mr. Freeman spoke quietly, but with a forcefulness behind his words that made Chase and everyone else know this was not play time in Atlanta.

"Each of you, just pick up one packet," Mr. Freeman said, "And read it."

"Me? Read?" said a boy near Chase. "I don't read nothing but numbers on dollar bills."

"I can't believe he's making us do this," said someone else.

Chase heard others, but none of them spoke up loud enough to challenge Mr. Freeman.

Chase watched Mr. Freeman watching them, but the man didn't seem bothered. He stood, his eyes focused on the group as if waiting for them to stop. Soon, all of the conversation stopped. Mr. Freeman then tapped a large pointer on his desk and everyone stopped talking. He cleared his throat. "A brief question for you guys before you go."

"Yeah, what now?" asked one of the kids, not aware that his voice had carried.

Freeman stared at him and raised a large, muscular index finger and pointed at the boy. "If you are asking for trouble, trouble is what you'll get," he said. "Don't play with me. One more outburst like that and you are in boot camp. Do I make myself clear?"

Chase felt the impact even though Mr. Freeman hadn't threatened him. So did the others. The offending boy sat up straight in his chair and lowered his head.

"Now, as I started to ask, what drugs on the street do you all think are killing most people today?"

"Cocaine!" one student yelled.

"Crack!" said another.

"Marijuana!" hollered one boy in the corner of the room.

"Just what I thought you'd say," said Mr. Freeman. "Those are all good answers, but they're wrong." He stepped forward as if to emphasize his answer. "Alcohol and tobacco are responsible for more deaths each year than all of those substances combined." He paused and said, "And there are a lot of other things for you to learn."

He allowed the silence to hang in the room. He looked at the ten kids who sat in front of him. Another group, another chance to make a difference. Sometimes they straightened out. Sadness filled his heart as he thought of those who hadn't made it. "Okay, you have your assignment. Read your material in your packet under Lesson 1, and you'll know the answer next time. See you next session." He walked out of the room.

Everybody took a packet. One of them said, "I can't read that stuff. Don't even know half the words."

"I didn't come here to read," said someone else.

Chase picked up his packet. Just as he opened it, he heard someone call his name. "Yeah, what?"

"Sorry about your boy Ernie," he said.

Chase turned around slowly, and looked at the boy who had spoken to him.

"How do you know about him?" he asked. "Who are you?"

"I know everything, man." His smiled, obviously pleased with this special talent. "They call me Brick. And there's a reason for that, but don't ask."

Three of the kids dropped their questionnaires and left the room.

"You know who did it?" asked Chase.

"I said I was sorry. That's it, man. I know what it's like to lose your boy. I lost mine, but I still ain't talkin'." He turned around and started to fill out his questionnaire.

Chase didn't know who this kid was, didn't know why he was even talking about this stuff. In a way, the awareness course they had all been sentenced to made them all equals. Chase watched him for a while, wondering whether to push it. Then Brick finished his questionnaire, tossed it on the desk, and Chase followed him out of the room.

Brick was aware that Chase had followed behind him, pleased about this too. "I hope they catch the guys that did it, man," said Brick, making small talk. "This gang initiation stuff—it's gotta stop."

Gang initiation? Chase hadn't heard anyone say that before. He wanted to know more, but he didn't want to press Brick. He knew he'd find out if he took it slow.

Once outside, Chase spotted his mom in their car. She honked the horn.

"Can we give you a lift?" Chase asked Brick.

"Not going your way," he said and gave Chase a high five. "See you round."

"Yeah, man, later," Chase said, but his mind wouldn't leave those two words: gang initiation. So that's what it had been. Just some stupid, stupid thing they had to do to get into their gang.

If his mother hadn't been there, Chase would have exploded with anger.

Chase didn't dream about Junior Saturday night, nor Sunday or Monday. By Friday, the stranger still hadn't appeared—in any form.

He felt really confused. Had the incident in the car with his mother just been a figment of his imagination? What had Junior meant about meeting with him? It had been more than a week since Chase had been given the note on Sunday morning. Where is he? What's going on?

"Somehow, I've gotta find him," Chase said. "There has got to be a reason for what's happening, for his coming to me on the street like that."

Junior became an obsession. Almost every waking moment Chase thought about tracking Junior. He'd heard about people who claimed to have the ability to enter into their dreams, stuff called astral projection. Chase tried the method, but it didn't seem to work for him. Each night before going to bed, he hoped that Junior would come.

One night he had an idea. While lying in bed, eyes closed, he focused his mind on the wall in his dream that he had leapt over before the darkness had turned into daylight. Again and again he visualized himself leaping over the wall and the brightness swallowing up the darkness. He envisioned the wall but nothing happened. Nothing magical transported him into the dream again. He felt helpless and defeated.

He gave up trying and picked up his biology homework and started to read.

The first yawn hit a few minutes before midnight, but Chase hardly noticed.

....

Chase spots Junior twenty yards ahead of him. He quickly narrows the distance. He feels lightning quick and imagines that he is a cheetah pursuing its prey in the night. Suddenly, he is right beside Junior as they leap over the wall together. Just as before, the deep blackness turns into bright sunlight. But Junior is gone. In his hand, Chase holds a piece of paper. He stares at it and reads the words twice. They make no sense to him.

He reads the words aloud: "What looks like death to a caterpillar, God calls _____." Angrily, he folds the paper and stuffs it inside his pocket.

"A riddle? Why did he give me a riddle," he asks. "What good is this? Man, this is strange. It doesn't tell me anything."

Frustration and anger burn inside him. Now confused and mad at himself, he strikes the wall with his right hand and feels a stinging pain.

At that point, he hears laughter—laughter so deep that it frightens him. Chase turns and sees the elusive figure a hundred feet ahead of him. "Wait!" he calls. "Hold up! I need to—"

Instead of an answer, Junior starts to run. Chase sprints forward. "I'm gonna catch you this time!" he screams as he gasps for air.

The more Chase runs, the greater the distance between them. But not only that, the intensity of the light is changing. At the wall, it had been a piercing hot, midsummer day. Now, every fifty yards or so, the light begins to lose its bright tone. Chase picks up speed and the darkness increases. As he pushes on, he realizes that the day has become night. Chase can no longer see anything ahead, beside him, or behind him, so he slows to a walk. This is the deepest darkness that he has ever experienced.

What is going on? he asks himself. Where am I?

He waits, hoping for a sound to guide him. After several seconds of silence in the total darkness, he stretches his hands in front of him and steps forward. Just then he senses that something is moving near his feet. At first he feels nothing, but then he hears a squashing sound, as if he has stepped on an animal. But most distressing of all he hears cries of pain.

"This is crazy," he says, but he keeps on.

With each step, he feels things crunch beneath his feet. Whatever they are, he knows that he is hurting them and he doesn't want to do that. Instead of stepping forward, he begins to slide one foot after the other.

Then one foot trips over something hard. He topples forward, his hands out to catch himself. The entire weight of his body lands on his right wrist. At the point of impact, he hears a pop and moans loudly.

It is obvious to him that he has broken a bone.

As he sits up, the night becomes even more terrifying. He notices objects, hundreds of them, crawling over his right hand.

"Spiders!" he screams. "They're all over me!" Fear grips him, and he screams once more as he frantically begins to brush the spiders away. He jumps to his feet. Many still cling to him.

Tears roll down his cheeks as he cries out into the darkness.

As if responding to his cry, a rumbling fills his ears and his body shakes. He realizes the rumbling is a voice—one so deep and loud that it sounds like none he has ever heard before. It is as if the forces of nature had joined together and formed a single roar.

The tears stop. The fear vanishes and he listens.

"Perhaps the way forward is the way back," he hears the rumbling voice say.

Before he can think about what he is doing, Chase turns and faces the way he has come. He takes a deep breath and starts to run. His right hand, now deformed, hurts badly. His left knee throbs, but there is no stopping him.

To his surprise, the pain in his extremities slowly lessens. After he has gone perhaps fifty yards, not only has the pain started to go away, but he also has the slightest glimpse of light ahead. He picks up speed. As he approaches the wall, the darkness diminishes. Light becomes brighter and brighter. Soon, he is back at the wall, and the day's sudden brilliance forces him to blink.

Exhaustion comes over Chase, and he slips to the ground, his back against the wall. He stares at his body, and to his surprise it looks as if nothing had ever happened. The pain is gone.

"Man, I am tired of this!" he says. "Let me go!"

As he speaks these words Chase realizes he holds a new piece of paper in his hand, folded in quarters. He stares at it without reading it.

"I mean it! I quit!" he says. "Let me out of this dream."

In the silence around him, he senses that nothing more will happen until he reads the message. "Okay, you win," he says. Slowly, reluctantly, he unfolds the paper. He reads the single sentence aloud: "Obstacles are those frightening things we see and feel when we take our eyes off the prize."

Now, even more frustrated, he leans his head against the wall and closes his eyes. He has had enough. "I just want out of this dream," he says.

He has no idea how long he has been sitting there. Long enough to become aware that his anger and frustration have melted away. For reasons unknown to him, he is slowly beginning to feel better. He opens his eyes and sees his surroundings with a new appreciation.

The bright sun doesn't feel hot, only warm and comfortable. As the rays embrace him, he feels a calmness flow through him and into his body. The grass around him is the most beautiful that he has ever seen and its fresh scent fills his nostrils. He breathes deeply and stares at an array of flowers with vivid hues. The sight mesmerizes him.

He turns his head to the right and sees a tree which seems to have just that instant appeared. Its color is dazzling. At first he thinks it is a strange kind of apple tree, but hanging from its branches are also large oranges, pears, cherries, and a variety of fruit that he doesn't recognize. Chase hears himself say, "A tree of harmony." He wonders from where these words have come.

He gets to his feet and starts to walk forward. Before him is a dirt path and footprints that lead to the tree. He follows the footprints to the backside of the tree and there he spots a cocoon on a bare limb.

"Check that out," he says aloud. Before him, a shuddering butterfly struggles to emerge from its cocoon. He watches in fascination as the tiny creature attempts to win its battle. He can't imagine how the tiny, golden-winged butterfly can possibly get out. "Aw, man, that ain't fair," he says, and reaches up and pulls it closer. With one finger he carefully widens the space for the insect to escape. He steps back to watch it emerge.

Hardly a second passes before the insect stops struggling. It is out of the cocoon. It makes several attempts to flutter its wings, but they move ever so slightly. The butterfly leans forward and falls to the ground. It convulses for several seconds, then lies unmoving.

"Oh, no!" He touches the butterfly as if his fingers could restore its life, but he knows that he can't. Sadness fills his heart and his eyes mist as he wonders what happened. Just then, the riddle flows through his thoughts.

"Butterfly! That's it!—that's the answer to the riddle. What looks like death to a caterpillar is it's changing into a butterfly."

He pauses to think more about what he has just said. "Butterfly! Please don't die on me, butterfly!" he cries out. "Come back butterfly! Come back!"

"Chase! Chase!" Some one has grabbed his shoulders and is shaking him hard.

....

The boy opened his eyes. His mother's hands were on his shoulders.

"What's wrong with you? You been having some kind of bad dream again," she said. "You okay baby?"

Chase lay stunned in his bed. He stared at the ceiling as perspiration ran down his face.

Chase was still thinking about the butterfly while he dressed for school. He knew that part of the dream was important, but why? And why did the butterfly die?

When he walked into his first period class, he was still pondering the meaning of the dream. All through his classes that day, he had to force himself to listen to the teacher. At noon, he took his lunch tray and sat down alone in the far corner of the room. What did that dream mean—especially about the butterfly? he kept asking himself.

During the afternoon, his mind still kept returning to the dream. Finally, seventh period came, his last for the day, and his favorite—Mr. Seymour's biology class.

For the first time, he wondered how old Mr. Seymour was. His hair had long turned white—what there was of it. His skin was ebony-toned. Although a tall man, Mr. Seymour seemed frail. All the kids at school knew that he was a sick man and had been hospitalized twice the previous year for an unknown ailment. Rumors went through school that this would be his last year of teaching and that he would go back to his home in Alabama.

Chase opened his book and reread the assigned lesson. For the next forty-five minutes, try as he might to keep his mind on the class, he kept drifting back into his dream.

When the bell rang, Mr. Seymour dismissed the class and said, "Will you stay a minute, Chase?"

Surprised, the boy sat at his desk and waited for everyone to leave. Then he went up to the teacher's desk.

"What's wrong?" Mr. Seymour asked. Before Chase could reply, he said. "You are the best student in this class. I have always counted on your interest and participation. But today your mind was elsewhere."

"I'm sorry, sir."

"I am not going to lecture you. I suspect that something is troubling you, and I am willing to listen." Mr. Seymour leaned back in his chair, put his thin arms on his desk and waited.

"Well, yeah, something is bothering me all right."

From the hallway, they could hear banging lockers and a few

voices yelling to others. From the street, they heard the steady stream of traffic.

Just then, Chase decided that here was a chance to open up to someone. He couldn't tell him everything, of course. But he decided to tell him about the butterfly, without saying that it had been a dream. "I'm confused by all of this," he said. He lowered his head. "I know it sounds silly, but—"

"Not at all," Mr. Seymour said. He got out of his chair, struggling as he did, and went to the chalkboard. He drew a diagram of the life cycle of the butterfly. He paused a few times to ask, "Are you with me on this?"

Each time Chase nodded.

The teacher dropped the chalk on the tray and came back to the desk. He sat on the corner and his dark eyes bored into the boy's. "I know about your love of nature. I assume that out of your love for the butterfly, you tried to set it free. Correct?"

Chase nodded again.

"That was the worst thing you could have done. You see, a butterfly needs that struggle. That's the way God designed it. During the struggle, the butterfly develops the necessary muscles to fly. By robbing him of the struggle, you rendered him too weak to live."

"I didn't know. I never thought—"

"Yes, I understand," he said. "Here's a case where the gift of life is in the struggle. The metamorphosis of the butterfly is a classic example of how parts of the animal kingdom have parallels applicable to human life. Next time, allow nature to take its course." He smiled and patted Chase on the shoulder. "You know, the same principles apply to your friendships and family matters too. You might think about that."

"Thank you, sir!" Chase picked up his books and started to leave the classroom. At the door, he turned around and looked back. "Really, Mr. Seymour, I mean it—thanks!"

Mr. Seymour smiled. As he did, he looked over his glasses and stared intensely into Chase's eyes.

Chase felt as if the penetrating stare looked right through him, as if the teacher knew something that he hadn't figured out yet.

"I think I really get it, sir," he said. "And I guarantee you that I'll remember."

"I know you will," the teacher said quietly. "Yes, Chase, I know you will."

He walked into the hallway and went to his locker. Something was happening to him. Slowly. Gradually, but it was happening all the same. He could feel it. He thought of a word he had read but never used before: Enlightenment.

Enlightenment.

Yes, that word fit.

five

Merchantville

WHEN HE ARRIVED HOME from school, his mother greeted him with a big hug. She seemed to be okay today, too. Chase didn't know what to expect from her of late. She was so up and down emotionally, and she never liked to talk about it. But he had over-heard the doctor talk about depression, so maybe that was the rea-son. He smiled as he thought, at least she's up today.

Dinner came, and once again Dad wasn't there. He helped his mother with the dishes and stored the leftovers.

"Is Dad on call?" he asked.

"Isn't he always?"

"Why don't you say something to him?"

His mother stared at him for a long time before she said, "This is an issue between me and your dad. You're stepping out of bounds."

"Well, I just thought——"

"Please. It's a parent thing, okay?"

"All right," he said and went upstairs.

As soon as he was in his room, Chase jumped on his bed. He opened his backpack. Stuck in the side of it were the articles from his Youth Awareness class. He pulled out the top one. Written in red ink was a message: "Glad you took a look. Just know the points highlighted in yellow."

Chase flipped through the article and actually read most of it. By the time he had finished, he thought, Ah, this ain't so bad. Then he carefully read the highlighted sections:

- Many individuals seem to inherit a genetic code that predisposes them to the development of alcoholism if certain biologic or environmental modifiers are present.
- 54% of adolescents who use drugs report doing so to relieve pressures at home.
- 88% of teenage substance abusers have friends who use drugs.
- Adolescents who report healthy relationships and open communication with their parents are less likely to use drugs.
- Lack of four elements of social bonding have been shown to be related to drug use:
  - Strong attachment to parents
  - Commitment to schooling
  - Regular involvement in church or religious activities
  - Belief in the generalized expectations, norms, and values of society.

Like the dreams, Chase pondered the meaning of all this. What did it have to do with him? He opened his books and pulled out his homework. As he always did, Chase flipped on the television.

He stared at the screen as a reporter interviewed the mayor's wife, Courtney Ewing.

"Now that you have been elected to head the State Committee on Healthcare Reform, what do you expect will be your first major changes in the system?"

"Of course we need to balance the budget," she said. "And I plan to do that first by assessing the need for certain hospitals in this city. "

The questions went on and on, and Chase tuned out. He finished his homework, and prepared to sleep. He lay on his back in bed with his hands behind his head. His mind was at ease.

....

Something is different. He is running beside Junior as he has before. Side by side, they reach the wall. This time, he feels more focused as he lands on the other side of the wall. The brightness begins to diminish before he takes his first step.

In the distance, he sees Junior running ahead. He is heading down the path that has led into such heavy darkness before. At first, Chase doesn't know what to do, and it seems natural to run after him. But he stops.

"No, not again," he says. "I'm gonna chill right here."

As soon as he speaks those words, he becomes aware that he holds a piece of paper in his hand. He looks down and reads the message: "Today is the tomorrow that you looked forward to yesterday."

He repeats the sentence several times, remains focused on his immediate surroundings and waits for his instincts to take over. He is amazed at the beauty and peacefulness of his surroundings. He bends down and inhales the pungent odors of the flowers. Somewhere in the distance, birds serenade the glory of nature. Once again, he follows the dirt path that leads to the back side of the tree of harmony. As before, he sees a bare branch and smiles at the struggling butterfly.

"Hold on," he says softly. "I'll help you by not helping you. You need to get through this by yourself, but soon you'll be free." He sits on the ground and watches the intense struggle.

Chase has no idea of the passage of time, but the butterfly finally breaks free by its own strength. Its wings batter the air and it soon lifts from the limb and circles the tree. It seems to dance back and forth in front of him.

It has gold-and-black markings. It is the most beautiful butterfly Chase has ever seen. He holds out his hand, wonders if it will land on his palm.

The butterfly comes close, turns a lazy circle, and goes three or four feet away from him. It circles and comes back toward him. Then it does the same thing again. As the butterfly gently drops its wings, Chase watches in utter fascination. Then he says aloud, "It's like Chilly the cat. It's acting just like Chilly did."

As soon as the butterfly brushes past him, Chase takes a few steps toward it. The insect loops and moves forward. Whenever Chase takes a step, the butterfly moves farther away. Soon Chase is following without hesitation. He is aware of a new energy inside him, and he thinks, man, I could walk behind this butterfly all day. He feels as if his feet no longer touch the ground. They seem to skim across the path that leads him down the deserted road.

Ahead, he sees a fork in the road. As he approaches, Chase realizes that the butterfly has disappeared.

"Just like Chilly," he says again, but this time he understands.

At his feet, he sees two piles of letters of the alphabet. Each letter is about four inches high. He stoops down and sees that under the two piles is an envelope. He opens the envelope. On a single sheet of paper are these words: "Reading is fundamental. The direction that you seek is in the words and how they meet. Have fun."

Have fun? He lays the letters out before him, but they don't make any sense. He moves them around a few times. Starting to grow inpatient, he asks, "Have fun? This is supposed to be fun?"

For a fraction of a second, he wants to get up and leave the letters, but he thinks, no, this is something I need to do. But what do I do?

"Just do what comes natural, Chase," he hears himself say, "Just do what comes natural."

He tries to figure out what to do, and nothing comes to him. So he stacks the letters back the way he has found them and decides not to do anything. Just then, he looks up and sees a road sign. It wasn't there when he arrived. The sign points in two directions, but there are no words on the sign.

"That's strange," he says. "How do I know where these roads lead?" He stares at the signs and back at the letters, and then he realizes what he is supposed to do.

He picks up the first pile of letters, takes the top one—a W. He kneels on the ground beside the first pile and lays out the letters. There is an H, N, E, O, R and another E.

He moves them around in an attempt to form real words, but nothing makes sense to him. As he moves the letters back and forth, Chase becomes aware of the rising temperature around him. He begin to sweat and his impatience is growing.

"Must be over 100 degrees," he says as he continues to move the letters around. Beads of sweat cover his brow and above his lip. He tastes drops of salty perspiration and wipes at his face.

"This doesn't make sense!" Just as he says those words, he pushes the second E to the end.

"That's it, I've got it!"

On the ground before him, Chase reads: N O W H E R E.

"I don't want to go there."

He stands up and places the letters against the sign that points to the left. They adhere as if glued. "Who wants to go nowhere?" he asks as he stares at the sign. Then it comes to him.

"I'll take the other path," he says.

He starts down the unmarked path, and after a hundred yards

it takes a sharp bend and then another. Ahead he sees a mud-and-thatch hut. From the pictures that he has seen on television, it looks as if the hut could have come out of Africa. Curious, he walks closer. He sees a man's face inside. The open door of the hut is about five feet high, and the man bends forward and comes out.

When he stands, Chase realizes just how muscular and tall he is. "He must be a giant," he says to himself. "I've never seen anybody that tall in my life."

The man is bare-chested with a brown cloth that runs from his waist to his knees. His cheeks are painted with red-and-blue markings. In his left hand, he carries a large skin-covered shield and a long spear in his right. Chase knows instantly the markings indicate that he is a chief—he is dressed to lead his people into battle.

I'll ask him where I am, Chase thinks as he walks close and smiles.

"Boy, I have a question!" the giant says as soon as Chase comes close. The sound of his voice has a force, and it stuns Chase still. "How does one choose sides on a round planet?"

"Huh? What do you mean?"

The chief glares at him as if waiting impatiently for a simple answer.

Chase feels awestruck at the warrior's presence. Not only is he tall, but he is handsome. Without an ounce of fat on him anywhere. The muscles on his arms and chest ripple when he moves.

"By being informed, little warrior," the chief says in the deepest voice Chase had ever heard. "Are you informed?"

"I guess not."

"Why not, little warrior?"

"I don't know."

"Ah, so you don't know why you don't know?"

Chase feels extremely stupid as he tries to conjure an answer, but nothing comes. Finally, he drops his gaze.

"Look at me, little warrior," the chief says. "Answers always come from above, not below."

Chase raises his head and when their eyes meet, the chief says, "We are most informed when we finish our lessons. Go back to the fork in the road." With his spear he points in the direction Chase has come from. "Go. Now."

The chief turns and goes back inside the mud-and-thatch hut. Chase stands motionless for a few seconds. Suddenly, he remembers that he hasn't done anything with the second pile of letters. It seems so obvious now, and he can't understand why he has hurried off on the path that was unmarked.

I've got to stop being so lazy, he thinks.

He turns around and goes back to the sign. The road seems longer going back than it had coming. When he reaches the fork, everything is as he left it.

He kneels on the ground and spreads out the second pile. To his amazement, they are exactly the same letters. He forms the same two words, but this time he realizes that the W is closer to the O, and he reads "NOW HERE." He places the letters on the sign that points to the right, the path he had followed blindly.

He stares at the sign and realizes that he has done it right this time. He smiles in satisfaction and a stirring sense of self-confidence fills his heart and mind. "This is the path to follow, and I know it this time," he says, and turns to the right.

Chase walks confidently forward. His steps quicken and he can feel anticipation in his heartbeat. The path makes two wide turns and, to Chase's amazement, it seems to be different this time. Further down the path, he sees the same hut and the same chief coming toward him.

Is he the same chief? he wonders. He looks like him and yet something is different. Chase curls his brow as he tries to figure out the difference.

"Or maybe I'm different," he hears himself say aloud. "Maybe my perception has changed."

The chief continues toward Chase until he is standing right in front of him.

"Wow! We're the same size," Chase says in amazement.

"That is correct, little warrior. We are equals," says the chief. "We always were."

"Yeah, I get it!" Chase says. "I was right in coming down this path the first time, but I just wasn't sure."

"Exactly, little warrior. And how did you change?"

"I went back where I started. This time I chose the right path—I was more confident before I started, that's all."

"That's all?" The chief laughs aloud and thrusts his spear into the ground. "That is an important discovery."

Chase smiles and then blushes. It seems so obvious now that he has done it. It's simply my perception that has changed.

"If you are so bright, little warrior, then I shall ask you another question."

"All right, ask me."

"Do you believe in a power greater than yourself?"

An even greater confidence flows through the boy. "Sure I do," he says. "That is, if you're thinking what I'm thinking."

"I'm sure I am, little warrior," the chief says. "Have you learned the value of patience?"

"Man, have I!"

"Explain that to me."

Chase tells him of the second leap over the wall, his journey into the darkness, as well as his first experience with the butterfly and its death. He tells the chief he found the butterfly the second time and allowed it to struggle.

"Very good, little warrior."

Chase grins at the chief. He knows he has done well.

"Impatience, as you have learned, leads to hasty decisions. Hasty decisions lead to chance." He pauses and steps closer. "Proper choice, not chance, determines one's destiny."

Chase nods as if to say he understands.

The chief's eyes bore into the boy's. Although the silence between them lasts only a few seconds, to Chase it feels as if it goes on for a long, long time.

"What do you know about honesty and truth?" the chief asks.

Unprepared for that question, Chase doesn't answer. He remembers a saying from his grandfather: "When you're in deep water, it's best to keep your mouth shut." He remains quiet.

"Are you afraid, little warrior?"

Chase opens his mouth ready to deny fear, but something tells him to be honest. "Yeah, I'm a little afraid—"

"Ah, you do know honesty, don't you?" He walks up to Chase and lays his muscular arm on the boy's shoulder. "Congratulations, the truth has set you free."

Chase feels his face beaming.

"Come," the chief says.

Together they walk down the path. Soon they come to a tall mountain with a small path that winds its way upward. Without a word, the chief begins to climb and the boy follows. The path leads to a higher peak, but the walking seems effortless. When they reach the top, the chief points on the other side of the mountain to a city below.

"Welcome to Merchantville. Go. There you will find your teacher."

"My teacher?" Excited at hearing these words, Chase waves to the chief and takes the first steps on the path leading downward.

"Not so fast, little warrior!"

Chase stops and wonders what he has done wrong.

"Before you go, you must answer one more question."

"Sure, what's that?"

"Where's your gift?"

"My gift?" Chase repeats and thinks, I didn't know that I was supposed to bring anything.

The chief laughs loudly again, this time waving his spear in the air. "Little warrior, the gift is in the struggle. And remember, the struggle is nothing more than the first part of something better to come."

Chase stares, amazed at the chief's answer. "Okay, I believe you. Now what?"

"Proceed down the hill. Once there, you will find a city of merchants. Look for the Center for Conscious Living. Your teacher awaits. Tell him that Chief Intimidator sends greetings."

What a strange name for an African warrior, Chase thinks, as he waves and starts downward. He walks carefully to make sure he doesn't fall and hurt himself.

"The Center for Conscious Living," Chase repeats to himself. He has heard of that place before—

After a few steps down the hill, Chase pauses and turns to look back at the African chief.

"You are correct in your thinking, little warrior," the chief says. "The Center for Conscious Living is a very special place. True, it is a shelter for the homeless, as you would call them. But you will find that the people who live there are very different. They are somewhat magical. In fact, you might call them superhuman. Don't let their outward appearance fool you. Remember, little warrior, character is what is inside, not what you wear on the outside."

"I'll remember!" Chase nods at the chief.

Although quite tired now, Chase keeps walking. Whenever he turns around, he realizes that the chief has not taken his eyes off of him.

"Chase!" yells the chief.

Chase turns around just in time to see the chief throw his spear in the direction Chase is walking. It lands about ten feet in front of

him. He turns to the chief once again but this time he has disappeared. Chase walks up to the spear and finds a deep-brown animal
skin cloth attached to it. Burned into the skin are these words:
"People don't ever fail, they just stop trying. Never be discouraged.
Every courageous attempt is a step forward. Good luck on your
journey."

....

Chase lay quietly with his eyes closed. He could still see the
words: People don't fail, they just stop trying.

Just then he heard a muffled noise. Voices? Crying? His mother's voice? He wasn't sure. He tiptoed into the hallway, careful not
to make noise. He walked down the hallway to his parents' bedroom. The door was slightly open. He peeked inside. His mother
was on her knees at the foot of the bed. She was sobbing and her
face was buried in a pillow to muffle the sound.

Sadness filled his own heart. He wanted to run into the room
and hug her and beg her not to cry anymore. But something
stopped him.

Suddenly, a loud pounding came from downstairs—the distinct
beating of fists against a door, of someone trying to get inside.

He was frightened and didn't know what to do. His mother's
sobbing frightened him, the pounding frightened him. His mother
got off her knees. With her back to him, she paused and yelled
aloud, "I should have done that a long time ago." She rushed into
her bathroom.

Chase heard the sound of running water in the sink. It was so
loud that it drowned the sound of her tears.

He turned and raced downstairs. He fumbled with the dead
bolt, and fumbled as he unlocked the door. He could hear a car
engine starting. He threw open the door and saw his father's Buick
pulling out of the driveway. It jerked at the end of the drive as his

dad shifted gears. Chase started to run after the car but realized he would not be able to catch up with it.

He turned around and went back inside. As soon as he closed the door behind him, he looked up and saw his mother standing at the top of the stairs. She had washed her face, but he could clearly see her puffy cheeks and the still-wet eyes. He tried to think of something to say.

"If you don't hurry," she said, "you will be late for school." She turned around abruptly and went back into her room. His first instinct was to run upstairs and question her, but he stopped again, thinking about his impatience in the still very real dream. He felt confused. "I just can't let her be alone like this," he said to himself.

He started again toward her room.

An inner voice said, "Don't forget the gift in the struggle."

Chase stopped. He knew what he was supposed to do. Although it hurt not to go to her, he realized that this was an issue for his parents to resolve on their own.

"I just need to chill," he said.

When he walked past his mother's room, he slowed down to listen. Again, he heard running water in her bathroom but this time he could hear her crying above the sound of the water.

six

Junior

HIS SOCIOLOGY TEACHER DRONED on and several of the kids slept. Chase stared into space and his body began to relax. Although this was new to him, he felt comfortable with it, because his daydreams had centered around the same topic as his night dreams—Junior.

In his mind, he and Junior race across a football field in a huge stadium with thousands of people watching and cheering them on as they run.

"Come on!" says Junior. "We have to move fast. There are so many things for you to learn and do."

"What things?"

"You will see," he says. "Meet me after school!"

"Where?"

"Chilly will show you."

Then it was over and he looked at the sociology teacher point to a chart on the board.

Not only did the daydream not make sense, neither did Junior's message.

When school was over that day, his eyes scanned the playground and the streets, but he never saw Junior or Chilly.

The following day he had the same daydream again. In this dream he was frustrated because he couldn't control what went on. He made several attempts to stop Junior and talk to him during the daydream, but it just wouldn't happen. He realized that he was becoming bombarded with images of Junior.

The next day was no different—another daydream.

Junior sat on the floor in a darkened room. There was just enough light coming in under the drapes for Chase to recognize him.

Junior looked up and called, "Chase."

But in this daydream—as in others—when Chase started toward him, his concentration broke. Either a teacher would say something or another student would nudge him. He could never get past that point.

On and on this went, taking Chase's mental concentration away from class. Finally, a girl behind him nudged his shoulder and handed him a note.

"Someone told me to give this to you. I haven't read it. I promise."

Chase looked at the note and read "Chilly will show you."

He turned to the girl and asked, "What else did he say? You spoke with him didn't you?"

"He didn't say anything. He just walked inside, handed me the note, and told me to give it to you."

The bell rang and the students raced from their seats and out of the classroom. Chase, suddenly aware of the activity, looked up at the clock and realized that he hadn't even heard the bell. He had lost all concept of time.

As he walked toward the door, his biology teacher, Mr. Seymour, looked at him quizzically. "Are you all right today?"

Chase nodded and started for the door.

"Lately you don't seem to be here. You look at me, but your eyes tell me that you are off on another planet."

"Sorry, Mr. Seymour," Chase said. "I'm trying to do better."

"Is there something wrong? Problems at home? You know, I can tell when something is bothering you—"

"Nothing, sir," Chase said, as he opened the door.

Once in the hallway, he hurried toward his next class. He just wanted the day to end. Something had happened and changed him, and he needed time to think about it. He knew he had been daydreaming a lot lately but there were so many changes going on that it was difficult to focus. And the fact was, he didn't understand most things that were going on. He had gone from nightmares of Ernie to nighttime dreams of chasing a stranger in the dark to daydreaming. None of it made sense. And then there was the added confusion of what was happening to his parents.

As soon as the final bell rang, Chase dashed out of the classroom and raced down the hall to the front door. He pushed open the door and stared into the afternoon sunshine. His heart sank again. There was no Chilly.

"Guess I was wrong to anticipate any of this would be real."

He slung his bag over his shoulder and started toward the sidewalk. Suddenly, a scratching sound to his far right caught his attention. He turned and saw Chilly trying to climb an oak tree.

"Hey, Chilly, what's up?" Chase called as he raced lightheaded toward the cat. When he was only three feet away, Chilly turned and ran toward the street. This time, Chase knew what to do. As he followed, he laughed aloud and called out, "Up to your old tricks again, huh, Chilly?"

The cat kept going; Chase followed.

Chase had no idea how long or far he followed Chilly, but he did notice that the neighborhood changed. They were no longer in the familiar southwest section of Atlanta. This section looked more like the inner city. With each block, the neighborhoods became increasingly more run-down. The buildings he passed were boarded with sheets of plywood. Graffiti was scrawled over the sidewalk and the walls, like a system of veins running through the neighborhood. He couldn't think of the last time he had seen so many trash Dumpsters. Stray cats and dogs lined the streets, quarreling and hissing if anyone came too close to their turf.

Chilly scurried past the other animals as if they didn't exist.

Chase kept following. The houses became smaller and more dilapidated. A few had windows covered with plastic to keep out the wind and rain. An indescribable odor of decay filled the streets. Homeless people, mostly men, sat on the curb. They talked, and drank from bottles inside brown paper bags.

As he stared at the blank faces, Chase realized how lucky he was. People just shouldn't have to live this way, he said to himself.

Ordinarily, Chase would have felt uneasy in this neighborhood, but not today. As he walked on, he just knew that this was something that he was supposed to do. There was no fear.

"I know where we're headed," he called to the black cat. Even though Chase had never been there, he knew their destination. "We're going to the Center for Conscious Living aren't we?"

Chase studied the three-foot-tall letters that covered one side of the freshly painted yellow house.

"This is it!" he said. He looked around, but Chilly had disappeared. He smiled; he had expected that.

He walked up three cement steps and knocked on the door of the Center for Conscious Living.

"Come right on in!" an elderly black woman called from behind the screen door. "Don't be standing out there all afternoon!"

He opened the door and walked inside. In contrast to the squalor of the neighborhood, the house looked very clean, and the faint odor of lemon filled the room. The woman stood at an ironing board and sang as she worked. "...I sing because I'm happy, I sing because I'm free. His eye is on the sparrow..."

Chase paused. The woman looked a hundred years old, but she had such a beautiful, clear voice.

She squinted and then asked, "What'cha need, boy? You don't look like you're from 'round here!"

He hesitated. "I'm, uh, here to see Junior?" It was almost a question.

"What do you need with him?"

Her response at once shocked Chase because she knew Junior and left him at a loss for words because he didn't know why he was there. He shrugged and remained quiet.

"What's your name, boy?"

"Chase," he said quietly. "What's yours?"

"Ledd. Leona Ledd," she said and put a fresh shirt on her ironing board. "Just call me Miss Ledd." The mysterious lady continued to iron. She began to sing the third stanza of the song and continued to sing as if Chase were not present. Then she finished the final chorus with the words, "...His eye is on the sparrow, and I know he watches me."

She hung up the shirt she had finished ironing and stared at the boy. "Why are you still here? Junior's room is down the hall. Last door on the right." She pointed.

Chase swallowed and took a deep breath before he headed down the hall. He looked around, and noticed there were several rooms. One room looked like a meeting hall, another like an arts and crafts room. As he continued on, he soon passed what he knew was a room for prayer. A Bible lay on every desk and the walls were painted with pictures of angels. The delicate stained glass windows reminded him of a church.

"Young man, why are you walking like that?" Miss Ledd called out from the end of the hallway. "You scared?"

"What do you mean?" Chase asked.

"Fear, boy. You feel it, don't you?"

"Not really," Chase said. Then he thought about it. "Yeah, well, maybe a little."

"'Course you're afraid. It's written all over your face." She pointed her finger at him. "Don't you worry none about this here place—it's safe—-everything is safe at the Center for Conscious Living. You got nothing to be worrying about, you hear?"

Chase nodded and tried to look confident, but he was beginning to doubt himself.

He thought about what he had just done. I wonder if I'm crazy. I've just followed a black cat that appeared from nowhere into a place like this where I don't know anyone. Is that crazy or what?

"Young man, you stop right there before you open that door. You shake off that fear, because we don't let fear live inside this place. Do you understand?"

Chase stared at her, not having any idea what she meant or what she expected him to do.

"Just do what I say, boy." She walked closer to him and stared into his eyes. "You need to move in one direction," she said. "Know which way that is? I will tell you—it's forward. Understand?"

"Yes, ma'am."

"Move only at one speed. Understand what I mean?" She paused and cleared her throat, but her eyes bore down on him. "And that one speed is constant."

Not knowing what else to do, Chase nodded.

She raised her finger at him and pointed. "Move only with one attitude—optimism. Do you hear what I am saying?"

"Yes ma'am, but—"

"No 'buts,' boy. You got that?"

This time, Chase thought about her words. They had an immediate calming effect on him. "Yes ma'am, I do."

"All right now, you can go on ahead."

Filled with a sense of anticipation, Chase opened the door and went toward Junior's room. In a whisper to himself, he repeated her three instructions: to move forward, to move constantly, to go with optimism. He felt even better.

He poked his head through the door and looked to his right. The soft fragrance of flowers sitting bunched on a table filled his nostrils as he stepped forward and closed the door. In the dimly lit room, he saw a figure sitting in the middle of the floor. The man's legs were crossed, and his hands rested on his lap, palms up.

It was Junior.

Even though calmness had replaced his fear, Chase tiptoed toward the figure from his dreams. Finally, no more running, he thought. I'm here with him, face-to-face.

A sense of overpowering awe came over him as he stood in front of the man. There was something special about seeing Junior in front of him—the feeling of the presence of something sacred came to mind. Chase now stood about four feet from the man

Junior was tall, muscular, and handsome. But something impressed Chase even more. It was Junior's face. Never had he seen such a look of peace on anyone.

He took a step closer, but Junior didn't move. What's he doing? Chase wondered. Is he asleep?

He shuffled his feet, but Junior didn't move. Next, he waved his hands in front of Junior's face, but that didn't disturb him either. Not knowing what to do, Chase finally sat down on the floor in front of the man. He tried to imitate his posture, but he was unable to cross his legs over one another.

After several minutes, Junior opened his eyes. His expression didn't change. As their eyes met, Chase sensed that Junior was aware of him, yet he appeared to be somewhere else at the same time. A chill went up Chase's spine as he realized that he was sitting face-to-face with the elusive one.

"Sometimes, the best way to see is to close your eyes," Junior said and smiled. He closed his eyes again.

Chase stared at Junior for three or four seconds and then decided to close his own eyes. They sat in silence. Without being told, he knew he was supposed to concentrate on what was going on in the room and block out all other noise and thoughts, but he didn't know how. After less than a minute, an argument going on in the street disturbed Chase. Far off in the distance, a police siren wailed as it raced through the neighborhood.

"Philippians 4:13."

Chase opened his eyes. "What did you say?"

"Philippians 4:13."

"I've heard of it—I mean I know it is in the Bible, but what does it mean?"

"That is for me to know and for you to find out."

"Come on, man, stop playing with me. Why can't you just come straight?"

Junior slowly opened his eyes. "I am not playing with you. That is the word of God. I don't play with that."

They stared at each other in silence before Junior asked, "Do you have questions for me?"

"Questions?" Chase detected a playfulness in the man's eyes as he said, "Yeah, plenty. I think about you all the time and——"

"Snap to it. That was a statement, not a question. You do not have much time before you must leave."

"Okay, then here's my first question. How did you come to me in my dreams?"

Junior chuckled. "You get right to it don't you?"

"Yeah. I want to know."

"Well, you must be patient. There are other things you must know first."

"What other things?" Chase asked.

"Continue to ask and you shall receive," Junior replied.

"All right, how come you ain't come forward for the money?"

Junior raised a brow. "Because I don't want it."

"Come on man, it's thousands of dollars!"

"Money is the root of all evil, son. More money, more problems. Ask anyone wealthy and they will tell you."

"Well they sure don't look like they have any problems."

"Ahh," Junior said. "But they do. They just have different kinds. Looks are deceiving, Chase. You can't judge a book by its cover. I know many people who are financially wealthy, but spiritually bankrupt."

"Yeah, I bet!"

"Let's move on."

"All right. It was you that saved that diabetic man, wasn't it?"

"Yes."

"How did you know what to do? And you saved that businessman too!" Chase raised his voice as his excitement grew.

"Wait, wait," Junior said. "Slow down." Then he laughed. "Let's just say that I am a good Samaritan, okay?" He stared at the boy. "Are you done?"

"No," Chase quickly replied. "Your name is Junior, right?"

"Yes."

"That's kinda an unusual name. Why do they call you that?"

"Why do they call you Chase? That is an unusual name."

"My father gave it to me!"

"So it is with me. My father—the Heavenly Father—gave me this name." Junior leaned forward slightly and smiled. "You were not expecting that answer, were you?"

Chase looked on impatiently. "Why are you toying with me?"

Junior waved away his question. "You see God is the senior member of this world as we know it. We are all juniors to him. I simply acknowledge that great truth. Thus, I am called Junior. Many of us on this earth are unaware and we do not give him his praise."

"His praise? What do you mean? We do, that is, we do that when we go to church."

Junior chuckled. "But what about after church?" He took in a few deep breaths and slowly let them out. "Philippians 4:13."

Chase stared at the man and realized he wasn't getting anywhere. He decided to try another approach. "So what were you doing just now? I mean when I came in? Were you asleep?"

"I was meditating. I was focused. Directed. I allowed no distractions. It appeared as if I were asleep, but I was not."

"Why do you do that?"

"A wise man named Sri Chinmoy once said, 'I meditate so that my mind cannot complicate my life.' That also applies to me."

"I don't understand that."

With his huge hand he patted the boy's shoulder. "Then try this. Have you heard the expression, 'A mind is a terrible thing to waste'?" His eyes bore into Chase's.

"Yes, but I don't misuse my mind."

"I did not say that you did. Why are you so defensive?"

Chase, embarrassed for his abrupt behavior, sat in a more slumped position than before. "I don't know," he said. "I thought you were talking about me. Guess I'm a little confused."

Junior took in another deep breath. He slowly exhaled it, making a loud noise when he did. "Meditation is the zone between that which is thought of and that which is soon to be." He paused, repeated the words, and added "That is, if you know how to meditate correctly. It is the bridge for you to become happy, joyous and free."

"You mean like not feeling alone?" Chase asked.

"Exactly." Junior nodded.

"Can you—-will you teach me?"

"I cannot teach you anything. I can only help you discover it within yourself."

"Okay—help me discover it. Come on—"

Junior sighed and Chase felt that the man had grown impatient with him.

"All right, all right," Chase said. "I'll chill. Go ahead."

"Tell me and I forget," Junior said. "Teach me that I may remember. Involve me and I learn forever."

"You're playing with me again," Chase said.

"No I am not," Junior answered slowly and deliberately. "Just get involved. The rest will take care of itself."

"See, you are. I don't understand."

Junior stood and stared down at Chase who got up as well. His 6-foot-4-inch frame overshadowed the boy by more than half a foot.

"Wait, please. Just one more question. The D.M. after your name. What does it stand for?"

"I wondered when you would ask. It is an abbreviation for what I am. You see, I am a Dream Merchant."

"A Dream Merchant?" Chase laughed. "See, you're toying with me again. I ain't never heard of such a thing."

Junior sat down again and crossed his legs as before. "Now you want me to explain." Chase stared blankly at Junior. "So it is more than one question that you have asked."

"Yeah, I guess so." Chase sat down in imitation of the man's position.

"A Dream Merchant is the highest level of human service in God's world. It is a physical and mental state that must be achieved before one can completely make the transition to the afterworld."

"The what? The afterworld?"

"Yes, the afterworld—where we go when we die."

"I don't get it," Chase said.

"I did not think you would. I shall say it this way: I am an earth angel—one who has been sent here on a mission. And if I complete this mission successfully, I shall receive angelship in heaven."

"All right, slow down. You're leaving me a mile behind. I mean, so you're saying like there are different stages to this—this thing—this afterworld."

"You are correct."

"If that's true, and you're a Dream Merchant, then what am I?"

"Although it means nothing to you now, you must understand that there are different levels of spiritual development. Before your journey is complete, you will have grown into so much more. To answer your question, at present you are a human doing."

"A human *doing*? A human doing what? What's that about?"

"My own terminology, actually. At present you are a human *doing*, but with dedication and hard work, you shall become a human *being*."

"I thought I was already a human being," Chase said.

"Yes, you are, of course, and no, you are not. You see, in this world, all of us are born human beings. Yet unless we are also deeply rooted in spirituality, our gift is lost. We then fall into the state that I choose to call human doing."

"But I—"

He held up his hand to silence the boy. "Tomorrow, you must observe—watch people. Listen. Be aware of how many people are occupied with doing, doing, doing. You will hear them say, 'I must do this. I must do that!' Do, do, do. People are obsessed with the doing of the journey, not the being of the journey. They have all forgotten how to be."

"Man, this is some deep stuff," Chase said.

"Listen and observe. You will find that most people think that growth in life is acquiring material possessions. It is sad that they are controlled with such an obsession."

"Yeah, I kinda know what you mean."

"Such desires drive us mad," Junior said, "and so do the regrets over yesterday and the fears of tomorrow. Just think of that. Regret and fear are evil elements that rob us of being."

"I don't understand all of that—"

"You will, Chase, you will."

Junior stood up and extended a hand and lifted the boy to his feet as if he weighed nothing. While he still clasped the boy's hand, he said, "My job is to show you the power within yourself. Within you is the dream. The dream world is only a medium by which you will learn. I am here to teach you. I can say only that sometimes I will come to you in your dreams. At other times, I will reach you in person. I do know one thing, however—"

"You do, what's that?"

"I have been given the honor of giving you all that I know." Junior's gaze searched his face, as if he could look inside the boy. "You see, it seems a little ironic, but for me to keep this wisdom, I must give it away. By teaching you, I teach me through reinforcement. That is how things truly work in God's world. I am certain you have heard the saying, 'When I help you, I help myself.'"

Chase nodded.

"The day you are transformed into a human being I shall gain access to new spiritual truths—truths that will make my transition less difficult."

"Your transition?" Chase asked and then he frowned as he realized what that meant. "You mean when you die?"

"If you choose to call it that."

"Then what happens to you?"

"After that, I shall reach guardian angelship."

"And I've gotta say you are totally confusing me, but I want to understand." Chase pulled out a crumpled up piece of paper and a pen from his coat pocket. "Can you, you know, repeat that?"

Junior smiled at Chase's effort to get it all down on a small scrap of paper. But he knew the power that was held in the word. "Chase, I want you to understand there is a divine order. We go from human doing to human being to spiritual being to dream merchant to guardian angel and then to full angelship." Several times he paused, waiting for Chase to write it all down.

"I got it," Chase said finally, and he read the words back to him.

"Yes, you do." He took Chase's hand in his and began to pray, "Dear Lord of Heaven and Earth, protect this young man for he knows not the difficulties of his journey. Preserve me, O God, for in you do I put my trust. Amen."

When he had finished praying, Junior slipped a sheet of paper into Chase's hand, opened the door, and walked the boy back through the house. "Go home now and have no fear as you walk these streets, for the Heavenly Father is protecting you."

Chase, confused and wanting to know more, sensed that this was the end of the lesson for now. He waved and walked back the way he had come. He saw the same neighborhood, the same homeless people, and the same run-down houses. But this time his mind was elsewhere. He felt a new sense of energy.

Suddenly aware of the paper he clutched in his hand, he unfolded it as he walked. He read: "We can do all things through Christ who strengthens us. Philippians 4:13."

Chase walked on absently, recognizing familiar sites as he got closer to his neighborhood. Lost in thoughts about Junior, he was suddenly jarred aware by the honking of a car horn.

An older model Lincoln Continental pulled up. Automatically, Chase tensed up, and then a voice called his name.

"Brick," he said when he recognized the driver.

"A little out of your territory, ain't you, bro?" Brick asked.

"Why do you say that?"

"Come on, man. I'm Brick, remember? I know everything. I know your daddy is a doctor. And trust me, no doctor lives around here."

Chase couldn't figure how Brick knew so much.

"Hop on in," Brick said. "We'll give you a lift."

Only then did Chase realize there were others in the car. One of the boys in the back seat opened the door. Chase knew he was late getting home, so he got in. He was supposed to have come straight home from school.

"Say, fellas," Brick said, "remember that kid that got smoked on the corner a few months ago?"

"Yeah, sure," one of the boys said.

"This is his boy, Chase," Brick said. "He's in that stupid Youth Awareness Class that I have to go to on Saturdays."

"Oh yeah," said another.

The boy in the front passenger seat then turned up the music. Chase could hardly hear Brick talk so he had to lean forward. "Hey, Chase, been doing your reading?" Brick asked and laughed.

"Yeah, doing your homework, little boy?" asked another boy and everyone laughed.

Chase didn't say anything. Chase had started sitting next to Brick at the Saturday Youth Awareness classes. He hadn't wanted to go, but he was glad he'd met Brick. Chase's street connections were limited but Brick knew things about Ernie's death—things he had hinted at but didn't say. He figured that maybe if he could get close to him, Brick would let out what really happened. Now he wasn't so sure.

The boy sitting next to Chase reached into his coat and pulled out what looked like a cigarette. "Hey, man, light this," he said and he handed it to Brick in the front seat. Brick arched his hips up as he drove with one hand and fished a lighter out of his pocket. It was neon yellow, and he tossed it into the lap of the boy in the front seat. The kid lit the cigarette, and Chase realized it wasn't an ordinary cigarette. He also realized this wasn't where he wanted to be.

The smell of dope filled the car.

"Say, Brick, this is far enough," Chase said. "You can let me out here."

"What do you mean, man? We ain't half way there to your place yet."

"Let me out, man," Chase said. "There's something I gotta do."

"Yeah, right, okay." Brick stopped the car.

As Chase opened the door to get out, Brick suddenly pressed the accelerator and laughed. Chase fell on the lap of the other passenger in the back seat. They sped down the street for another half mile, the open back door swinging out like a broken wing.

"Look, man, I want out," Chase said, "I mean it, *let me out!*"

A pedestrian, who carried a stack of newspapers, had almost reached the middle of the street—he was crossing with the Walk light. The Lincoln was almost on him when Brick slammed on his brakes and barely missed the man who jumped, tripped, and fell to the street. He dropped his stack of newspapers and they fluttered all around him.

"Move off the street you idiot!" Brick yelled.

"Yeah, get a life!" yelled the boy next to Chase. "Did you see that dude's face?"

"Yeah, I really shook him up," Brick said and then he laughed.

Chase turned around to look out the back window at the man they had almost hit. Newspapers were scattered everywhere and then to his horror Chase recognized the man on the ground who stared back at him.

It was Junior.

How could that be? he thought. I just left him a few minutes ago at the Center for Conscious Living.

They were nearly half a block away, but he could see Junior now standing and bent over, picking up the papers from the street.

"Brick, let me out! Now!"

"Hey, come on—"

"*Now!*"

Brick pulled over and Chase jumped out of the car and ran back toward the intersection, now two blocks away. He ran faster and faster until he reached the intersection.

Junior was gone.

Instead of seeing a pile of newspapers in the middle of the street, he saw a single copy of *Street Smart*. He picked it up and looked around. How could Junior have disappeared like that? And so quickly. What happened to all of those newspapers?

He started back across the street to throw the newspaper into a trash container. Just then, his eyes fell on the "Words of Wisdom" section.

There he saw the new message. He had no doubts that it was meant for him. The passage said: "Our greatest asset, second only to God, is the company that we keep." It was signed, "Junior D.M."

He wasn't aware of the car that had pulled up close beside him. "What are you doing standing in the middle of the street like that?" It was Judge Dunn.

"Uh, just picking up this newspaper—"

"You could get hurt. Hey, what are you doing in this neighborhood?"

"Just—just walking."

"Get in, boy, I'll take you home." Two blocks further down the street, Judge Dunn came toward an intersection when the siren and lights of an ambulance made him pull over. A small crowd of pedestrians had gathered just ahead, drawn like moths to a patrol car's flashing blue lights.

Chase saw Brick's Lincoln. "Stop," he said.

The judge pulled his car up alongside the crowd.

Brick stood outside his car. The emergency medical technicians were putting some kind of splint on his arm—he was obviously in pain.

The Lincoln had apparently hit a lamp post as well as another car and looked like it had been totaled; the engine was still smoking. Chase didn't see the other boys.

"Ah, that's too bad," Judge Dunn said. "Someone had an accident."

Chase stared and just then Brick looked up. Chase couldn't

hear him, but he could see his lips moving. "I'm all right, man," he said, his dark eyes hollow.

During the rest of the ride, Judge Dunn talked about Ernie, and reminded Chase of the good times the four of them had had.

"You understand, don't you?" Judge Dunn said as he wiped tears from his eyes. "Ernie was all I had."

Chase nodded.

To his surprise, this time Chase found it easy to listen to him talk. He could hear about Ernie now without wanting to cry or to die himself. That must mean I'm better, he thought. Maybe I'm finally putting the pain of Ernie's death behind me.

Judge Dunn pulled into Chase's driveway. "Thanks for listening." He looked up at the soft yellow glow in the window at the front of the house. "Tell your dad that I'd come in, but I've got a meeting, and I'm already running late."

"Okay, Judge," Chase said, but the judge's reason didn't sound very convincing.

seven

Double Vision

"BOY, WHERE HAVE YOU BEEN?" his father angrily shouted. "Are you out of your mind, coming in late like this?"

"Don't you know we've been worried about you?" asked his mother.

As soon as he had walked into the house, his mother and father assumed what he called the parent-posture—they sat stiffly in their chairs, arms folded, and stared straight at him.

Before he could answer, they bombarded him with more questions and didn't wait for answers. They both talked at the same time and each seemed to want to talk louder than the other. Chase found this somewhat amusing and would have laughed, but he knew that it would have only made things worse.

"It's 7:45. Do you see the numbers on that clock?" said his father.

"You know better than to stay out like that," his mother said.

Chase hung his head until the bombardment stopped. He really didn't want to lie, but he knew that he couldn't explain where he had been, especially to his father. Dad seemed to have a low tolerance these days and he doubted he would believe his story anyway. Finally, they stopped and waited for him to speak.

"I'm sorry—"

"Sorry is not good enough, boy!" his father said.

Chase looked at his father. Who was he to talk to him about coming home? He was never there. Chase felt defensiveness rise up within him.

"I stopped by a friend's house. We talked and, uh, you know, before I knew it, it was 7:00. Look, it's not even dark outside—"

"Listen, young man, it's not that 7:45 is late. The issue is that you didn't report home right after school. Your mother and I have been worried sick about you."

"We've been over this before," his mother said in a quieter voice. "If there is no pre-planned activity, you're to come home immediately after school. You know that—right from school!"

"Yeah I know—"

"If your mother doesn't need you," his father said, "then you can hang out or do whatever you want. We just need to know where you are and what you're doing. Got that?"

"Yes sir, but I really wasn't doing anything bad. I know my restrictions. I was only with a friend—"

"Just for that back talk, you're under a week of house arrest."

Chase stared at his father and frowned. That's not fair, he thought. He just hated being a prisoner in his own home. Besides, he wasn't doing anything wrong.

"You hear me, boy?"

"Yes, I hear you." Chase walked over to the recliner and sat down. In an attempt to lighten the air, he looked at them both, hesitated, smiled and asked, "How about a work-release program instead?"

His mom walked over to the bottom of the staircase and pointed upstairs to his room. "For that smart remark, it's now two weeks."

"He's playing with us. He thinks this is funny," Dad said. "Chase, go to your room."

"No sense of humor," Chase mumbled under his breath.

"What?" asked his father angrily.

"Nothing."

By 9:15, Chase had finished his homework and decided to watch television. He was hungry, but he wasn't going to go downstairs and ask for food. He'd just go without it. He'd show them he wasn't going to beg for anything. He also decided that he wouldn't talk to them either, at least not for a while. Chase knew that he wasn't being reasonable, but he was angry at two weeks of house arrest when he felt he really hadn't done anything wrong.

A gentle tap on his door startled him. "Yeah?"

His mom opened the door and the aroma of macaroni and cheese followed her into the room. It was one of his favorite meals. He smiled at her. Mom had the neatest way of orchestrating a truce while still implementing the punishment.

Despite his resolve not to talk to her for weeks, he looked up and said, "Thanks, Mom."

She bent down and kissed him on the cheek, and quietly left the room.

Chase was hungrier than he thought. He gobbled down his food and then lay on his bed. "This situation sucks!" he said, "Two weeks of house arrest. I can't believe it."

He got off the bed and picked up his backpack, flipped through it looking for something to do. Then his eyes fell on the newest assignment from his Youth Awareness Class. He hadn't finished it.

"Aw, man, I almost forgot about this." He pulled the article out of the bag and scanned it. Although Brick and the others had laughed at him earlier, he knew he needed to read it. He didn't want to get caught unprepared for the class.

No boot camp for me, he thought as he began to scan the article. He once again concentrated on the highlighted sections. As he skimmed it, he noticed the following:

- 80% of high school tenth graders have tried alcohol.
- 20% of twelfth graders smoke cigarettes on a regular basis.
- One out of three high school seniors has smoked marijuana, with the sixth grade being the time of initial use for most students.

Then his eyes fell on the last statistic. He was astonished because this one he didn't know:

- High school students in the south typically have the lowest incidence of drug use. This has been found to be due to a higher proportion of African-American students who report lower use for most substances than any other ethnic group.

He'd never heard that before. Then he thought about how the media always seemed to misrepresent that fact. He wondered why.

He finished reading the rest of the article and then skimmed it again. Soon he began to feel tired, so he got ready for bed.

....

He is back in the now familiar dream. He looks around and slowly recognizes where he is—in front of the Center for Conscious Living. He sees a three-foot-high sign, painted in red letters, that he had not seen when he visited before. It hangs over the door and the bold letters read:

HOMELESSNESS IS A STATE OF MIND.

What do they mean by that? he asks himself. Then he remembers what the African chief had said, "Don't be alarmed by what you see." While he stares at the sign, Chase senses there is something new for him to learn. The words on the sign excite him as much as they puzzle him. How can being homeless be a state of mind? He wonders what the people who live on the streets think of that.

Chase sighs and moves on. Just as before, he walks into the house. He sees the gray-haired Miss Ledd. She sits at a table writing a letter. When he comes inside, she pauses, looks up at him, and says, "You don't look frightened today. Good. So you are teachable."

Chase smiles and heads for the door to the hallway.

"Strive to remain teachable," she says. "You can never be too old or too young, too rich or too poor, too healthy or too sick, too wise or too ignorant to learn a lesson."

Then she turns back to writing her letter, as if she hasn't seen him.

"Thank you," he says.

Chase opens the door and goes down the hallway to the room where he had met Junior before. And just as it had been the previous time, Junior sits in the meditation position. Chase tiptoes in and sits directly across from him. This time, although he doesn't know exactly how to do it, he decides to close his eyes and give meditation another try.

He tries not to force it, tries to allow his mind to do whatever it wants. It surprises him that, for perhaps a minute at a time, he is able to lose awareness of the world around him. Outside noises, however, keep pulling him back. He readjusts his position, and becomes aware of a woman in the next room. He can hear a variety of muffled sounds; most of them sound like sobs.

What's wrong with her, he wonders.

As if he has spoken the question aloud, Junior says, "How soon you forget the lessons you have learned."

Chase opens his eyes.

Despite the rebuke, Junior's face is kind.

"I don't understand what you mean," Chase says.

"Have you already forgotten the gift of the struggle?"

He shakes his head slowly.

"Good. Then you can allow her to be in her own space. Nothing in God's world happens by mistake. She is exactly where she needs to be today. Grant her that. Her situation will change. For change is the only constant in this world. Her moments of pain will soon pass. In time, greater clarity will come to you. Then and only then, will you know when to respond."

Chase doesn't understand, but he chooses to accept what Junior has said. Someday I'll get it, he thinks.

The boy and the man sit for a long time in silence. Chase has no idea how long this goes on, but it feels as if twenty minutes has gone by.

"Open your eyes," Junior says.

Chase does, but Junior's eyes are still closed.

"Your eyes are not open until your mind is open," Junior says in a whisper so soft that the boy has to lean forward to catch the words. "Do you understand?"

Chase ponders the statement several seconds before he says, "No, I don't think so."

"That is fine. I did not expect you to." Junior opens his eyes and smiles. "It is better to be ignorant of the truth, than to know the truth and ignore it."

"I get that!"

"Good." Junior pauses and takes a deep breath through his nose. He holds it for a few seconds and then slowly releases it through his mouth. "Your mind is either your greatest limitation or your roadway to infinite possibilities. To make the transition from human doing to human being, you must transform your mind into a reservoir of positive thoughts. Out of that reservoir, meaningful answers occur which then yield positive results. You know, one of my professors once said—"

"Your professor? Did you go to college?"

Junior ignores the interruption. "You see what you look for and you recognize what you know. That is what my professor used to say."

Chase stares at him as he thinks about that. He starts to ask another question, but Junior shakes his head.

"Never assume that the obvious is true in what you see. Also, never assume that what you hear is reality without understanding the heart from which those words come. To do so requires a unique intuition; an intuition that has its foundation and understanding in your own heart. Understanding what is in the heart of others first requires that you understand what is in your own heart."

He pauses to allow Chase time to grasp what he has said. "Do you understand what I mean?"

"You mean that if I know myself, I can begin to understand other people better?"

"Yes, in a way. You see, your own internal clarity reveals the true intent of others, and therefore gives feeling and understanding to their words. This is a difficult concept to use in daily life, but it is the quintessential step of your transformation from human doing to human being. It is called the principle of Double Vision."

"Double Vision? Okay, you've lost me again."

"You will get it. Double Vision is a very difficult concept to grasp. It forces you to take notice of a person's character—not the person who is a character. It requires a second look at every situation and teaches you to incorporate both the heart and the words of the person you interact with. For example, did you get in trouble when you arrived home last night?"

"How did you know that?"

When Junior doesn't answer, the boy says, "Yeah, I sure did." He explains what happened.

"What does that situation mean to you?"

"I guess that my parents were angry because I broke a rule of the house, so they punished me."

"On the contrary, they were showing you love," Junior says.

"Love? By yelling at me? by grounding me?"

"You did not see with Double Vision." He pauses and stares deeply into Chase's eyes. "The principles of Double Vision that link the eyes, ears and heart with the open mind will reveal that what took place there was parental love in action."

"Some love!" Chase replies. "Grounded for two weeks for just a little thing like that."

Junior takes in another deep breath, then closes his eyes. He releases the air even slower this time. "Do you know the story of Sarah Smith?"

Confused by the abrupt change of the subject, Chase answers, "No."

"Well, let me tell you. Two years ago, when Sarah was fifteen years old, she was taken from this world in a tragic way. I interject here to tell you that she is doing very well now as an angel in God's world. She will soon get her wings."

"Get her what?"

"Wings," Junior says. "I will explain."

Chase shifts his position on the floor. "I hope so."

"Before she left this world, she did a very unusual thing. Can you guess what it was?"

Chase shakes his head. "I have no idea."

"Sarah was abducted on the way home from school. They found her clothing in a dumpster, but her body was never recovered. Unfortunately, I must tell you that she is dead. But before she died, she asked God to help her parents deal with their loss of her. That simple, unselfish request planted a seed of goodness on this earth that propelled Sarah from the state of a human doing to a guardian angel in a matter of minutes. Her transition was one of the fastest ever noted. In her brief Dream Merchant state, she planted a solid foundation for her parents during their times of pain."

"Really? I mean, how? What happened?"

"They have since learned constructive ways to channel their energy. Because of Sarah, they founded an organization called PIA, which stands for Parents In Action. It is a support group for parents who lose children by means of violence. The support group that started in their home has grown to international proportions. Through helping others, Sarah's parents have been helping themselves. They have gained something positive out of the loss of their daughter. But what I want you to grasp is that Sarah's single gesture elevated her to guardian angelship."

"Man, what an unusual thing for her to do."

"Yes it was," says Junior. "Now, your mother read about Sarah's story in the newspaper two years ago. Do you remember how upset she was about the girl's death?"

"Sort of. I mean, I remember that she talked about some girl who had disappeared in broad daylight who lived about four blocks from us. I guess that was the same one."

"Yes, that is the one. Now if you think back, it was about that time that the rule came into effect in your home."

"You mean to come home directly after school?" asks Chase. "I can't remember exactly, but, yeah, I guess, that's about right. I was thirteen then, so yeah, it must have been."

"Think about last night again and their words to you. What you perceived as anger was really their deep concern for you and the fear that something like that might have happened to you."

"Why didn't they just say so?"

"They are parents and they are human. Sometimes they just do not explain their fears or concerns. But I assure you, it was love in disguise. Two years ago, they added the rule to protect you. The house arrest was instituted to teach you to honor the rules. That decision to ground you is love in action. The principle of Double

Vision would have allowed you to understand what they did instead of becoming angry and resentful."

"Yeah, maybe, but they yelled at me—"

"Don't try to justify yourself! The principle of Double Vision sometimes calls for patience until more of the situation is revealed. This principle takes a long time to learn. It will require all that you have learned thus far and much more. As you move toward integrating this principle, you will make mistakes. At times, you will rush to judgment. For now, that is acceptable. It is part of the process. Learn from your errors and continue to search for answers." Junior pauses and stretches his body as if he is yawning.

"Okay, I'll try."

"So far, you have learned the significance of the belief in a power greater than yourself, the value of patience, the gift of the struggle, and now you are beginning to learn the principle of Double Vision."

"But Junior, it seems like—well, I'm not sure that I'm learning anything. I mean, not really."

Junior nods. "But you are learning. Again, be patient. As you incorporate these principles into your belief system, you will learn how to look into others' eyes, hear their words, feel their sadness and yes, share in their joy."

"All right, if you say so," Chase says reluctantly, as if he is beginning to doubt what Junior is saying. At the same time, he thinks, I can't believe all of this stuff is coming from a homeless man.

"Homeless? Where is this homeless stuff coming from?" Junior asks.

"You read—you read my thoughts?"

"No, I read your face."

"I'm sorry, I didn't mean to—"

"Don't lie to protect yourself. Dishonesty has no place here. Speak the truth, even if you think I will not like it. Are you with me?"

"Yes."

"Okay. Now, what does the word homeless mean to you? Do you mean, he was home less than he should have been? If so, I agree. In fact, if you think about it, most people today, black and white, rich and poor, should be home more instead of home less."

Chase snickers at Junior's play on words.

"But, my little friend, if you mean homeless in that I have no home, then you are very wrong. You see, homelessness is a state of mind."

"Like the sign on the door," Chase says. "I knew there was more to it."

"Yes, you are right. Everyone on this planet has a home—the earth. Our heavenly father provided the earth as a place for us to dwell and learn spiritual principles. I may not own a house, but I have a home. The ground beneath me is my hardwood floor; the trees around me are my walls; the clouds and the stars above are my roof; and the wind that surrounds me is my air conditioning—" Junior pauses and smiles. He seems to be having fun with the boy.

"I hadn't thought of it like that—"

"So never, never say that word to me again. I do not consider myself to be homeless, do you understand?"

"Yeah, I understand."

"Good." He pats Chase on the shoulder. "You must go. When you wake up, you will be just in time to eat your mom's cheese eggs."

"But I'd like to ask you about—"

"No more questions, you must go. I leave you with the Word of God. A prophet of old named Isaiah spoke these words to the people: 'I have called you by name. You are mine. You are precious in my sight and I love you.'" He looks deeply into the boy's eyes. "Remember that." He takes his hands off the boy's shoulders. "Have a great day, son."

....

The smell wafted upstairs from the kitchen. The combined aroma of cheese and eggs floated into Chase's bedroom. He opened his eyes and lay there. "Love that smell," he said to himself.

Once showered and dressed, Chase hurried downstairs. His mother had already set his plate. She smiled and said, "I hope you like these."

"I always like your cooking, Mom."

As he gazed into his mother's face, he felt a warmth spread inside himself. He realized how much he loved her, and how he appreciated her cooking a special breakfast for him.

Just then, a moment of insight struck him: Junior's teachings were getting through. Things were becoming clearer to him.

He was still under house arrest, but as he stared deeper into his mother's eyes, he saw nothing but love.

He had begun to develop Double Vision.

eight

Word Perfect

ON HIS WAY TO SCHOOL, Chase rummaged through his gym bag to find a new CD for his Walkman. His mind stayed mostly on his dream and the words of Junior. As he approached Savannah's house, he slowed his pace, hoping that she would run out and join him.

Of all the girls that he knew in his neighborhood, Savannah was the one he thought about the most. Funny, but a few years ago he would have considered her too skinny and too silly, but not now. She had changed, and he felt undeniably attracted to her.

When did all of this happen? he asked himself. He didn't know and didn't care. Right now, he just wanted to be with her, to touch her, to know what it felt like to call her his own.

"Hey, you! Get up from there!"

Chase looked up to see a crowd of people gathered at the corner. A policeman stood over a man on the ground. "Get up!" Seven or eight school kids surrounded them.

Chase moved in closer.

"Listen, buddy, you need to find another neighborhood to pollute," said the policeman.

A second policeman knelt on the ground and was trying to arouse the man. When he pulled back his hands, they were stained with blood. "Come on, fella!" he said with new urgency. "Speak to me."

"What's going on?" Chase asked one of the kids.

"They found this guy unconscious. Blood coming out of his head. I got here just a second or two before the cops showed up."

"I think the man on the ground hit his head," said another kid. He pointed to the bench at the bus stop. "I think he was sleeping over there and fell off."

"Sleeping?" said another kid sarcastically. "Yeah, real heavy-duty sleeping, all right. What's the matter with you, can't you smell the booze?"

Just then, Chase became aware of the heavy odor of wine. He looked closer but he couldn't see the man's face because of the crowd. He could see that his tattered sports jacket and pants were stained. The man was lying on his back, his gangly arms and legs making him look like a fallen puppet. Next to his body, Chase could clearly see a quart-sized bottle inside of a brown paper bag. The neck of the bottle stuck out. He recognized it as Turkey Wine—the cheapest kind you could buy in the neighborhood.

"Come on, big guy! Can you hear me?" the policeman asked.

The man raised his hand and waved it as if trying to say yes.

Chase stared in disbelief. There was no mistaking that large hand with the long fingers. He stepped closer. "Junior, is that you? You're not drunk. No way!"

Chase brushed past three onlookers and yelled at the policeman. "Why don't you just leave him alone? He's hurt! Can't you see the blood?"

"He's also drunk!"

"No, he's not," Chase said. "He's my friend, so leave him alone!"

He knelt beside Junior and clasped his hand. Then he placed both of his arms around his friend's upper body. He pressed his head hard against Junior's chest as he struggled to lift him. Then it happened again. As he heard the pounding of Junior's heart, he was instantly back in the dream—the nightmare—listening to the beating of Ernie's heart on the street corner that night. It was as vivid as ever. Chase saw himself as he held Ernie tightly while bullets flew overhead. With sweat pouring down his face, he cried out to his friend.

"Don't die, man! Don't die!"

The kids at the bus stop looked on in disbelief.

"What's he talking about?" one said.

"Man, he's freakin' out," said another.

Chase cradled Junior's head and shoulders; all the while he whispered words of encouragement. As he envisioned himself holding Ernie close, he relived the moment when Ernie's heart stopped.

"Look up!" he heard Ernie say. A car blew its horn as it passed by the bus stop. The noise snapped Chase out of his trance. He felt a hand on his shoulder, and as he looked up, he stared in the face of one of the policemen.

"It's okay, kid, he's not going to die."

As Chase forced himself back to the present, a familiar sound hit his ears. It was a loud car muffler. It was unmistakable. He knew that car. It was the same car from which the bullets had come that night when he lost his best friend.

Chase stood up and faced the street, but by then the car had gone. Everyone was staring at him. He dropped to his knees again beside his friend.

Junior's eyes fluttered open and he smiled.

"Junior, are you all right?"

He brushed Chase's words aside. "Help me," he whispered. He reached out for Chase's hand and used it to pull himself from the ground.

Junior released the boy's hand, took two or three steps forward, stumbled, and fell. As he did so, he involuntarily grabbed the leg of one of the policeman. Startled, and thinking that he was being attacked, the policeman swirled around and knocked Junior backward with a body kick. Junior fell to the ground, striking the back of his head on the pavement. The wound opened up even more. Blood stained the sidewalk.

"No, stop! He wasn't trying to hurt you!" Chase screamed.

Junior struggled and got on his knees. His eyes focused first on Chase, then the policeman, and finally on the crowd. He lifted his hands in front of his face, palms together, and began to pray, "Dear Lord, I admit before you that I am powerless today. I turn my will and life over to you. Grant me the serenity to accept the things I cannot change. Give me the courage to change the things that I can. And most of all, reveal to me the wisdom to know the difference."

A silence descended on the entire crowd. Several of them stepped closer.

With his palms still together and his eyes closed, Junior said, "Grant that these people be not conformed to this world, but that instead they be transformed by the renewing of their minds so that they might find all that is good, all that is acceptable, and all that is the will of God."

"He's praying," someone whispered.

"Yeah, and he's praying for us," said another voice.

"Check that out!" yelled another one of the kids.

Junior paused and stared at the crowd. "I ask of you, through the grace so humbly given to me, that all of you here think not more highly of yourself than you do of your fellow humans and that you think seriously in accordance with the mind of God, the Almighty."

The policeman, caught off guard, stepped backward.

A blanket of silence had been thrown over them; no one spoke.

Chase saw the deep cut on his friend's head. "Man, you're really hurt." He took the two large hands in his own. "What happened?"

"Life is like a card game," Junior said. "God is the dealer and the stake is your soul. You must play the hand you are dealt. That is all anyone can do. Last night, I played my hand poorly. I did not know my enemy. More important, I have embarrassed you, and I am sorry. Please forgive me."

"Don't worry about that, let me——"

"I am not drunk," Junior said softly, as if the idea had just occurred to him. He looked up at the crowd and then back at Chase. "I am not drunk. I was attacked here by someone who was. That bottle of wine belongs to the man who assaulted me. It broke during our struggle."

Every eye stared at the brown paper sack.

The policeman examined the sack. "Guess that's right. There are strands of hair and blood stains on the package." He turned to Junior, cocked his head as if he were looking at him from another angle. "Sorry, man. We thought you were drunk."

"I understand." Junior touched the back of his head. When he pulled back his hand, the fingers were moist from his own blood. He used his other hand to help himself stand.

"Let me help you," said one of the policeman as he got on the other side of Chase. From the expression on his face and the softness of his voice, he obviously felt bad about the way they had treated Junior.

Together, Chase and the policeman slowly lifted Junior to his feet. They held him steady for several seconds. The other policeman asked the crowd to disperse, which they did.

"Thank you," Junior said to the two policemen.

He stuck his hands into his pockets and pulled out a folded

piece of paper with each hand. He handed one to each of them.

"What's this?" one of them asked.

Chase looked on, smiling because he knew.

"Read it," Junior said.

The policeman's eyes fell on the paper and he read aloud, "Once life—the chess game—is over, both the kings and the pawns always go back into the same box." He stared at the paper in confusion.

"Now you," Junior said to the other policeman.

"You are no better or no worse than those you associate with," he read. He looked at the other policeman, then back at Junior. "Wait a minute. You're the guy everybody's looking for aren't you?"

"Yeah—Junior!" said the other policeman. "Why don't you collect the money?"

Chase saw Junior's face fall. These police were more interested in their discovery of the mystery man than they were in the message he wanted to deliver to them.

"All I want is to be left alone. Is that too much to ask?"

"All right, man," said one of the officers. "If that's the way you want it. But I don't understand."

"Maybe it's not for you to understand," Junior replied.

"Yeah, maybe so."

Chase had been closely watching what was going on around him. Now in the awkward silence, he took a towel from his gym bag and held it against Junior's head. "You want a doctor?" he asked.

"No."

When Chase looked up, the two policeman were getting into their patrol car. Tenderly, he helped the large man walk over to the bench by the bus stop.

"Ready for the next lesson?" Junior asked.

"You're hurt and you want to teach me? I don't know, I have to get to school. If I don't, I'll be late."

Junior momentarily leaned on the bench as if he received strength from it. Then he let go and started to walk. "I'll go with you." With his right hand, he kept Chase's towel pressed against the back of his head.

As they headed toward the school, Chase thought they must look strange together. From the corner of his eye, Chase realized people were staring. To take his own mind off the people, he said, "Hey, Junior! That prayer. What did it mean?"

"It is my interpretation of Romans 12:2. When you get home, you can read it for yourself."

Chase remained silent as he walked.

"Do you remember the other verse that I gave you?" asked Junior.

"Yeah, Philippians something. 'I can do all things through Christ who strengthens me.'"

"Yes, that is correct. Philippians 4:13. I see I am going to have to stay on my toes with you."

"And, uh, the notes you gave the policemen. What did they mean?"

"There is nothing like a good reality check for some people."

Chase laughed. "Yeah, guess so. And that prayer. I mean, it blew them away."

"Prayer always works in times of need, particularly when there is a crowd. It taps into the spiritual side of everyone present whether or not they are aware."

As Chase stared at him, he realized Junior's voice had grown stronger. He walked straighter and taller.

"In prayer, their spiritual energy then becomes a part of the process and miracles occur. The key is having the humility and courage to pray on your knees before others." Junior folded the towel and flipped it into a trash can. "That is a real test of your belief—being willing to get on your knees."

They were half a block from the school building; Chase realized Junior was going to leave him, so he said, "Just one more thing. The story about Sarah Smith really got to me. But you know, I don't understand the part about how she transformed so quickly. Can you explain that?"

"Sure, spiritual transformation is a dynamic process, but there is a flow of energy that sometimes gets trapped at certain levels. In most instances, however, the rate of transition depends on the quality of the life lived or the act in which the person is taken." He looked at Chase and smiled. "Yes, I know I am using heavy words, but you are smart enough to follow."

Chase nodded.

"One more thing. You see, in Sarah's case, as she faced terror head-on, she thought not of herself, but of her parents' grief. In God's eyes, that lack of self-centeredness at a time when it was certainly warranted, propelled her through her transition. Self-sacrifice for the good of others is the greatest gift on this earth. Sarah exhibited that quality in a most gracious way."

"Yeah, I'm with you there."

"Okay, I want to be certain. Another example is that of Dr. Martin Luther King, Jr. Because of the dedication to his work, and his mission to elevate the consciousness of all humanity, his transition was also a rapid one. His work was so powerful that he was allowed to visualize his transformation before it occurred."

"Really, how's that?"

"In April of 1968, Dr. King journeyed to Memphis, Tennessee, to come to the aid of people of all colors involved in a garbage strike. He was a man who dedicated his life to civil rights. Because of his long record of enormous self-sacrifice for others, God allowed Dr. King to peek at the promised land—the place where we all go when God sends for us. At Memphis, in his speech called, 'I've Seen the Promised Land,' he told about his vision. It was one of his most powerful and eloquent deliveries." From an inside pocket, Junior pulled out an old newspaper enclosed in plastic. He took out the article, unfolded the paper and began to read it aloud.

Chase listened and something strange happened—something he didn't understand then and was unable to explain later. As Junior read, his voice changed. It was no longer his voice, but that of Martin Luther King, Jr. himself. Chase had heard that voice in recordings many times.

"And then I got into Memphis. And some began to say the threats, or talk about the threats that were out. What would happen to me from some of our sick white brothers?

"Well, I don't know what will happen now. We've got some difficult days ahead. But it doesn't matter with me now. Because I've been to the mountaintop. And I don't mind. Like anybody, I would like to live a long life. Longevity has its place. But I'm not concerned about that now. I just want to do God's will. And He's allowed me to go up to the mountain. And I've looked over. And I've seen the promised land. I may not get there with you. But I want you to know tonight, that we, as a people will get to the promised land. And I'm happy, tonight. I'm not worried about anything. I'm not fearing any man. Mine eyes have seen the glory of the coming of the Lord."

Junior stopped reading, carefully folded the newspaper clipping and reinserted it inside the plastic. "The next day—the very next day—Dr. King made his transition through the hands of an assassin. You see, once the promised land is seen, all the answers become clear and the transition must take place. His life's work was so powerful that God gave him a peek. Even today if you listen to his speeches, you can hear it in his voice. That was one of the finest gifts that God can give any person—a peek at the promised land. I share this story to point out that the process of the transition has no definition. Anyway, you must go now." He pointed to the school. "That is where you belong now."

"All right, later," Chase said.

"Oh, wait a second." Junior then reached into his pocket

again and pulled out a sheet of paper that contained a list of words. "Study these words. When you have finished, I will come to you."

"Finished? I don't know what you—"

"When you have unlocked their meaning, I will come to you."

Chase stared at the words. All of them were simple, everyday words, and he shrugged. "What's the big deal?" He looked up at Junior.

"What's the big deal? The big deal is the words. Words are one of the most important forms of communication today. The better you understand them, the more effective a communicator you become. This is simply an exercise to demonstrate the power of words."

From the paper, Chase read the words: "Understand, live, power, history, dog, disease, momentum, awareness." He looked up and said, "All right, but I don't really get it." He tucked the list inside his shirt pocket and hurried to class.

The day went fast, but Chase was especially interested in his second-period class, Physics, that Mr. Seymour also taught. As far as Chase was concerned, Mr. Seymour could make the most boring topics seem interesting. Today's lesson was an introduction to Newton's Laws.

"Newton's first law is the law of inertia," the teacher explained. "It states that a body at rest remains at rest, and a body in motion remains in motion unless acted upon by an outside force. The second law states that the total force acting on a body is equal to the mass of the body times its acceleration."

Newton's third law, which Chase found the most interesting, stated that for every action there is an equal and opposite reaction.

After school, Chase slowly walked home, although he no longer feeling like a prisoner. He might have moved faster, except that he kept turning and looking, hoping to see Junior. He also looked back at the school several times, wishing that Savannah would come out and walk home with him.

Savannah was such a nice name. And sweet. Yeah, he thought, Sweet Savy.

Lost in thoughts that moved from Junior back to Sweet Savy, Chase looked up and realized he had reached his house. As soon as he entered, Mom greeted him with a kiss. To her question about whether he wanted a snack, he called over his shoulder, "No, got some things to do. Homework."

His homework was the list of eight words Junior had given him. He pulled out his dictionary and began to look up the words and wrote down the definitions. He made notes that looked like this:

Live: to have life.

Power: an ability or faculty, physical strength, control.

History: a record of past events.

Dog: a common quadruped of many breeds.

Disease: an unhealthy condition.

Momentum: a measure of the quality of motion, a product of the mass and the velocity, the force built up by a moving body.

Awareness: consciousness, to be informed.

Inadvertently, Chase hadn't noticed the first word, *understand*, so he didn't write it down or look up the definition.

Chase stared at the list, repeated the definitions, and shook his head. He understood each word, but together they didn't make any sense. How were the words connected? "Think of this as a puzzle," he said to himself. "Junior's really into puzzles and riddles."

He rearranged the words in columns, side by side, and tried combining them. Nothing fit.

Wearily, he went downstairs at dinner time. As he started down, the aroma of fried chicken filled his nostrils. He detected also the more subtle scent of collard greens. It was going to be a great meal, and he knew Mom's mashed potatoes with her special red-eye gravy would be the best ever.

He hugged his mother. "Thanks," he said and went toward his chair. "Where's Dad?"

"He's not eating with us tonight. Let's start without him." Without waiting for his reaction, she took his hands in hers and prayed a simple blessing for the food.

Chase thought little of his father's absence at first. He was used to having his dad walk in after the meal started. Once in awhile—especially lately—he and his mother finished before Dad came home.

They ate in silence. As he took his final bite of collards, he looked up, ready to thank his mother again. He saw a pained look on her face as she stared out the window.

"Mom, what's the matter? Did I do something wrong?"

"Oh, no, nothing," she said and attempted to smile. "I have a slight headache. Just finish your dinner."

Chase thought about the call mom received from the doctor. He knew she was on medication and he was worried. He took two bites of mashed potatoes and gravy and said, "You sure it's, you know, just a headache?"

His mother didn't answer for several seconds, but stared at her plate. She hadn't eaten very much. Then she began to talk in a low voice, as though she wasn't really aware of her son's presence. "I'm not very happy these days, and it's nothing that you've done. I think it's just me." She sipped her iced tea before she said, "I'm proud of you, and I have a lot to be thankful for. But I can't seem to shake this—this feeling."

"What feeling?"

"Well, the truth is, I am a little depressed. But that's not all. Sounds strange to talk about, but I've been having dreams...the kind of dreams that stay with me, and fill my thoughts throughout the day. And they're, well, they're dreams about your father mostly."

111

"Really?" Chase tried not to sound too eager. "What kind of dreams?"

"I'm not sure...I'm not sure I should be saying all this, but..."

"Come on, Mom. I wish you would stop treating me like a kid."

His mother stared at him and then nodded. "Yes, you have grown up quite a lot."

"So tell me."

"They're dreams about your father's faithfulness, his love for me. At times, I doubt his love. Then I pressure him to show it, but that only seems to push him away." A troubled expression spread across her face. "I'm also worried about him—really worried. I don't know where he is a lot of the time. I don't know when or whether he's coming home." She paused and stared at her son. "I'm sorry for saying these things—"

"Why would you be worried about things like that?"

She dropped her fork on the plate and pounded her fist. "Why? I'll tell you why!" She spoke with a force Chase had never heard before. "Your father didn't come home last night. That's why. And it wasn't the first time." She dropped her head into her hands and started to cry.

For a moment Chase was completely stunned. He had never seen his mother's mood so volatile before, her reaction so unpredictable. He reached timidly across the table and touched her hand. He waited. Then he got up, went to her, and hugged her. Instead of trying to think of a lot of words of comfort, he remained quiet.

His mother hugged him and more tears flowed.

As he held her, Chase realized it wasn't his problem to solve. What could he do? It was an issue between his parents and beyond his control. Although he hurt inside, he sensed he was doing the right thing by holding her and allowing her to talk. Double Vision was really beginning to make sense.

But what's going on with Dad? he asked himself.

"Thank you for being here and for listening," she said and

pulled herself free. She went into the other room for tissues to blow her nose and to wipe her eyes. "You're a good son. You're really growing up. You know that?"

After she had calmed down, Chase went back upstairs to his room. He lay on his bed and looked at the list of words again. He repeated each of them, trying to make sense by spelling them backward. He couldn't figure any way to make a sentence out of them. Nothing helped.

Sometime in the middle of the night, Chase heard a banging downstairs and his father's voice. He couldn't catch the words, but he heard the angry tone.

He went to his door and cracked it half an inch. He could hear his mother trying to quiet Dad, but she couldn't.

Then he heard Mom scream at Dad in a way she'd never done before. Now he could hear their words clearly. "If you don't stop this, our marriage is over. I've been quiet long enough!"

"What do you mean?"

"I mean, we are leaving you, and yes, I will go to the authorities."

"Don't threaten me!" said his father.

"No threat, baby. This is definitely it. I mean it!" Chase could hear his mother start upstairs. He closed the door. He heard another set of feet pounding up the stairs, and the bedroom door slammed. A moment of silence, and then his father's voice exploded from the darkness. He couldn't remember ever hearing such anger from him before.

After a while, their voices lowered. Chase lay on his bed, frightened about what was happening to his family. It was 2 a.m. He closed his eyes tight against it, but the blood kept beating behind his lids.

Chase is sitting in front of Junior at the Center for Conscious Living.

As they face each other in silence, he realizes how comfortable sitting in meditative silence has become. For several minutes at a time he is able to block out his own thoughts and empty himself to the inner space. He doesn't yet have words to describe it, but he knows he is at peace.

"It is good to see you," Junior's voice says softly. "Have you done your work?"

"I tried, but I couldn't figure it out." He drops his head, feels his sense of failure keenly.

"No, no, son. I did not expect you to solve the puzzle."

"You didn't?"

"It is the effort that counts," Junior says. "Did you look up understand?"

Chase knows the surprise on his face answers for him. "Okay, I forgot that word. How did you know?"

"Sometimes I do not know how I know. I just do. Now, if you had looked up *understand* you would have seen that it means simply 'to seize the meaning of, to be thoroughly acquainted with, to be expert in the use or practice of.' Do you think you understand?"

Chase nods.

"I want you to learn a concept that I call Word Perfect. It will unlock the mystery for you and show you how to dissect words in a different way. You will learn the hidden essence behind their meaning." He takes a deep breath and exhales. "For example, understand is actually two words, under and stand. At its root, it means to stand under." He pauses and smiles when he realizes Chase is listening closely.

"Word Perfect teaches us to transform words into their roots and visualize their meanings. It gives words more clarity. To stand under is to provide support. Thus, in order to truly understand someone or something, you must—based on your own experiences—support the person or concept. Through the centuries, many words such as understand have lost their true meanings and become diluted. When you hear or intend to use that word again, remember its root meaning. Use it only if it is applicable. If you have not lived through or felt another person's experience, then you cannot truly understand. Believe it or not, when you listen, you can detect such experiences. In your subconscious you grasp what the other undergoes. If you truly do not understand, the feelings that you intend to transmit get lost. The communication between you becomes diluted. Subconsciously, without either of you being aware, a weaker bond is formed."

"I'm not sure I get that."

"All right, try this. If you want to strengthen the bond between you and someone else, you would simply speak the truth. That is, you would voice a similar experience of your own or you would say, 'I don't really understand because I haven't had that experience.' Even so, you can empathize." He pauses and studies the boy's face. "Now, do you understand?"

"I hope to."

"You have given me a true answer."

"It just seems too much for me—"

"You will learn. Now, to *live* is what your higher power intended for you to do—to have life—to be, not just to do. In Word Perfect, if you spell live backward, you get the word evil. In many ways in God's world, evil is the opposite of the good life. When we do not live our lives to the fullest as God intended, evil ensues. Often, evil is simply internal unhappiness with life. Evil persists in the heart long before it is acted on in the real world. Unhappiness with life also easily occurs when we begin to fear life, or when we begin to walk through life with caution. You see, Chase, God wants us to live life large, to stamp out evil, and not just to skate cautiously on thin ice. Instead, dance on it. God wants you to rock and roll! Do you know what I mean?" He laughs and his whole body shakes.

"Yeah, I'm beginning to see," Chase says and joins him in the laughter. "Each of the words is a puzzle for me to play with and find the hidden meaning. Right?"

Junior nods.

"Okay, what about power?"

"Slow down. I will get to all of them soon enough. First, take the word history. It is made up of two words—"

"Yeah, I can see that. His and story. Right?"

"That is totally correct. By definition, history is a record of past events of humanity. History is composed not of humanity, but of individuals. Every individual has a story. You have your story; I have mine. What we fail to remember, or what has been lost is the recognition that the same hands that have written history—God's hands, of course—are the same hands that have written your story and mine. Therefore, we are history."

"I see that but—" Chase scratches his head. "But, well, I don't get the importance of what you mean."

"It means that what you do and what I do are important in this world. If you generate one spark of happiness within you, it affects another person. That in turn, affects another and so on. It all starts with you. None of the people in your history books at school knew they were making history when they did what they did. That was for God to decide. History is His will. If you make your will God's will, then your life will be a part of history."

"Man, that's deep stuff. I never heard anything like that before. Keep going."

Junior laughs. "Enough for now. I have started you on unfolding your puzzle. Study the other words I have given you, and we will discuss them another time."

"Ah man, you always get me going, then cut me off."

"No back talk. Take the cotton out of your ears and put it in your mouth."

Chase smiles because he realizes that Junior wants him to stop talking and listen. He sits quietly, waits for him to speak again.

Junior closes his eyes, lifts his hands to his chest and places his palms facing each other. "May God's love shine through you. Remember, it is the father of the children that shall make thy truth known." He pauses and adds, "That is from Isaiah 38:19."

....

Chase lay on his back in bed. One arm had arced over his head, like a swimmer's stroke, and had come to rest against the wall. Chase's father stood in the doorway of his room, and watched him sleep, his face smooth chestnut where the warm light of the hallway fell on him.

He stood there a long time.

nine

The Five P's

SINCE DAWN, HE HAD BEEN sitting beside Chase's bed, trying to figure out a way to say all the things he had needed to say for years. Even now, after hours of waiting and struggling, he couldn't force himself to express what he really meant. The feelings were in his heart, but he couldn't put them into words. He had never learned to express his emotions to anyone. He had made a career out of giving advice, and he was good. As a doctor he had learned to listen to people talk about their problems. Had been good at encouraging them to talk.

Physician, heal thyself.

For several seconds, his eyes searched his son, as if seeing the boy's features for the first time. People had often told him how much Chase looked and behaved like him. The tall, angular features, the quickness of speech, the bright mind. But there was a difference. Chase felt things and was able to show his feelings. How ironic he thought: to watch his son rise into a man as he, himself, slowly sank into shame. He hadn't been there for him—couldn't be there for him—for some time now. He looked at his sleeping face for a long time, as though Chase's sleep could hold back time, make everything somehow stop.

When Chase fully opened his eyes, his father stared at him and the boy smiled.

"What's wrong, Dad?" Chase said and got out of bed.

The two faced each other, Chase was a few inches shorter. Then his dad did something foreign to himself. He stretched out his arms and embraced his son. He held the boy tight for a long time.

"You're crying, Dad. What's wrong? You don't cry. I've never seen—"

The man, aware that his cheeks were moist against the boy's face, couldn't speak. He felt that if he spoke now, he would lose total control. Instead he shook his head and hugged the boy again.

"Why don't you——?"

He let his son go, pulled back, and moved out of the room.

Chase listened to his father's footsteps going down the hallway. He had never seen his father cry before. He didn't know if it was him, or the thing that was happening with his mother. He just didn't know.

A knot of pain curled around his own insides. In a way he couldn't ever explain to anyone, he felt the pain of his father. It was a totally new experience for him.

Chase left for school at his regular time and walked his normal route. He approached the corner where the policemen had fought Junior. No crowd had gathered today, but he did see a man sitting at the bench. As he grew closer, he recognized Junior.

"Junior!" Chase raced toward the bench.

Junior stood up. He was clean shaven; his jeans and tee shirt were clean. He looked over his shoulder at the traffic as he chatted absently with the boy.

"Something wrong?" Chase asked. "You're acting kind of nervous or something."

"No." Even as Junior said the word, his eyes glanced toward the left, and then he turned to look toward the right.

"Come on, Junior, I'm your friend."

An Oldsmobile slowed down at the curb. All the windows had a dark tint and Chase couldn't see inside. Junior waved to the car as if to say, "I'll be right there."

"Junior, you don't have to—"

"I have an important meeting," he said and gave the boy a quick hug. "I'll see you tonight." He walked to the car, opened the back door, climbed inside. It was like Chase was watching him leave his world and step through a dark door into another world, one that didn't include him. As soon as the door slammed, the car started off.

Chase watched the car move away from the curb, a silver and blue bumper sticker flashing in the sunlight, off and on, like an eye winking in secret. It said: *One day at a time.*

Chase felt his patience being tested. He also felt a keen sense of disappointment because Junior had left him behind.

Chase faced few challenges in school that day, which gave him time to concentrate on his Word Perfect. Did dog, spelled backward, stand for God? No, that couldn't be. Too easy. He moved to the next word, power, but no meaning came to him. He tried to turn his mind back to his class, but he caught himself wandering back to the Word Perfect list.

Dad. How long had Dad's problems been going on? What were his problems? Had these difficulties between his parents always been there?

Abruptly, his mind shifted to Junior. What was he doing now? Why had he acted so odd at the bus stop?

Several times during that morning, he had spotted Savannah

and either waved or smiled. What a fine body she had. And he loved to watch her laugh, which she did so readily. Why hadn't he been aware of those things about her before?

Now in his Biology class, Chase sat at his desk, his textbook opened in front of him, but his mind traveled beyond the walls of the classroom.

He was in Mr. Seymour's class and, at the same time, he was able to see himself sitting in a large classroom with students who must have been at least ten years older . All of them had their attention focused on the lecturer, a fat, balding man who wore a white coat. Chase had trouble concentrating on what the man was saying because he used odd words, many of them Latin sounding.

"Observe this patient's right leg," the man in the white coat said in a boring, droning voice. As he spoke, he clicked the remote control for the slide projector. He showed several pictures of a man's leg and then snapped to a list of five words called "The Five P's."

Chase, still caught in his daydream, grabbed the pencil from his pocket and started to write the five words in the margin of his book:

Pain.

Pallor.

Paresthesia—whatever that meant.

Pulselessness—another strange word.

Paralysis. I know what that is, Chase thought.

The teacher flashed the next picture. But then he heard laughing around him.

Chase opened his eyes. Someone's hand was resting on top of his head.

"Ah, you are still alive," Mr. Seymour said, and dropped his hand. "Good."

Several kids laughed. Chase wanted to turn around to see if Savannah was laughing too. He didn't dare.

"Sorry, sir."

The bell rang and the students hurriedly left the room.

Mr. Seymour stopped Chase.

"I am very much concerned about you, Chase, as I tried to express before. Until recently, you have been one of the best students I have ever taught. But lately, you have not shown the aptitude and brilliant mind that I have come to depend on."

"I'm really sorry—"

"You have been drifting. Oh, your work is among the best in your class, but your attention span has diminished; your participation has become scarce. Get honest with me. What is going on with you?"

Chase wished he could share his experiences. As much as he liked Mr. Seymour, he was sure that the teacher would think he was strange, childish, or say what he'd heard adults say about young people's behavior: Oh, it's just a phase.

"Well, things could be better." Mr. Seymour waited. "I guess I'd rather not discuss it now."

"As you wish," he said and patted Chase on the back as usual. With a smile he dismissed him.

When Chase got home, his mom kissed him and asked him about school. Even as she asked, he sensed the struggle in her voice, how she forced the words out. He saw pain in her eyes, but he didn't know how to respond to her. He remembered the cocoon and the gift of struggle, so he said nothing.

He had been home about half an hour and had just put away his homework when his mother tapped on his door. He invited her inside. She sat down on the chair next to his bed. For a while she stared at her hands and turned the rings on her fingers.

Chase sat quietly on the corner of his bed. He was willing to wait.

"It's about your father and me. Your father—"

Is this it? thought Chase, and he let out a breath he'd seemed to be holding forever.

"—well, he's having some personal problems. He needs time alone to work them out."

"All right, Mom."

"He's a good man, and wants to be a better man—"

"I know."

"You see, at some point everyone has serious challenges. He's facing his now."

Ordinarily, Chase would have asked a dozen questions, but the lessons from Junior had begun to sink in. He sensed that he could be most helpful if he just listened.

"Your father is going to be staying with his friend Mike for a while, at least until he figures out what he needs to do."

She stared at Chase, waiting for a response.

He opened his mouth to speak, and an inner voice whispered, "Double Vision." He leaned forward, hugged her, and said, "I love you, Mom, and I love Dad, too."

She looked at him oddly for a moment, and then her arms tightened around her son and she said softly, "Thanks for being such an understanding young man."

A minute later, she was gone. Chase could tell by the way she walked that she was feeling better.

Although he couldn't explain it to himself, he felt that by his understanding the situation and telling her, he had given her the support she needed. He wanted to know everything that was going on, but Double Vision told him he didn't need to know more right now. Her explanation was an expression of love and protection. She was doing her best to inform him about what was happening.

He knew his mom loved him, and he knew he loved both his parents. "I was dealt love and returned it," he said aloud. "Not as my mind told me to do, but as my heart felt she needed it." He realized the power and meaning behind hugs. Such a simple gesture, but when he put his arms around her, his actions had spoken more powerfully than any words he might have used. And her embrace had been just as powerful.

"What's happening to me?" He laughed as he realized how much Junior had taught him over the last few months. "I'm changing—I'm really changing."

After dinner, Chase called Savannah and talked to her about an assignment in a class they had together. He wanted to say more, especially to tell her how much he liked talking to her, but he felt self-conscious and hung up after a few minutes.

Yet he couldn't seem to stop thinking about her. When they had talked earlier that day after the economics class, he had finally asked about her perfume. "What do you call it?"

She laughed and her face lit up. "It's called 'Dream Song.' It's my favorite and it's the same name as my favorite song." She winked at him. "Come closer and get a better smell."

He closed his eyes and imagined waves of Dream Song filling his nostrils. He took in a deep breath, exhaled, and smiled.

As Chase moved closer she turned and walked away with a bounce more exciting to him than usual.

That night as he lay on his bed with his eyes on the TV set, his mind stayed on Savannah. He wished she was his lady. He wanted to touch her tender skin. Then he laughed aloud, "Man, I need to cool out with this. I'm getting obsessed."

....

Chase is dreaming of Junior again. They are in the same room at the Center for Conscious Living, but this time there is a chalkboard. Junior stands in front of it with a piece of chalk in his hand.

He ignores Chase and writes in large letters: The Five P's. He turns around and says, "What I am about to share with you is from the heart. Actually, the idea is not my own. In medical school, I once heard a lecture on the Five P's and—"

"Medical school? *You* went to medical school? Are you a doctor?"

Junior takes a deep breath, then says, "Tonight the lesson is not about me. It is about you. There is little room left for wisdom when one is full of judgment."

"I'm sorry, I didn't mean to make it sound like it was impossible. You just don't look like a—I mean—how could you be—Okay, I'll shut up."

"Fine, then listen and you will hear what is intended for you to know." He rattles the chalk in his hand for a minute and then says, "The Five P's stand for symptoms and physical findings associated with an acute vascular insult to an extremity. They are pain, pallor, paresthesia, pulselessness, and paralysis." He stares at Chase. "That is the lecture you were seeing in your daydream today."

Chase nods, but he still has no idea what the words mean.

"Forget their definitions. I am using the Five P's to share with you my personal guidelines for you to be successful and happy as a young man in this world. This is particularly important to you, because you are an African-American male at a time when the world receives you with hesitation. These principles, however, apply to us all, male or female, black or white, rich or poor." He pauses. "Any questions?"

"What are they? The principles, I mean?"

"Before I tell you, I want you to think of them as the principles that provide steps to acceptance of life on life's terms. When mastered, the transition from human doing to human being has been made."

Cool, Chase thinks, but he says nothing.

"The principles are Presence, Positivity, Patience, Perseverance and Powerlessness."

Junior insists that Chase repeat the five words aloud several times.

"Remember them, but remember them in the order you heard them."

The boy repeats them once more.

"The hands that wrote the history of the world as well as the history of your life wrote those five words especially for you. I am simply the Dream Merchant delivering them to you. Understand?"

Before Chase has a chance to answer, Junior turns and begins to write on the chalkboard. He is speaking without notes and without turning around. The lecture—and it sounds like a lecture—goes on for a long time.

Junior tells him that the first word, *Presence*, by definition refers to the fact of being present, available, seen or a quality of poise or effectiveness. He then writes Psalm 16:11 on the board: "You have made known to me the path of life; you will fill me with joy in your presence."

He pauses and waits for the boy to read the words aloud and then he continues, "It has been said that 80 percent of success is just showing up. No go, no show! No show, no go! There can be no success without attendance. Many of our homes today are without the presence of a father or father figure. It is very difficult for a man to be a good parent or leader if he is not available. He cannot be a role model in absentia. That is why it is so important that we, as people, take a hearty interest in what goes on at home, work, school and church. Parents must attend PTA meetings, the sporting events their children participate in and any other performances or activities. Just think of how you feel when you know your parents are interested in what you do. As a young man, this translates to your being present at all that they do too. Understand?"

"I think so."

"They look for you. Parents also need support."

Chase thinks of his mom and dad.

"You must also be available for siblings and friends in need," Junior says. "Be understanding and supportive. One day you will be in need. Remember this principle: The more you give, the more you receive. Rewards come pouring from the heavens when we put in both quantity and quality time with those in need. Service work is the work of the Lord through you. That reminds me of the Law of Fringe Benefit, which we will discuss later."

Law of Fringe Benefit, Chase repeats silently, wondering what that means.

Junior clears his throat, "You will learn and it will become ever-present to you that giving and receiving are one and the same. They simply manifest themselves in different ways. Are you following me?"

"Yes, sir, I mean, I think so."

"Good. We must set a visible example for everyone around us. The statistics in your neighborhood are alarming. Over 50 percent of the homes in your community are single-parent homes. In many of the other half, there is a male figure only by virtue of a physical body. This brings me to the other significance of presence. This is defined as having quality of poise; an effectiveness that develops closeness."

Chase looks confused, but Junior doesn't stop or allow him to ask questions.

"We must not only be present in body, we must also have presence with empathy and understanding. We must show compassion and love for all whose lives we touch. So I ask of you tonight, from this day forth, that you be present, have presence and strive to be gentle, compassionate and understanding on a daily basis."

Chase nods.

"The second P is *Positivity*. That is not simply the lack of negativity or a motion in the right direction. It is, on our most intimate level, the act of conquering our fears. It has been said, and I agree, that the basis of all negativity is fear.

"The word fear is an acronym for many things. Some of us allow fear to control us, so we Feel Everything And Run from it. Those with wisdom acknowledge their fear and Face Everything And Respond. We all have a choice. In our world, fear manifests itself mostly as the word can't. To me, can't is an acronym that stands for Crying About Not Trying."

Junior turns around and faces Chase. "That reminds me of a poem by Doris Beason titled, 'I Can't' and it goes like this:

> "I Can't" lacks in nerve; he's too faint of heart
> To pitch in like a man and do his part
> He has none of the spirit that fights and wins;
> He admits he is beaten before he begins.
>
> "I Can't" sees as mountains what bolder eyes
> Recognize as molehills: ambition dies
> And leaves him complaining in helpless wrath
> When the first small obstacle blocks his path.
>
> "I Can't" has a notion that, out of spite,
> He's being cheated of what's his right
> The men who succeed by hard work and pluck
> He envies and sneers at as "fools for luck."
>
> "I Can't" is a loafer, who won't admit
> That his life's the mess he made of it
> The treasure that's sparkling beneath his eye
> He thinks he can't reach—and won't even try.
>
> "I Can't" has a feeling the world's in debt
> To him for the living he has failed to get
> But given a chance to collect, he'll rant
> About past failures and whine, "I Can't."

Junior pauses to take a drink of water. "Are you still with me?"

"Oh, yeah, but—"

"Good. I am on a roll, so listen. Whenever negativity surfaces, you must ask yourself, 'What am I afraid of?' By acknowledging it, fear is before you, and you have a chance to conquer it. We all know negative people. Right?"

Chase nods.

"From this day forth, think of them not as negative, but as fearful. If God calls on you to offer help, address their fears in non-intimidating ways. Help them learn to trust and respect themselves. Only then can they trust or respect the process."

While Chase reflects on those words, Junior says, "That reminds me of another poem. It is called "The Looking Glass" and was written by Edgar Guest:

> When you get what you want in your struggle for life
> And the world makes you king for a day,
> Then go to the mirror and look at yourself
> And see what that guy has to say.
>
> For it isn't your father, mother, or wife
> Whose judgment you must pass
> But the guy whose verdict counts most in your life
> Is the guy looking back in the glass.
>
> You can fool the whole world down the path
>   of the years
> And get pats on your back as you pass,
> But your final reward will bring heartaches and tears
> If you cheated the guy in the glass."

"Yeah, I like that," Chase says.

"So do I. Now, learn to respect yourself and treat yourself

respectfully. You see, Positivity leads to power and awareness. Word Perfect reveals the word *owe* in power. That is to remind us that with power comes responsibility—a debt to repay your Higher Power by service and kindness to humanity. Awareness shows us the battle within." He stares at the boy and asks, "What does awareness mean to you?"

"I—I'd have to think about it—"

"Okay, think about it. Use what you have already learned. Talk aloud to yourself. It will come to you."

Chase writes the word on a piece of paper and stares at it. This is like a puzzle.

He writes Awareness and says the word aloud very slowly. "Oh, now I get it. It's A-War-En-Ess! Yes, that's it. It means a war in us."

"Very good." Junior laughs. "And the war in us, Chase, is the battle between positive and negative. On a deeper level, this is the struggle between good and evil. For with every good deed, there was first a thought, and with every wrong doing there was first evil intent. If all thoughts can become positive, then the will of God can be shown. There will be peace on earth and good will toward all." He stops and looks at Chase for a moment. "Are you tired?"

"Yeah, but so what? Keep on. Besides I've got no place to go anyway."

"Very well, the third principle is that of *Patience*. You have had an introduction to this with your experience at the tree of harmony. You learned that impatience can lead you into the darkness, the kind you experienced when you chased me in haste. In the darkness you found terror—an unnecessary terror that led to further internal turmoil. It was then that you fell and injured your wrist. You see, Chase, the physical manifestations of disease occur only after the mental manifestations of disease. You could have avoided the pain simply by being patient and making the appropriate choice to walk to the tree instead of into the darkness. Had you not gone into the darkness, you never would have fallen. Had you not fallen, you would have never broken your wrist. Understand?"

"Yes."

"Nonetheless, your inner voice saved you because you listened to it, and you turned around."

"Yeah, that's right."

"To elaborate further, by definition Patience is bearing pains or trials calmly or without complaints. Psalm 40:1 says, 'I waited patiently for the Lord and he inclined unto me and heard my cry.' You see, patience is God. It is through patience that God can intervene. Without it there is no order. Without patience, we simply react and not respond. Word Perfect will tell you that to react is simply to re-act. That is, to do the same act again. You don't put out fire with fire, you do it with water. Water is the solution, the response. Fire is the problem.

"Patience teaches us the correct response. It takes us out of the problem and puts us into the solution. The answers, then, come without our trying to acquire them. You have heard the saying, 'Don't just sit there, do something.' Listen carefully because I want you to hear it differently. 'Don't just do something, sit there.' Most situations clear themselves up with the passing of time. That is how your Higher Power works. It teaches us that lessons cannot be learned in a day. Trouble did not start the day you first saw it and solutions do not come on that day either. In many ways, every person is a problem in search of a solution. All of us are on our way somewhere, but there is no way to happiness. Do you know why?"

Chase shakes his head.

"Because happiness is the way, that's why. We arrive there through the vehicle of patience. When we fuel our limousines with patience, God becomes the chauffeur. Another thing I want you to grasp is this: there are no mistakes in God's world, only learning experiences. The principle of positivity will turn stumbling blocks into stepping stones. The principle of patience allows your will to become that of God. With this unity comes the defeat of the ego."

Chase nods. He has learned about ego in school. It means the self.

"Ah, yes, you understand. The ego does nothing more but Ease God Out. It is the number one hindrance to spiritual growth."

Chase loves hearing Junior speak, but he is starting to tire.

"Yes, I know you are tired, but stay with me a little longer," Junior says. "The next principle is *Perseverance*. By definition, it means to go on stubbornly in spite of opposition. Here on earth, we are aware of its importance, but we often fail to practice it. We toss around sayings such as, 'Hang on in there!' 'Don't give up!' 'When the going gets tough, the tough get going.' 'It ain't over until the fat lady sings.' 'Don't throw in the towel,' and on and on. Now hear what I am saying: Never give up on the dream."

Despite the tiredness, Chase nods and forces himself to concentrate.

"I share with you words from two great former Dream Merchants. First, Dr. Martin Luther King, Jr., who once said, 'The greatest measure of a man is not where he stands during time of comfort and convenience, but where he stands during challenge and controversy.' He was aware of the gift in the struggle and also that struggle is the first part of reward. Perseverance is simply the training program before the true test that is yet to come. Booker T. Washington also had a similar awareness and said, 'I have learned that success is measured not so much by the position that one has reached in life, but by the obstacles one has overcome while trying to succeed.'"

"Yeah, I'm down with that," Chase says.

"Excellent. Here is something else I want you to understand: perseverance strengthens character. Character is an extension of God. Our ability to dodge adversity is luck. Our ability to live in adversity requires perseverance. I asked you to stay with me a little longer because I wanted you to hear a poem by an anonymous author, as you would call him or her. Later in your training, I will tell you who Anonymous really is. This poem is titled: 'Don't Quit.'

> *When things go wrong, as they sometimes will,*
> *When the road you're trudging seems all up hill*
> *When the funds are low, and the debts are high,*
> *And you want to smile, but you have to sigh,*
> *When care is pressing you down a bit,*
> *Rest, if you must, but don't you quit.*
>
> *Life is queer with its twists and turns,*
> *As everyone of us sometimes learns,*
> *And many a failure turns about*
> *When he might have won had he stuck it out:*
> *Don't give up, though the pace seems slow*
> *You might succeed with another blow.*
> *Often the goal is nearer than*
> *It seems to a faint and faltering man,*
> *Often the struggler has given up*
> *When he might have captured the victor's cup.*
> *And he learned too late, when the night slipped down,*
> *How close he was to the golden crown.*
>
> *Success is failure turned inside out*
> *The silver tint of the clouds of doubt*
> *And you never can tell how close you are*
> *It may be near when it seems afar;*
> *So stick to the fight when you're hardest hit*
> *It's when things seem worst that you must not quit."*

Chase tries to listen, but his attention span is fading.

"I apologize that this lesson is taking so long tonight," Junior says, "but with the acquisition and subsequent application of these principles, your transition to human being is guaranteed." He pauses and asks, "Can you stay with me just a little longer? Just one more principle?"

"Sure," Chase says, and he resolves to stay alert.

"The last principle is *Powerlessness*. I have found this to be the most difficult. It teaches us that we must accept and embrace the insecurity of not being in charge. This principle exemplifies that, in reality, we are all juniors, because God Almighty is the most senior of beings. It has been said that one can make decisions out of God's will, but one can never be out of God's reach. We must pray for our will to be God's will.

"Make no mistake about it, Chase. This is God's world. We are only a small piece of the puzzle. We must graciously and humbly accept the divine power. I know that I have told you the value of perseverance and never to give up. But for you to understand powerlessness, you must first surrender. That is the greatest contradiction in life.

"You must surrender to win. God is the only game in town that allows you to throw in the towel and win the boxing match. When you admit powerlessness, you become truly free. You recognize that you are never in charge, so that there is no real value in the concept of being in control. The concept is only an illusion—and that leads to stress, which subsequently leads to dis-ease—a state of mind more than a state of body."

"Like the stress and dis-ease with my broken wrist in the darkness?" Chase asks.

"Exactly! Incorporate powerlessness into your life, son. It is the only way to serenity and peace of mind. As you leave here tonight, I ask you to practice these principles. Think about them. Make progress with them. Do not seek perfection—"

"Why not? I mean, isn't that what I should want?"

"To seek perfection only sets you up for failure. Nothing and no one is perfect except God. Have presence, be positive, practice patience, exhibit perseverance, and most of all, accept powerlessness. My little friend, happiness is a choice. May you choose wisely. Or to sum it all up, strive to become a human being, not a human doing."

"Junior, I've been listening and trying to understand. Now I have one question. Why Me? Why did you choose me to teach?"

"If not you, then who? If not here, then where? If not now, then when? Sweet awakenings," he says.

And then morning arrives.

Chase was awake again.

ten

Fringe Benefits

THE HOUSE SEEMED DIFFERENT to Chase. He decided it was because he knew his dad was no longer living with them. Although he usually didn't see his father every morning anyway, it still gave him an odd feeling to realize that his father wouldn't walk out the door or start the car outside.

Chase realized how much he loved him. It was something he hadn't thought about much before. The fact that Dad wouldn't be home—might never come home again—brought sadness, pain and fear to his heart. Then he thought about one of the lessons he had been taught about fear—F E A R. Yes, he could Face Everything And Respond.

"I just need to deal with it," he said to himself. "I wish I knew exactly what the problem was."

Then something occurred to him. Even if he knew the problem, he was powerless to do anything. That made him feel even worse.

Chase dressed and went downstairs for breakfast. Mom was cooking blueberry pancakes, bacon and grits. She had her back to him and was singing a song he didn't know, but it reminded him of church.

"...Silver and gold! Silver and gold! I'd rather have Jesus than silver and gold..." On the table lay her Bible. It was opened and the highlighted verse in yellow stuck out. Curious, he flipped the Bible around and read it. It was Romans 8:28: "And we know that all things work together for good to them that love God, to them who are called according to his purpose."

Chase read the verse twice. After his dream last night, he realized what his mother was doing. It was her way to surrender the problem to God. Yesterday, I wouldn't have understood that, he thought, but today I do.

"Almost ready," Mom said as she flipped a pancake high into the air. Chase watched and laughed—her spirits seemed lighter and he was glad. Over her shoulder she said, "Baby, would you get the milk out for me?"

As he took out the milk carton, he noticed an ornamental magnet on the refrigerator door. He paused to read the words. It was a saying by Confucius: "The gem cannot be polished without friction, nor man perfected without trials." He'd never noticed it before. Suddenly a thought came to him—a revolutionary insight he wouldn't have considered before. That applies to Dad. He's going through his difficult times for a reason. Could that be part of his polishing and perfecting? He looked at his mom and realized that it applied to her as well. This didn't affect just Dad; it was a necessary struggle for her too.

Chase sat down and poured his milk and he played back the ideas that had been running through his head. A smile came to his face. Man, I'm different, really different. Junior's getting to me and I'm beginning to think and sound like him.

He liked that part a lot.

"Hey, Mom, do you agree with that?" He pointed to the saying by Confucius.

"Very much so," she said. Then she pointed to the highlighted verse he had read. "I agree with this too. To my thinking, those words by Confucius are another way of saying what the Bible says."

Although she spoke like the mother he had always known, there was a sadness in her eyes and on her face he hadn't noticed before. Maybe those signs of depression had been there all along. Perhaps he had just been too concerned about himself and had never noticed. Until recently, he hadn't thought about his parents having problems. He continued to stare at her—glad that she was his mother. He loved her more than anyone in the world.

They ate in silence. "I love you, Mom," he whispered, but his words were so soft she couldn't hear them. It didn't matter. He had said them and meant them. That mattered. Her gaze had fallen on the Bible and she read for several minutes. Chase inhaled the sweet smell of syrup and chewed the blueberry pancake. His mother's lips were softly forming and moving around the invisible words, as though each word had a palpable taste, as though the words themselves were her sustenance.

He thought about the words polishing and perfecting. In a doubtful tone, he thought, I don't know, not really, if this even makes sense. Some of this stuff sounds good, but when it is happening to me, it just hurts.

And he was hurting. The daily pain on his mother's face and the absence of his father bothered him. While his parents tried to work through their pain, they had brought more pain into his life as well.

Chase swallowed his last bite of the pancake and took a final swig of milk. "Everything is going to work out," he said to his mother.

She didn't look up.

He got out of his chair and went to her. He hugged her and

looked deeply into her eyes. "It'll be all right. I know it will."

She patted his hand as if to say, "I know, baby."

As he left the room, he turned and looked at his mother. Unaware that he was watching, she continued to read her Bible, her lips barely moving now as she breathed in the words. He didn't know how it would happen, but he knew the words she read would comfort her.

Chase once again headed toward school, lost in his thoughts and unaware of anything going on around him. He was looking at the sidewalk as though it contained answers.

"Hey, don't you know me today?"

Chase looked up and saw the most beautiful girl in the world standing at the corner, Sweet Savy. She smiled and waited for him.

He ran to catch up with her. "Why that serious face?" she asked.

"Just thinking about, you know, some things at home," he said.

"Yeah, that can be tough." They crossed the street.

They had gone less than twenty yards down the next block, when she stopped and stared at Chase. "I've been thinking about you a lot lately," she said. "You're one of the nicer guys around here."

"Thanks, Savy." Her words took him by surprise; he wasn't sure what to say and didn't want to trip over his own nervous words. "I kinda feel the same way about you and—"

There was silence as he studied the sidewalk again.

"So I'd like to talk to you," Savy said. "I mean, I need to talk to someone, and, well, do you mind? I mean, will you listen, even if what I have to say sounds strange? You know, really weird?"

"Okay, sure."

"Chase, well, do you ever have strange dreams?" Chase, surprised, looked fully into her face. "I mean," she said, "you know, sometimes you have a dream and you wake up in the morning, and the dream felt so real that for a moment you're not sure that it didn't happen. I mean, like it's hard to tell the difference between the dream and reality."

Chase smiled at her warmly and some of her nervousness melted away. He didn't know how much to tell her. Finally he said, "You know what? I've been having the same kinda dreams myself."

"What? Really?"

"Really."

She stopped and stared and gazed into his eyes. "You're not just saying that to make me feel good, are you?" She put her hand on his. Her touch made his body tingle all over.

"Oh no, I wouldn't do that to you." As he spoke he stared at her. Savy was much lighter in complexion than he was. And her eyes, although brown, had tiny flecks of green in them. They were the most captivating eyes he had ever seen. As they stared at each other, he was sure that both of them felt an intense connection. Time seemed to momentarily stop. They heard nothing, and felt themselves being drawn into each other's world.

"You are so sweet." She stood on her tiptoes and kissed him.

Chase stared at her in shock. Her lips had touched his. Without thinking, he put his hand on her cheek. It was as soft as he had known it would be.

And then there was the sharp intrusion of the school bell. He was late for class.

Chase forced himself to pay attention for the rest of the day. He felt focused even though he was bored. Throughout the day, he thought about the teachers and other students and not just about himself. In class he asked questions. He volunteered answers and spoke up. It made the time go by faster, he decided. Plus, he helped the teachers feel they were getting through to him.

After his seventh period class, Mr. Seymour asked, "How is it going, Chase?"

"Much better, sir, I really am."

"You seem somewhat better today. More relaxed and more like your old self. No, not quite like that. Almost as if—"

"As if what?"

"You seemed to have grown up the past few weeks, matured. Changed in some way. I know there has been a struggle, but I like what I am seeing," Mr. Seymour shook his hand. "Keep it up."

By the time he left the classroom, Chase felt a lightness in his step that hadn't been there before. He stopped at his locker, grabbed his books for homework, and walked down the hall. Through the glass doors at the end of the hall, he saw a man sitting at the corner of the bus stop. Although he couldn't see much of his body, he knew it was Junior.

Chase ran down the hallway, excited to see his friend. He had just reached the steps at the entrance when someone's leg came out from behind a corner. Chase tried to dodge it, but he was moving too fast to change directions. He tumbled down the stairs, dropping his books as he did. He landed on his hands and broke his fall. But he still felt pain.

Lying at the bottom of the steps, he turned over and looked upward. At the top, five boys stood with their arms crossed. They were laughing at him.

"Thought you had better footwork than that, Chase," one boy sneered.

"Why you kissing the cement like that?"

"Yeah, you need to be kissing Savannah not the ground."

"He ain't man enough," said another. "He doesn't have the right stuff."

They laughed even louder.

Chase ignored his books and got to his feet. The palms of both hands hurt, and he knew he had skinned his left one. He stared at the laughing boys above him. Filled with anger, he raced up the steps. "I ought to take you out!"

The gang members stood together as a unit, ready for action.

"Is that right?" Sammy said. "You and who else?" He was shorter than Chase, but broad shouldered.

"Yo, Sammy," Chase yelled. "Why you trying to hurt me, man?"

"I ain't trying to hurt you," Sammy replied. "I'm just trying to get through to you. You need to come on board."

All five of the boys closed in around Chase.

"Think about it, man," said another. "Because if you don't, you'll have lots of accidents like this one."

"Like I said before," Chase replied, "I ain't—"

"Don't answer now," Sammy said and slapped him on the shoulder. "Just think about how lucky you were today and how you caught yourself before busting your—"

"Yeah, coulda been a bad fall," said one of them, "the end of that sweet jump shot of yours."

"Yeah, the end of your basketball career," said another. "But by the looks of your arm, it might be over already."

"And we're going to step up the pressure next time," said the boy closest to Chase.

Sammy leaned forward so that his face was only inches from Chase. The tobacco breath made Chase draw back. "Now go on over there with your little street rat!" He gestured toward Junior, who had now started to walk toward them.

"Street rat! Who you calling a—?"

"Chase!" Junior shouted.

A strange thing happened when he called out. Chase's name echoed loudly in the air several times and then faded away. Everyone on the steps and within hearing range stopped as if momentarily frozen in place. The ground shook, and the metal railings of the steps rattled.

"An earthquake!" one of the boys yelled.

Just as quickly as it had begun, the shaking of the earth stopped.

Chase stared into Sammy's eyes and he clenched his fists in anger.

"Violence is not the way," Junior said.

Chase wanted to strike Sammy but he knew Junior was right. Still staring at him, he slowly unballed his fists. He turned and looked at the others, then walked down the steps and picked up his books.

The others yelled at him, but Chase ignored them. Once he had his books, he hurried after Junior.

"Who is he? The new Ernie?" Sammy yelled. "Go over there with your boy!"

Chase turned and looked back at Sammy. "That's cold, man. That's cold." He walked toward Junior.

Junior stopped, turned around and smiled. "Greetings." Today he wore a clean pair of jeans and a bright orange tee shirt.

"Man, why didn't you let me take them out? At least Sammy. I could've handled—"

In a millisecond, Junior's bright smile turned into a frown. "Never talk to me that way. Do you understand? I am here only to help."

Chase blinked.

"Your anger is with Sammy. Not me. Just pray on it."

"Pray on it? Five guys are ready to jam me and you say to pray? Get real, Junior," Chase replied, aware he was still filled with anger. "Prayer ain't got nothing to do with this."

"Why do you say that?" Junior asked. He smiled but it was what Chase would have called a sad smile. "They pray!"

"Give me a break! They wouldn't pray if their lives depended on it!"

"On the contrary, they just do a different kind of praying."

Chased was confused, but then he saw the faintest twinkle in Junior's eye. It diffused his anger. "All right," he said. He realized a new lesson was coming.

"You are learning much quicker these days," Junior said and paused. He pointed to a stone bench across the street. Silently they walked over and sat down. Junior leaned back and stared at the students' cars whizzing out of the school parking lot.

After several minutes of silence, Junior turned and faced Chase. "Yes, they *prey*. They use anger as one kind of bait to make others play their way." He pointed to the boys. "Look over there. You were outnumbered five to one. You would have gotten whipped. You almost let your anger allow you to play with fire. Had you done that, they would have beaten you. The beating would have heightened your fear of them. Each time they beat you, you would have become more afraid. You see, that is exactly what they want. They *prey* on people like you."

"Yeah, I get it," Chase said. He lowered his head.

"I'm proud of you." He placed his arm around Chase's shoulder. "You may not realize it, but you won today."

"Won? How can you say that?"

"Look at the big picture. You are still on probation. Fighting in school would definitely have sent a message to your probation officer that you are not staying out of trouble. That would have sent you to boot camp."

"You're right, man," he said. "I forgot."

"Yes, but they did not. They knew exactly what they were doing. They are not as stupid as you think, especially Sammy. If they had won today, you would have been in more trouble and would have been in a boot camp detention center. Everything in your life would then have changed. Not everyone in boot camp has a positive experience. After completing it, you might have felt that there was no future for you—and that would make the gang more attractive."

Chase nodded in understanding.

"You see, that entire encounter was a serious test of your Double Vision."

They got up and walked side-by-side to Chase's home. Even without asking, Chase knew Junior had more for him. And he was ready.

The day turned warm, so they took a small detour and went inside Burger Mania, a popular local fast-food restaurant. Most of the kids had gone home, but two couples sat in the corner, holding hands and sipping Cokes.

"I'd better call Mom," Chase said. He found the pay phone, called his mother, and told her that he had stopped for a Coke. He was walking back to the booth where Junior waited when he heard someone call out his name.

"Hey, Chase!"

He looked up. He hadn't noticed the four boys who came in and sat at a booth. It was Brick and three of his friends. He walked over and gave them each a high five.

"I heard the Skin Tight boys were on your case," Brick said and smiled. Skin Tight was the name of a street gang. Many of its members shaved their heads bald.

How does he always know?

As if Brick had heard his thoughts, he said, "Hey, man, I'm Brick. I know everything, remember?"

Chase noticed a cast on Brick's left arm. One of the other boys had a walking cast on his leg and scars across his face.

"Man, I saw the accident, I mean a few minutes afterward," said Chase. "It looked pretty serious."

"Yeah, I totaled my ride, but that's all right."

"You're lucky to be alive, man."

"Brother, every day is an adventure for me. See, they don't call me Brick for nothing. I'm hard, man. I always come through." Brick sipped his drink. "Listen, Chase. Stay away from those boys, man!

They are dangerous—real dangerous."

"What are you trying to tell me? You think I want to walk with them?"

"Just hear what I am saying. They don't play. The word is that they are trying to expand, see, and that means they need new blood. But they ain't for you. Plus, their initiation process is crazy."

Chase suddenly became more focused. That was the second time that Brick had mentioned the word initiation. What was Brick trying to tell him?

Brick finished his drink and put a dollar bill on the table. "Later," he said and got up.

Chase walked back over to Junior, who was fumbling through his pockets looking for money.

"Any change?" Junior asked.

"Yes, plenty. And speaking of change, I've gone through a lot of change recently." Chase smiled proudly. It was his first test of using Double Vision and Word Perfect. He reached into his pocket, pulled out two quarters, and said, "Maybe this is the change you were looking for."

"You know nothing of change, my friend," Junior said. "I do not say that to cut you off or offend you. However, as I said to you before, change is the only constant in this world. It is a prerequisite for a peaceful life, yet it is one of the most feared concepts in decision-making today."

Chase stared in confusion and sat down in the booth.

"Change is action, not simply a thought," Junior said. "It is a mental and physical manifestation. You are beginning to grasp the mental portion. You are making great progress, and I commend you for your work thus far. But do not accept reward or give praise to yourself without completing the process. Be careful. As you have heard, a little knowledge can be very dangerous."

Chase lowered his head. He had hoped for praise.

"Sorry again, I must have sounded a bit harsh. Let me explain change." Gently he tapped Chase on his hand. "One of my professors used to say, if you keep doin' what you been doin', you're gonna keep gettin' what you been gettin'. Although simple, it is a very powerful statement. You see Chase, when faced with life's challenges, people regularly change their minds. But more often than not, they do not change their ways. They have become victims of habit—addicted to behaving a certain way. Like the boys in the gang—they are the kind of people who are unable to take mental change to a physical realm. In other words, there is a lack of action. Word Perfect will tell you that action is really ACT I ON.

"Yeah, I got that," Chase said after he scribbled the words on a napkin.

"Action must involve YOU in a physical sense." Junior waved for a waitress and signaled that he wanted two Cokes. "Although our brains have the potential to perform telekinesis—"

"Telekinesis? What is that?"

"That refers to the ability to move matter with your thoughts. Our brains are not fully developed yet in that ability. So, at this point in our development, we must settle for the hands-on approach. That reminds me of a poem by Anonymous. Have you heard of him?"

Chase burst out laughing. "What do you mean? Anonymous means that nobody knows the author. I thought everybody knew that—"

"Shame on you for your closed-mindedness. Anonymous was a great poet. He is not remembered because he is never seen. He is the Almighty One who writes history. Anonymous is God. All that is written is the Word of God. Our Higher Power simply uses the name of Anonymous when He does not want to take credit. It always makes God feel good to act in that way. You want to know how good it feels?"

"Yeah, sure, I guess so." Chase sat back in his chair. He wasn't quite buying this one.

"If you do a kind deed for someone and do not let that person know you did it, you then become anonymous. Correct?"

Chase nodded.

"If you have done it properly, you can watch the joy in the recipient's face. It is overwhelmingly powerful. It is God-like."

Chase grinned.

"Now I want you to listen. It is called 'Change.' With his deep, resonant voice, Junior recited the entire poem:

> *If you always think what you've always thought*
> *Then you will always feel what you've always felt.*
> *Then you will always do what you've always done.*
> *If you always do what you've always done,*
> *Then you will always get what you've always gotten.*
> *If you always get what you've always gotten*
> *Then you will always think what you've always thought.*

Chase laughed, but he thought, that's just silly, man. You're losing it.

"It is not silly and I'm not losing anything."

"You're in my head, man. How do you do that?" Chase demanded.

Junior held up his hands. "Never mind and listen. You still have much to learn." He recited the poem again and then said, "It is quite a clever poem, and true. Now, here is what you need to consider: Change puts into action a series of universal events." He leaned forward and stared intently at Chase. "What does universal mean?"

"The world. The whole world."

"Not quite. We need to shift into Word Perfect. It comes from the word universe which is uni-verse. Uni verse means one song.

That's harmony. No matter how difficult, change brings about harmony in some way. Harmony then opens you up to the world of infinite possibilities. There is where you see, examine, and choose all the gifts of God for your life. Do you recall that I mentioned Fringe Benefits?"

"Sure, but you never explained."

"Correct. This is what I meant when I spoke about Fringe Benefits. It is the Law of the Fringe Benefits."

"Wait a minute, you're going too fast," Chase said.

The drinks came. Junior sipped his Coke as if he had plenty of time. "You see, Chase, once you master the Law of Fringe Benefits, life becomes an ever-owing dynamic process of reward. Rewards come in many ways—often entirely different from what we expect, but after all, change and growth are not about our will anyway, are they?" He leaned forward once again and softened his voice as if to emphasize his next words. "The whole world of infinite possibilities is available to you and to everyone. It requires only the desire to change. There is only one catch."

"Okay, so tell me."

"The change must be one of Positive Momentum."

"What is Positive Momentum? I've never heard that before."

"Correct. You are paying attention, good. Positive Momentum refers to a change within you that carries the intent to help others more than yourself. Your personal satisfaction comes from the gratitude of helping others, not in the receipt of material things or personal recognition. It is like the difference between being NOWHERE and NOW HERE. Do you remember?"

"Uh huh."

"It is a change both of heart and mind. Change is universal— one song! Do you remember your first leap over the wall?"

"How could I forget that?"

"Do you remember the footprints you saw?"

Chase nodded.

"They were placed there for you by your Higher Power."

"Really? Why? Where did my Higher Power want me to go?" As soon as Chase asked, he answered his own question. "To the tree—the tree of harmony."

"Precisely. It is symbolic of infinite possibilities. All different kinds of fruit live peacefully on the same tree, under the same sky, nourished by the same God."

"But I didn't get it right at first."

"You encountered obstacles," Junior said. "Obstacles are nothing more than God leading you in life. Think of it this way. Obstacles exist to promote change. You must exercise your power of choice to implement those changes. If you do that, you will then be open to all the Fringe Benefits offered by the Heavenly Father—"

"That's the second time you've mentioned Fringe Benefits, but I still don't understand what you mean."

"Fringe Benefits? That is simple to explain. I refer to friends, opportunity, success and satisfaction. You see, they are not what you strive for. They come to you when you strive for the right things."

Without giving Chase an opportunity, Junior got up, gulped down the rest of his drink and led the boy out of Burger Mania.

Chase looked at his watch. "Man, this is really getting deep, but I've got to go. I promised Mom I would be only a half hour late."

Junior smiled and reached into his back pocket. He pulled out two things. The first was a white plastic coin with a gold triangle. Engraved inside the triangle was the letter A, although the engraving had become quite faded. "Keep this. It is the most valuable piece of change I own. Later you will learn its significance."

"Okay," Chase said and stared at the coin, which was the size of a quarter.

"One other thing," Junior said. He handed him a sheet of paper. "Add this to your collection." As Chase took the paper,

Junior glanced at his own watch. "I am late for an appointment. I must leave you now."

Chase opened the folded piece of paper.

"People don't tell you how much they know until they know how much you care."

He turned to wave to Junior, but he was already gone. Chase walked the final four blocks alone. He stuffed the paper into his bag and walked inside the house. As soon as he closed the door, he saw his father sitting in his stuffed chair. His head lay back as if he were asleep, but his eyes were open. He didn't move.

On the floor next to Dad lay a half-empty bottle. Even from that distance, Chase recognized it as Jack Daniels whiskey. Chase walked closer to his father and saw the glazed look in his eyes, saw his chest rise and fall with each breath. His dad seemed to have no idea that Chase was there.

Then Chase saw four suitcases at the bottom of the steps. Two of them were his. He quickly figured out that his mom had packed them. Dad had returned home and Mom didn't like the conditions.

In the background, jazz music played and the captivating and melodic voice of Billie Holiday swelled and filled the room.

Just then, his father began to sing the final words of the song. "...God bless the child that's got his own . . . that's got his own." He bowed his head and stared at the floor.

eleven

Just Say Yes

WITH EFFORT, CHASE'S FATHER RAISED up his head and gazed into the eyes of his son. He blinked several times as if he were unable to focus. Slowly, the glazed look diminished and he smiled faintly.

"Hi, Dad," Chase said. Automatically, his eyes followed his father's hand as it reached for the bottle of Jack Daniels. As he stared at his father, Chase tried to define the look he saw on his face. Guilt? Yes. Shame? Definitely. Remorse and embarrassment? Absolutely.

"About time you're home."

Mom came down the steps and sat across from Chase's father.

Dad nodded to her. "Now we're all one, big happy family." He reached down to pick up the whiskey bottle. He unscrewed the top and held it up. "We can celebrate that." He took a long drink.

Even though Chase stood several feet away, the odor from the bottle seemed to gush out and fill the room. He stared as his father upped the bottle and drank until he emptied it. Dad threw the bottle on the floor and it broke, sending pieces of glass throughout the room.

Mom jumped, as if she had been interrupted from her private thoughts. She glared at her husband as she obviously worked to control her emotions. Tears slipped down her cheeks, but she didn't seem to care. She twisted and wadded a pink handkerchief in her hands, sighed deeply and cleared her throat before she said in a controlled voice, "Chase, we're leaving." She walked to the stairs and picked up two suitcases.

A shocked Chase watched her, but he seemed unable to move.

"*Now*. We're leaving right this minute!" she said. She walked toward the door.

"Wait, just let me talk to him. I'll be out in a minute—"

"Don't try to talk to that man. He's drunk! Can't you see that? Dirty, filthy, drunk. And it's not the first time. I can't stand it anymore. Come on—"

"Mom, please, one minute."

She wrestled her two suitcases through the door, as though they were big stupid dogs. She left the front door ajar. After a moment or two Chase could hear her opening the trunk of her car.

Chase closed the door and went back to his father's chair. He knelt beside his dad and laid his hand on his father's hand. "Dad, I'm sorry—"

His father's hand jerked up to flip off Chase's touch. "Stay away."

And then suddenly his father seemed very lucid. He looked up at Chase; his eyes eerily clear as they stared into Chase's own. It was like an altered state of reality that his father could control at will. Chase didn't know what was real anymore.

"Son, I'm in no condition to explain. Any discussion right now will just make things worse. Just remember what you saw today." He reached for the bottle of Jack Daniels, forgetting that he had broken it. "Oh yeah, it shattered didn't it." He began to laugh as though it was a joke he had played on himself. Then he began to cry. "I need help, son. Don't ever let this happen to you. Promise me!"

Chase got off his knees, scared. "I promise." But he didn't leave. He looked down at the sad face, and felt the torment of his father.

"One more thing," his father said. His lucidity was now gone. His speech was slurred and he spoke with his face only inches from that of his son. "I'm sorry, and I love you." He then burst into a strange, forced kind of laughter. "Hey, I guess that was two things, huh?"

"Yeah, two things, but that's okay." Before Chase walked away, he said, "I don't like what you're doing, but I love you back."

"No, you don't. How could you? I haven't been a good father." He slumped in the chair. Within seconds, he was snoring.

Chase picked up his suitcases and went out. He kicked the door shut as he walked to the car.

His mother stared straight ahead. "Put them in the trunk," she said.

As soon as Chase had gotten into the car, she drove off. She had stopped crying, and there was a hardness in her features Chase hadn't seen before. Yet even through all the hardness, he could see the pain.

On the way to his Aunt Marissa's house, not a word passed between them. Chase wanted to talk, but he realized that his mother needed the privacy of silence right then. He wanted to talk to somebody. If he knew Savannah a little better, maybe he could have confided in her. But if she knew about Dad's drinking, she might not want to be around him anymore.

I wish Ernie were here, he thought. The only other person he could think of was Junior. Where are you when I really need you? he silently asked.

Just then, his mother pulled into the driveway of a small bungalow in Riverdale, a suburb on the south side of Atlanta. Aunt Marissa hurried outside and helped them carry in their suitcases. She showed them to their rooms efficiently, the way a hotel steward might, and Chase realized she knew.

Chase laid on the bed and watched the news and a game show. By then, Aunt Marissa called them for dinner.

"You've grown quite a bit," Aunt Marissa said as she served dinner.

"Yes, ma'am."

"Your mother says you're bringing home good grades."

"Yes, ma'am."

After the fourth attempt at conversation, Aunt Marissa began to speak to Chase's mother. She, at least, tried to carry on her end of the conversation.

They talked about church, the weather, and mutual friends. No one said anything about what had happened earlier, almost as if it were a forbidden topic. It was as though speaking about it would make it too real, and so each withdrew into a quiet, private space.

Around nine o'clock, Chase excused himself and went to his room. He opened his biology textbook and tried to read for a long time. He resigned himself to the change in his life. "Change is action, not simply a thought," Junior had said. How could Chase possibly act upon this change? This was something between his mom and dad.

"God, if you're up there, please help my dad..." The words came slowly to Chase because he had never done much formal praying. But tonight, he talked to God about both his parents and the sadness of his own heart. As he talked, he could still see his dad in the chair in the living room. He could hear the breaking of the empty whiskey bottle.

"God, where are You?"

....

"Chase, I'm here."

Chase knows he is dreaming. He is standing once again inside a building. It is the Center for Conscious Living, and he stands just outside a room he has been in before. "Chase, in here." It's Junior's voice. The door is slightly opened, so Chase peeks inside. A group of people—five men and four women—sit in chairs in a circle. Their heads are bowed. They hold hands. No one says a word.

After several minutes of silence, Junior lifts his head, but his eyes are closed. "Our Father, who art in Heaven..." he begins and the others join with him.

Chase closes his eyes and quietly intones the prayer as well.

After everyone says, "Amen," a woman whose back is to Chase says, "God's gift to us is life. Our gift to God is what we do with it!"

"Yes," someone else says.

Quietly, everyone gets up, hugs one another, and speaks in such quiet tones that Chase can't understand most of what they say. Within minutes, all of them are gone except Junior, who remains seated in one of the chairs.

Chase walks inside and smiles.

"Greetings, my friend," Junior says and holds out his hand. "Troubled tonight, are you?"

"Yeah, real bad." As Chase shakes Junior's hand, he says, "I need to talk with you about something."

"I already know about your father." He points to a chair. "Sit down and relax." He waits until the boy sits down. "Have you prayed on it, Chase?"

"Yeah, some."

"Then have faith. The unforeseen help is already on its way."

"What do you mean by that?"

"Faith is the belief in things unseen. You have heard something like that before. Am I correct? Trust is the belief in things that are. Matthew 21:22 says that all things—whatever—we ask in prayer, if we believe, we will receive. Prayer answers all. All is answered in prayer."

"I've prayed, but nothing has changed."

"Just have faith and trust the process." Junior pauses and stares into space for several seconds before he asks, "You do believe in the process?"

"I guess. Yeah. Yes, I do," Chase says. "I never thought about it much before, but, yes, I do."

"Well, then, let go and let God!"

"Let go of what?"

"Of the problem. Release it. You have handed it to God, so it is no longer in your hands. Your guardian angel has heard your prayer and the messenger from God is on his way. His journey is long, so you must be patient."

"I've never heard anything like that before."

"Trust me. Trust what I am saying."

"Okay, so where is the angel coming from?"

"Good question," Junior says and smiles. He leans close to the boy. "It is coming from your heart. Did you hear that? From your heart. The angel must peel away the layers of protection that surround your heart so he can see your soul."

"That doesn't make sense. I mean, I don't understand what you're saying."

"I know. I did not expect you to," Junior says. "Right now you are confused and you are feeling much pain. That is a normal place to be after such a traumatic experience. When human doings undergo such stress, they usually become defensive. Protective. They are not ready to hear healing words. Chase, you cannot help feeling pain because that is simply part of being human. The issue is how soon you can accept the pain for what it really is, how quickly you let go of it, and allow God to work for you."

"I hear you, man, but I still ain't getting it."

"Try this. Accept your powerlessness. Does that make sense?"

"Wait a minute! You mean, I can feel the pain, but I can't do anything to change the situation?"

Junior clamps him on the shoulder. "Yes. Exactly."

"I have. I mean, right now, or a minute ago—"

Junior leans closer. "Do not just talk the talk," he whispers. "You must walk the walk."

While Chase thinks about this, Junior gets up, leaves the room, and goes back to where Chase had met with him before. The boy follows. Without saying anything, Junior sits down in the meditation position and Chase does the same.

After what seems like ten minutes of silence, Junior begins to speak in a quiet voice, "What you must learn today is the true meaning of one word. It is the word *detachment*."

"Detachment? I don't get it. What's detachment got to do with—?"

Junior puts his index finger to his lips as if to command silence. He takes several deep breaths and silence fills the room before he says, in a far-off sounding voice, "Detachment means being

> Objective, but not indifferent
> Flexible, but not indecisive
> Firm, but not hard
> Wise, but not clever
> Patient, but not resigned
> Strong, but not overbearing
> Resolute, but not stubborn and
> Compassionate, but not indulgent.

Master these concepts and the process will work for you. Be otherwise and you will only get in the way."

Once again silence fills the room. "Now, Chase, your father has a dis-ease. His personal story is one of great triumph and disaster. In God's eye he has done a wonderful job, but your father does not think so. Out of displeasure with his life and grave disappointment with himself, he acts as he does. His dis-ease manifests itself through drinking alcohol. Others with the same dis-ease overeat or overwork or overreact or exhibit violence or rage, show anger, become depressed and some commit suicide. They develop a deficiency-motivated existence. That means they live only to acquire what they do not have. Some live in a malignant entitlement state because they believe that they deserve whatever happens to them. Others acquire authorized blame projection."

"Wait. You're throwing a lot of new stuff at me. I don't get that—"

"Put more simply, they blame everyone for their problems. It is a vicious cycle. Then comes more rage and more blame and more—"

"So Dad keeps repeating his cycle and he can't stop?"

"Precisely. Your father needs to see his dis-ease, and at that point, without his knowing or understanding, his guardian angel will come to his aid and help him recover."

"Why can't Dad see what he's doing?"

"Because he is in denial. Hear that word again, Chase. Denial. As one of my friends often jokes, denial is not a river in Africa."

Chase laughs. "Yeah, I got that."

"Good. Now I want to tell you a story." Junior gets up and points to the door. "I prefer to walk as I tell you this story."

They leave the Center for Conscious Living. Although it is night and there are no street lights, they have no trouble seeing where they are going. Soft clouds crawl lazily across the sky, allowing the moonlight to guide them. Chase hears a soft humming in the background that soothes him.

Junior places his arm on Chase's shoulder and they walk side by side. "Do you remember the time when one of your friends turned sixteen, and you and seven others had a birthday party for him?"

"Yes, it was about a year ago."

Just then, Chase stares at the building in front of him. "Yeah, it was here in this place."

The large, flashing red-and-blue neon sign reads: Li'l Walter's Food and Spirits.

"Read the words on the sign to me."

"Li'l Walter's Food and Spirits."

"What do they serve in there?"

"Food and beverages."

"Oh? Food and beverages or food and spirits? The sign says food and spirits."

Chase stares at Junior uncomprehendingly.

"You see, son, they do not call them food and spirits for nothing. The beverages they serve—mostly alcohol—are intended to substitute for your spirit. Human doings come here to get rid of their problems. Alcohol, or so they think, frees them from their problems. Little do they know that alcohol is merely a temporary substitute. Their problems are still there when the bottles are empty. In fact, in many cases the alcohol only compounds the issue by creating other problems. Lives are lost because of those who drive when they are drunk. People die in domestic quarrels."

"But my dad wouldn't do that!"

"No, not if his spirit was in control. That is the point I wish to make. You see, over time, the use of alcohol becomes a habit. Once it becomes a habit, a chemical begins to substitute for the person's spirit."

"Like my dad," Chase says.

"Yes, and I shall explain the reason. Instead of searching their souls, they seek to find answers in the drink. It is easier."

Chased nods and says, "It sorta makes sense now."

"You also need to know that alcohol is only a symptom of a far deeper problem. The problem is one's self. Are you following this?"

"Yes, I think so."

"They slowly drown their spirits inside the bottle. As one of my friends says, 'They are dead, they just ain't laid down yet.' That is how it is with your father."

"I understand," Chase says. A deep sadness fills his heart.

"Now, I want to talk to you about the little party that you and your friends had here."

"You know about that?"

"Yes, and you lied to Judge Dunn. You do drink. Remember how you and your buddies felt the next day?"

Chase avoids eye contact. "Do I? Bad, man, it was bad. We had gotten hold of fake IDs so we could buy the stuff. Then we partied a little bit."

"Yes, I know. Thus, the lesson in honesty and truth with the African chief. Had you not gotten honest with him, I would not have come to you. One cannot teach a dishonest person. Anyway, that is in the past. Let's move forward."

"I'm sorry I lied to Judge Dunn and sorry for the drinking."

"Yes, I know. Remember that next morning after you drank? Each of you felt rotten, and even though each of you got into big-time trouble with your parents, you guys glorified the experience to yourselves. And to your friends. Do you remember that as well?"

Chase hangs his head. "Yeah, we did."

"Now I shall use the very words you boys spoke. 'It was dope!' 'I was trashed.' 'I got wasted.' 'I was ripped.' 'I was stoned!' Am I correct?"

"Yeah, we said all those things."

"Since when has being a dope, being trashed, feeling like waste, being ripped and getting stoned been a good thing to brag about?"

They walk on, but Chase keeps his head down because he feels ashamed. Even though it had happened months earlier, the shame and guilt are still there, particularly since Junior knows Chase had lied to Judge Dunn.

"Now you understand the idea of denial. Each of you vividly described the way you felt. As accurately as you spoke, you did not feel or accept the true meaning of the words. You had been conditioned to think of those things as something manly, something macho."

Junior pauses and they walk in silence. Shame clothes Chase so fully he feels nausea crawling around in his stomach.

"Alcohol and drugs promote false courage. They create an illusion. They blind your judgment and if you continue down the same path, you self-destruct. Hear this: The day you start drinking is the day you stop growing emotionally. That night you buried your spirit one layer deeper within you."

"But I don't want it to be that way—"

Junior puts his arm around the boy. "And it does not have to be. Let me share a poem by my dear friend, Ella Wilcox, called 'The Two Glasses'."

There sat two glasses filled to the brim
On a rich man's table rim to rim
 One was ruddy and red as blood
And one as clear as the crystal flood.

Said the glass of wine to the paler brother:
"Let us tell the tales of the past to each other;
I can tell of banquet and revel and mirth,
And the proudest and grandest souls on earth
Fell under my touch as though struck by blight
Where I was king, for I ruled by might;
From the heads of kings I have torn the crown,
From the heights of fame I have hurled men down

I have blasted many an honored name
I have taken virtue and given shame

I have tempted the youth with a sip, a taste,
That has made his future a barren waste

Greater, far greater than king am I
Or than any army beneath the sky.
I have made the arm of the driver fail
And sent the train from the iron rail.

I have made good ships go down at sea,
And the shrieks of the lost were sweet to me,
For they said, 'Behold how great you be!
Fame, strength, wealth, genius before you fall
For your might and power are over all.'
Ho! Ho! pale brother, laughed the wine,
Can you boast of deeds as great as mine?"

"Man, that wine was pretty dangerous," Chase said.
"Yes, but listen to the water," Junior said.

Said the water glass: "I cannot boast
Of a king dethroned or a murdered host;
But I can tell of a heart once sad,
By my crystal drops made light and glad;
Of thirsts I've quenched, of brows I've laved
Of hands I have cooled, and souls I have saved,
I have leaped through the valley, dashed down the mountain,
Flowed in the river and played in the fountain,
Slept in the sunshine and dropped from the sky
And everywhere gladdened the landscape and eye.
I have eased the hot forehead of fever and pain;
I have made the parched meadows grow fertile with grain;
I can tell of the powerful wheel of the mill,
That ground out the flour and turned at my will.

I can tell of manhood debased by you,
That I have lifted and crowned anew.
I cheer, I help, I strengthen and aid;
I gladden the heart of man and maid
I set the chained wine-captive free;
And all are better for knowing me."
These are the tales they told each other
The glass of wine and the paler brother
As they sat together filled to the brim
On the rich man's table, rim to rim.

After Junior finishes, they walk quietly and stand once again in front of the Center for Conscious Living.

"Remember this little story, Chase, for one day it may serve you too. You see, this dis-ease often runs in families. There is a saying, 'The fruit never falls far from the tree.' You need to have concern for yourself. You must not worry too much about your dad. He can be saved, but he must first ask for help. When he does, God will work with him. God can move mountains, but your father must bring his own shovel. As for you, involve yourself with the issues within, and the answers will come. Remember the Law of Detachment. Contribute only through its principles. The enemy that your father faces is cunning, baffling and powerful. The enemy is himself, not the substance. Do you understand that?"

Chase nods. "Sure. Just taking away the alcohol won't help, right?"

"That's right," Junior says. "And when your father realizes the truth of what you have just said, on that day he will be on his way to salvation."

"Let's hope so."

"Yes. Now, Chase, I want you to be strong. Do not allow your father's troublesome situation to get you down. But if it happens, let that down be down on your knees in prayer."

Chase stares at Junior. Tears are rolling down the man's cheeks, and he makes no effort to stop them. He wonders why Junior is crying so intently. It is almost as if Junior feels his father's pain too.

"Such tears are good," Junior says. "You will understand this later." He lays his arm on the boy's shoulder and gently hugs him. "It is time for you to go back."

"Thanks. I feel a little better now."

"Go back with this thought. Stand under your father. Support him by allowing him to discover his own dis-ease. Today there is so much hype about the slogan, 'Just say no.' Often times we try to find solutions through the negative—by telling people what not to do. This clearly sets them up for failure. As you have learned, real solutions come through positive thoughts and desires."

"Positivity!" Chase says.

"Yes. And it yields infinite possibilities. Young man, you can only take care of yourself, and if ever again you are faced with the issue of whether to indulge in chemical substances of any kind, think of this: Don't just say no! Say yes."

"What?" the boy asks in surprise.

"Say yes to God. Say yes to keeping your spirit. Say yes to keeping your soul. Say yes to mental clarity. Say yes to being physically fit. Say yes to good grades. Say yes to college. Say yes to a prosperous career. Say yes to a family of your own someday. And finally, say yes to Heaven. By saying yes, you will receive eternal blessings."

They stare into each other's eyes and Junior starts to pray the Lord's Prayer. Chase joins him.

"...Thy kingdom come, Thy Will be done, on earth as it is in Heaven..."

....

He was in bed in his Aunt Marissa's house. At the foot of his bed, his mother knelt. The morning light had come in the window and gotten caught on her pale blue collar. He heard her say, "...Thy kingdom come, Thy will be done, on earth as it is in Heaven..."

Chase got out of bed and knelt beside her and they prayed in unison, "Give us this day our daily bread, and forgive us our trespasses..."

twelve

The Dream Team

CHASE CHECKED THE CLOCK on the back wall. He was ten minutes late. He walked toward an empty desk.

Mr. Freeman stopped speaking in the middle of a sentence and stared at him. So did all the other kids in the substance abuse class.

"We don't tolerate being late around here, young man," Mr. Freeman said.

"I know, sir, but I couldn't help it. We had car trouble. I tried to call, but all I got was an answering machine."

"Just what number did you call?"

Chase reached into his back pocket and pulled out a small sheet of paper. "686-1190," he said. "The Juvenile Probation Board."

The teacher stared at him as if trying to decide what to do.

"You can call my mom if you don't believe me."

"Sit down."

Mr. Freeman went back to shuffling papers on his desk until

Chase found a seat. "I don't know if you have noticed," Mr. Freeman said, "but there are four people missing today."

Chase looked around; he noticed the vacant seats. He stared at the chair where Brick usually sat. Where's Brick? he wondered.

"What happened to the other guys?" yelled one of the kids.

"Yeah, where's Brick?" barked another.

Mr. Freeman walked down the aisles of the classroom and distributed the next assignment. He stopped beside the last boy who asked a question. "Three of the other boys in here were found to have previous felony records. They are now in a juvenile detention center doing time. Brick had a car accident and the police found dope in the car." He stood up and looked at everyone and said, "Using any kind of dope while you're here is against the rules. That puts him out of the program."

"Where is he?" asked Chase.

"You break the rules, you go to boot camp," he said. "Brick has been sent to Missouri. He'll be on a work detail cleaning up the damage from the flood. It's going to be hard work, and he's going to be there for a while."

Chase wondered why Brick hadn't mentioned anything. He must have known the day they met at Burger Mania.

All the kids began to whisper among themselves and Mr. Freeman tapped his desk with his pointer.

"As I was saying before our latecomer arrived, here is some more food for your brains. According to the latest figures:

- 20% of kids between the ages of 14 and 17 are problem drinkers.
- It is estimated that over three million adolescents are alcohol abusers in this country.
- An alcohol-impaired driver, ages 16 to 17, is 165 times more likely to be involved in a fatal collision than a sober child the same age."

He paused and cleared his throat after the last fact. "Hear this clearly. TV is not your friend. It is the most frequent source of information about drugs and alcohol today. Do you kids know that for one year in the early '90s more than 600 million dollars was spent on beer advertisements on TV alone?"

"Wow! That's a lot of cash," said one student.

"Yes, and another 300 million was spent on wine and wine cooler ads," Mr. Freeman said. "But, let me share one other thing with you before we go on." Mr. Freeman looked up and caught Chase staring out the window.

"Chase," he called. "Read the fifth fact."

Chase focused on the notes before him. He flipped through two pages and saw the highlighted section. He began to read.

"One study has shown that whether a man considered himself 'a drinker' depended on his perception of drinking by his father or best friend."

Chase was startled at that statement. Immediately, he thought of his father and what affect this could have on him.

Throughout the remainder of the class, his mind kept turning to his father. Although he was careful not to gaze out the window, he heard very little of the lecture. Before he knew it, class was over and Mr. Freeman walked out the door.

Many days passed in which there was no Junior, no dreams and no lessons.

"Maybe this is the way it is supposed to be," Chase said to himself. But he knew that Junior still had more, much more he needed to teach him. "He'll be back. I know he will," he said to encourage himself.

A small part of him was glad he was having fewer dreams. He had taken in so much information during the past few months that he needed a break. He called it sensory overload, a term he had picked up in school.

Chase hadn't heard from his father lately either, and that bothered him. He thought of his father every day and many times throughout the day. When he did, he prayed as Junior had instructed him to. I guess no news is better than bad news, he thought.

After they moved in with Aunt Marissa, Mom began to speak more openly about family problems. She told him his father's drinking had been going on for years. She traced the beginning to the death of his dad's brother, Alexander.

"What really happened?" Chase asked. He had never heard any details. He knew there had been a brother who died, but it was one of those things that his parents never talked about.

"Yes, it was very mysterious," his mom said. "Alexander died from knife wounds inflicted during a quarrel in someone's apartment. You were four, maybe five at the time. Your dad was devastated by it, but he didn't deal with it. He needed counseling—someone who could help him understand something so traumatic." She sighed deeply, "I wished he could have talked to me about it."

"He didn't talk to anyone? Not even to you?"

Mom shook her head. "I tried to get him to open up, but he wouldn't. Or maybe he couldn't. Like a lot of men, he keeps his feelings locked inside. Whenever I brought up Alexander's death, he would say, 'It's over, I have dealt with it. We have to let go of the past and move on.' But I knew it wasn't over because he was still in so much pain. He couldn't hide that from me."

Mom stared into space and Chase knew she was remembering his uncle's death. "Everything, all the details, were left to your dad. He was the one who had to identify Alexander's body. Then he organized the funeral and planned a memorial service for relatives who later came from Michigan. Not once did he cry or show any sadness. Everyone called him a 'rock of strength.' And, of course, he also had to go through the trial."

"What kind of trial?"

"Oh, they caught the woman who killed him. The City of

Atlanta tried her, but she got off by claiming self-defense. Your father went to court every day the trial lasted. He sat and mostly he stared at the defendant. He never showed any feeling and never spoke to anyone. That went on every single day for two weeks."

"He just sat there? No tears? No anger? No nothing?"

"That's right. I was there too, but I couldn't stop crying—it was so sad. But your dad never showed any of his pain."

Chase remembered back to his own day in court with Judge Dunn. His mother—sitting in the courtroom with tears rolling down her face. But his father, absent, and then coolly reserved when he did show up.

"Did you say anything to him?"

"I tried. Once I called him out on trying to be so tough, and he said to me, 'I'm taking care of business in the only way that I know how.' Now I see he was taking care of it through the bottle."

She paused and wiped her eyes with the handkerchief. "It was very unnatural, you know, not crying. The two brothers had been so close. It was as if your father took pride in not showing his feelings."

"That must have been tough," Chase said. "And then the woman got off. I would have really been pissed—"

"Chase, don't use language like that. Yes, her getting off made a lot of people angry, but your dad never said a word. Not one word. He just walked out of the courthouse. The next day he started to drink—"

"I'm sorry—"

"And he has never stopped drinking all these years." She burst into tears.

As Chase listened, he thought about his Uncle Alexander. He wished that he had known him. He'd always felt lonely because he didn't have a brother, someone to grow up with. He wondered what it would have been like to lose a brother if he had had one. Maybe he had lost a brother when he had lost Ernie. Even more, he wondered why his father didn't talk about Alexander.

171

"Mom," Chase had waited until her tears had subsided. "I've been wondering about something. How do you feel about what's happened recently? You know, leaving Dad and us moving here?"

"Well, baby, sometimes you gotta have it out before you can work it out," she said.

Chase sensed her answer had been rehearsed, as if that's what she told everyone who asked. But then maybe that's how she needs to deal with it, he thought. Yet he felt she wasn't dealing with this any better than his dad did when Uncle Alexander died.

Each day he watched as Mom's eyes lost their glow. She seemed to walk with a much slower, deliberate pace. All of the emotional trauma seemed to be taking its toll on her.

It was the night of a full moon, and Chase thought it looked unusually radiant. It made him think of Junior, of the night races of his dreams. He wondered what Savannah was doing; whether she was moon gazing too. He decided to phone her. Just the sound of her saying the first word—"Hello"—sent tingles throughout his body. Nobody had a voice as soft and sweet as Savy.

Savy was a dreamer as well. Ever since that first day she hesitantly spoke about her dreams, some kind of wall had been knocked down between them. She trusted him; he respected her. Took her seriously. She liked that; in fact, she really needed a person like Chase in her life.

He did realize that sometimes it was hard for him to listen and hear at the same time. It was hard not to jump into the conversation and take over as soon as she paused. In the past, he always prepared his answers while he waited for others to stop talking. Tonight he didn't think about answers, only about what she was saying.

"So I guess that's all," Savy said. There was a long pause, a deep cup of silence that each expected the other to fill. So Savy said, "Chase, there's something I'd like to read to you. I got it off the

Internet. The author is anonymous."

"Anonymous?" he asked and stopped himself from telling her what Junior had taught him.

"You know how it is on the net. Somebody finds something, likes it, downloads and forwards it, and it goes everywhere and nobody really knows who wrote it."

"Yeah, I know about that."

"So let me read this to you. Okay? It's called 'Listen.'"

"I'm listening!" he said and they both laughed.

"When I ask you to listen to me and you start giving advice you have not done what I ask. When I ask you to listen to me and you begin to tell me why I should not feel that way, you have trapped my feelings. When I ask you to listen to me and you feel you have to do something to solve my problem, you have failed me, strange as that may seem. Listen. All I ask is that you listen. Not talk or do, just listen and hear me. I can do for myself. I am not helpless. Maybe I'm discouraged and faltering, but not helpless. When you do something for me that I can do for myself, you contribute to my fear and weakness. But when you accept as a simple fact that I do feel what I feel, no matter how irrational, then I can quit trying to convince you and get about the business of understanding what's behind this irrational feeling. When that's clear, the answers are obvious, and I don't need advice. Irrational feelings make sense when we understand them. Perhaps that is why prayer works sometimes for some people, because God is mute and doesn't give advice or try to fix things. He just listens and lets you work it out for yourself. So please listen, and just hear me. And if you want to talk, wait a minute for your turn, and I'll listen to you."

"Cool. I like that!" Chase said.

"You do? Really?"

"I wouldn't lie to you," he said. The words sounded much like what he'd heard his mother say. Or like something Junior would say to him.

They talked a little while longer, and then Savy suddenly said,

"Wow! It's almost two o'clock. We lost track of time."

Chase smiled quietly and thought, No Savy—we're just in dream time. But Chase said goodbye and hung up. He lay down and pulled the sheet over his body. As he fell asleep, he saw the round moon arc over the magnolia tree, and drop into a basket of branches.

....

Chase sits in the second row of the Omni—the indoor stadium in Atlanta where the Atlanta Hawks play. The scoreboard says it's the third quarter of a basketball game. Around him, people are cheering and applauding, yelling words of encouragement. He looks at the players, and realizes the team is made up of the top professional basketball players in the world. He recognizes them as the Dream Team.

Hey, this is great, he thinks, and joins with the others in cheering them on. Chase wonders if time is shifting—if this is the Atlanta Olympics again.

"Time doesn't really matter, Chase."

Until then, he hasn't been aware of Junior. Now the man sits next to him.

"I know this is your favorite sport. What do you think of the game?"

"This is a dream come true—a chance to see the Dream Team in person."

"You have made an interesting statement." A twinkle appears in Junior's eyes. "Dream Team in person."

Chase laughs. "Hey, that does sound far out."

"I did not say far out. I said interesting. And they are in person," Junior says. "So tell me then, why do they call them the Dream Team?"

Chase laughs and shakes his head. "Everybody knows that. Because they're the best in the world! The greatest!"

174

"Oh, I am not so sure they deserve that name."

"Of course they do! Why would you say that?" Chase asks.

"Simple. There is only one true Dream Team. If everyone knew about it, their lives would be filled with peace and joy."

"Okay, you've lost me," the boy says.

"My son, in the game of life, the team you pick to lead you determines whether you achieve your determined destiny. God, of course, is the commissioner of the league. That is obvious, but there are other crucial members who are almost equally as important, like your guardian angel, your senior advisor, your friendship council, your coat of arms." Junior stops talking and turns to watch the game.

The third quarter ends and the teams leaves the floor.

"As usual, I don't have any idea what you mean," Chase says.

Junior smiles as if to say, "I know that." For several minutes, he says nothing. Then he points to the officials who are talking in a corner of the room. "God, being the commissioner of the league, controls everything, particularly the picking of the officials. As you know, the officials dictate how the game is played. They control the tempo. You understand that much?"

"Of course."

"Good, because that reminds me of a little story. Once there were three umpires who had just finished calling a baseball game. They were hungry, so they decided to grab a bite to eat. While they ate, each began to talk about his relative importance to the game. The first umpire said proudly, 'I call the plays like I see them.' The second umpire finished his sandwich, wiped his mouth and said, 'That's fine, but I call them as they are!' The third umpire, who had already finished with his food, raised his hand for the check, paid it, then sat back, crossed his legs, and very calmly said, 'There is no call until I call it.' With those words, he excused himself and left."

Chase laughs. "Where do you get these stories? That's funny, but what's the point?"

"The moral of the story is that one person ultimately makes the call and that is God. He is umpire number three in this story and plays many roles in other stories, too. Always acknowledge to yourself that God is a teammate, an official, and the commissioner too—if He so desires. He is in everyone and in everything. God is all. Everything. Got it?"

"Not really—"

"You will. Now, the next thing." Junior is interrupted by the sound of the horn for a time-out on the floor. "Your guardian angel is more accessible than God. During difficult times, human doings tend to abandon the spiritual principles they have learned. They will often be aware of the existence of a Higher Power, but lack faith in Him. Sometimes that is because of an inability to place a face with the name or concept. Human doings begin to doubt the process. They ask questions."

"What kind of questions?" Chase asks.

"The kind whose answers are none of their business."

"Now you've really lost me."

"You know the kind. 'God, where are you when I need you?' 'God, if you are really there, won't you come to me?' The worst is, 'God, why me?' God is quite aware of this and thus He developed the concept of guardian angels. A guardian angel is usually someone you once knew well—someone who has already made the transition to the afterlife, someone who watches over you. It may be a friend or relative. Sometimes God will designate the person you least expect to be your guardian angel, just to get the most out of that angel's heart. After all, it is only with the guardian angels' best service to humanity that they receive their wings."

"Okay, I think I understand that, even though I'm not sure I believe it."

"That is all right too. Now, do you know your guardian angels?"

"Wait a minute—angels? More than one?"

"Yes. And I will tell you the names of yours. They are your Uncle Alexander and a fellow by the name of Ernie."

Chase feels his eyes fill with tears. Something about hearing Ernie's name and knowing that Ernie has been taking care of him in heaven is totally overwhelming. "Yeah," Chase says sadly. "Ernie was—was my boy."

"By *boy*—do you mean best friend?"

"Yeah, sure."

"I did not exactly know the connection," Junior says, "but I know you two were close."

"I can figure why Ernie would be up there helping me, but why Uncle Alexander? He died when I was a kid."

"The time of his death does not matter. Many years ago, long before you were born, Alexander and your father made a vow to each other. They vowed that if anything ever happened to one of them, the other would take care of their children. Now, as I said, that was a long time ago, long before either of them thought of getting married and having children. Little did they know that God would honor these terms and that the person in the position to offer the most service would be the one in the afterlife."

"So you're really saying Uncle Alexander is my guardian angel? That he, uh, looks over me and helps me?"

"You heard me correctly."

"Awesome," Chase says. "Just awesome."

"Something else, Chase. Your father and I are alike in many ways."

"Oh, no, you're wrong there," the boy says. "You're nothing alike. You don't look alike, talk alike, think alike—nothing. No way."

"Trust me on that one, then. I know this is difficult. It is beyond the scope of tonight's lesson, but I shall discuss this later as I teach you about the significance of the Mirror Image."

"Okay, but I have to tell you that if you really knew him, you'd

177

say there was nothing—not a thing—you and Dad have in common."

Junior holds up his hand. "I choose to move on. For now, I want you to know that you have two guardian angels and that your uncle is the one with greater authority. Get to know him. Grow to understand him."

"Okay, I believe you because you've been straight with me on everything else. But that's impossible. How do I get to know Uncle Alexander? He's dead."

"Of course, but you can still get to know him. Ask your mother for pictures of him. Ask her to tell you about him. Talk to people who knew him and your father when they were boys. When he was overseas in the army, he made two audio recordings and mailed them to your parents. Your mother kept them, and she can give them to you. It is important for you to learn who he was—who he still is. In the process of learning to know about your Uncle Alexander, you will grow in understanding your father as well. They are of the same blood. Most important, as you become more familiar with him, pray to him and visualize him standing alongside God and as a part of your team."

Chase is mentally exploring the idea of a Dream Team. He doesn't understand all of what Junior has said—which is as usual—and yet he feels the guardian angels are real. "That's something," he says aloud. "It's awesome to think that there's someone up there working for me."

"Chase, it is not just 'up there.' It is all around you."

There are five seconds left in the game and the Dream Team is up by one point. The opposing team is at the free throw line. Chase looks on as the player misses both free throws and the game ends. "They lucked out."

"No, not luck. The Dream Team was just supposed to win. That's all. It's all part of a bigger plan, you know—even things like basketball games."

"Oh, come on, man, you can't be serious. Are you?"

Junior smiles. "Let's move on. Look around you, Chase. You see, on earth, you must develop support systems of your own. Part of your own dream team is what I call a 'senior advisor.' This is an elder in your neighborhood—someone you look up to."

"Who is mine?"

"This you must learn for yourself by seeking him out. Just go look. Find anyone. It will seem as if it does not matter. The one you choose—once you have made your decision—will be the right one. You will ask, but God will choose him for you in such a way that you won't know until after you have made a decision."

"Kinda sneaky," Chase says and laughs.

Junior laughs as well. "That is how it works. You must search until you find the person God has already chosen. You need to do this as an essential part of your growth. To work with a senior advisor will demand love and kindness from you. You will learn that as you give, your senior advisor will share unique wisdom about life. Oh, yes, and something else. Word Perfect will tell you that you will discover in the middle of the word *gold* is the word—"

"Old! I'm ahead of you on that one."

"Correct. And to be old is to be rich—rich with insight and understanding. When you have selected your senior advisor, he will provide a bridge between generations. He will allow you to see how it was in his days and how things are really no different today."

"No different?" Chase asks. "Seen any computers lately? The new TVs? Or the souped-up engines in these cars?"

"Sure, technology has changed, and it will continue to change. That is not eternally important. What your senior advisor will do is help you see that the moral and spiritual issues are just as present today as they were at the beginning of time. In the book of Genesis, when Adam and Eve plucked fruit from the tree against the will of God—in deliberate disobedience—that was no different from our trying to live our wills today. Times may change, all right, but the core issues remain exactly the same. Here is a little tip: the most powerful senior advisors are those who are closest to making the transition into the afterlife."

"You mean I should go out and look for someone who is dying?"

Junior smiles. "Here is the only direction I will give you. Go and look. Find someone in your neighborhood who needs you. As you experience the gift of giving, you will receive far more than you can give. As one of my friends has said, 'What we shovel out, God shovels in, and God has a bigger shovel'."

"Okay," Chase says. "So I have Ernie and Uncle Alexander looking out for me. And I can understand finding someone, uh, some older guy in my neighborhood, who I can learn from."

Junior picks up a large plastic cup of water on the bench next to him and takes a long drink.

Chase looks around. They are the only ones still left in the indoor stadium.

"But the Dream Team, these guys that play here are real. Where's the rest of my team?"

"It says in Proverbs 18:24 '...there is a friend who sticks closer than a brother.' I call them your 'friendship counsel.' I am talking about friends—males and females, brothers and sisters—who care about you and support you. Henry David Thoreau used to say of friends, 'They cherish each others' hopes and are kind to each others' dreams.' You see, friendship is a relationship of love. I like to say it this way: True love in its fullest sense is friendship on fire. Never forget that."

"I've got a few friends, but I don't know," Chase says. "I mean this sounds like serious stuff."

"And it is. Therefore, you must choose your friends wisely. When you best exercise this God-given choice and do it correctly, you will find that the friends you pick will become an extension of you. They will care about you and wish only the best for you. They will listen and become the council that you seek for advice. True friends are gifts from God. They will be honest with you, even when it hurts. There is no better place to seek refuge from your hurt or pain than in friendship."

Chase thinks about the guys he had tried to hang around with. Some of them weren't good choices. He can see that now.

"It is nearly time for you to wake up, and I must leave soon, but before I depart, I must equip you with the final component of the Dream Team." Junior gets up and leaves the stadium.

When he returns he is holding a book and a small jewelry box in his hand. He opens the book, which is the Book of Psalms from the Bible. He opens it to Psalm 121.

"Read this aloud with me," he says and points to the first verse.

Together the two voices blend in reading:

"I lift up my eyes to the hills—where does my help come from? My help comes from the Lord, the Maker of heaven and earth."

"Now read it again. Just you," Junior says.

Chase repeats the words aloud.

Junior opens the jewelry box. "This also is for you," he says. From inside, he pulls out a glittering cross on a gold chain. "Bend forward." He hooks the chain around Chase's neck and tucks it inside the boy's shirt so that it rests against his bare chest.

Chase feels the cool metal against his skin. He opens his shirt and stares at it. The gold glistens brightly as if it drew energy from the bright lights in the stadium. Its coolness evaporates and he feels a warmth inside his chest, a warmth that seems to move deep inside.

"This is your coat of arms. Wear it proudly. In your times of weakness, it will surface and shine brightly, and you will feel the warmth all the way inside just as you do now. That is not an accident or coincidence. Pay attention to it. Its powers are insurmountable. It will, by its simple presence on your chest, screen the people who approach you. Those that live by the word of God will find you and feel drawn to you, even though they may not know why. Those that do not so live will shun you. That is its greatest gift."

"It's—it's awesome. Thanks!" Chase holds the cross up to his eyes and stares at it. He has ever seen anything so beautiful in his life.

....

When Chase awoke, he was in bed, his right fist balled tight on his chest. But when he opened it, there was no cross. A sadness came over him.

"It was only a dream," he said, and for the first time he doubted the reality of any of his dreams.

Chase showered, dressed, and had his breakfast. His walk to school was twenty minutes and he knew he had to get going.

"Chase, wait!" his mother called.

"I'm going to be late if I don't hurry."

"Then I'll drive you. This is something important." She asked him to come into her bedroom. "I have something for you. I've kept it here with Marissa, because your father didn't want it in the house. He said he didn't want to see it again, ever." She smiled and hugged him. "I waited until you were old enough. I thought when you graduated from high school I'd give it to you. But, I don't know baby—you've grown so much, and we've been through so much . . . ."

Her voice trailed off. From deep inside the top dresser drawer, she pulled out a small, velvet-covered jewelry box. Chase stared at the box, and thought, I already know what's inside.

"I want you to have this. It actually belongs to your father, but he doesn't want it. You see, it was a gift from your Uncle Alexander. When you were tiny, maybe a year old, he gave it to your father and me. He meant for you to have it when you'd grown. I think now is the right time to give it to you."

He bent down and she put the cross around his neck. He hugged her tightly. As he did so, he felt the warmth of the cross against his chest. He smiled. His protection was complete.

thirteen

The Man in the Mirror

THE FOLLOWING WEEK, CHASE and his mother moved back home. She gave him no explanation except to say, "It's time. Don't worry about your father. He won't be around for awhile."

He liked being back in his old room and in his old neighborhood, but he still longed to see his father. He hadn't seen him now in three months, and his memory of him mingled with what he thought he really knew of him—how could Junior think they were anything alike?

Over the next few weeks, Chase continued to grow emotionally; his faith was greater now. He had surrendered himself to the changes in his life. It felt personal, as if God had a special plan for him.

Chase spent time learning about his uncle. He asked his mother and his aunt Marissa questions, and even talked on the phone to an elderly woman who had once been a neighbor.

He selected his senior advisor. The choice had been obvious—

Mr. Seymour was his only candidate. Chase didn't explain anything, but he began to spend a few minutes after school with the teacher, just talking. He did little errands for him and helped clean the biology lab.

Over the next few weeks, Chase opened himself up to other kids he admired because of their positive outlook on life. He never told them that—he didn't think they would understand. It would take time, but the friendship would come.

Not a day passed that he didn't lay his hand against his coat of arms and use that as a time to pause and give thanks for being helped through such a difficult time in his life. He thought back to the night on the street corner with Ernie. He reflected on his day in court with Judge Dunn. Then he thought about his father.

"It's all going to work out," he said to himself. And to his surprise, he believed those words. Somewhere along the way of this journey he had acquired faith.

Chase had actually seen his Dad once during this time. He showed up at school one afternoon and took Chase for a pizza. They talked for a while, but it was mostly Chase who talked. But his dad listened and that surprised him. He told his father about his dreams and about trying to better himself through his associations. Although he knew his father was skeptical about the dreams, he didn't argue or tell him to stop. He did, however, smile when Chase asked, "Do you believe in angels, you know, like guardian angels?"

"Yes, son, I do."

"Well, you will be happy to know that Uncle Alexander is my guardian angel."

His father laughed aloud. "I don't know about that part," Dad said. "But I'm glad you want to know about him." For several minutes, he told him childhood stories about Alexander. His father became quite animated at times, as though the stories had transported him back to better times.

At one long pause in the conversation, Chase said, "I thought I'd be seeing you more often."

"I planned to," his father said. "I really did, but, you know, work, things like that—"

"No, Dad, I don't know, but that's all right. I'm just glad to know you're okay."

"It ain't easy, Chase," he said.

"Okay," Chase said, feeling more like a father than a son. "Tell me more about you and Uncle Alexander."

Although Dad didn't say so, Chase felt as if the family had faced a lot of problems—the kind no one spoke about. When Chase tried to probe into them, Dad shifted around in the booth and said, "Uh, well, they did the best they could, you know."

It all sounded familiar to Chase—more of hiding the truth. But he didn't probe any further out of fear of alienating his father.

"Thanks, Dad," Chase said. "I feel happy that you'd tell me all this."

"It just seems right to tell you," he said.

Chase took a deep breath, "Something else, Dad. I know about your substance abuse problem. I say that because I care." His father was holding the salt shaker, turning it around and around in his hands.

"Are you getting any help?"

With his head down his father nodded, as if unable to trust his voice. Chase knew that if his father raised his head, he would see tears streaming down his cheeks. He knew that was unacceptable to his father, to let his son see him that way. Chase remembered the lesson about denial and didn't want to push any of his own ideas or offer solutions. "I just want you to get well, Dad. We miss you."

"I miss you a lot too," his father said. He got up from the booth and went to the men's room. When he came back, his dad looked pale and a sadness seemed to fill his face. He didn't make eye contact with his son.

Chase wondered if his father had been crying, or drinking.

Summer vacation came and went. School would soon start again.
It had now been almost a year since Chase had first met Junior in
a dream. For the past five months he had heard nothing from his
friend. He missed Junior and wished he could see him, even if just
in a dream. But Junior had given him so much that he knew he
would continue to grow even if he never saw his Dream Merchant
again.

He and Savy had had their first date a month earlier. They sat
in a movie and hugged each other tightly. The touch of her felt so
good that he paid little attention to the screen. When he took her
to her door, he kissed her lightly on the lips and said, "I've always
been crazy about you."

With a blushed look on her face, Savy said, "Me too. . ."

The last Saturday afternoon in August, Chase sat on the front
steps. He had been reading a book that Mr. Seymour had given
him. It wasn't a book about biology; it was about listening to the
inner voice. He had read the entire book and was now going
through it a second time.

Just then a man appeared, who wore white pants and a green
surgical scrub top. He unfolded a sheet of paper and stared at the
numbers on the house. "Does Chase live here?"

"Yeah, I'm Chase."

The man handed him a single sheet of paper folded into quarters. "This is for you." He smiled, and left.

Chase opened it and read it aloud:

Deep peace of the running wave to you,
Deep peace of the flowing air to you,
Deep peace of the quiet earth to you,

Deep peace of the shining stars to you,
  Amen.
  And so it is!"

Below that was a message from Junior:

Dear friend, I am bedridden with personal dis-ease. In my present state I have lost the ability to come to you. I graciously request your presence at my bedside. I am in Room 314 at the Touchstones Institute. Peace!

Chase read the letter again and suddenly he understood the reason for Junior's silence. He raced inside the house and found his mother.

"Mom, I have to go someplace. Please, it's important and I'll be fine."

She nodded. "You know, I just don't worry about you anymore. Be safe and do the right thing."

"Thanks, Mom." He embraced her and kissed her cheek. "I've got the best mom in Atlanta. Maybe even the best in the world!"

Chase raced out of the house. Three blocks away, he caught the train that would take him to the northwest side of town. He knew approximately where the Touchstones Institute was. From the rapid rail line, he asked for directions and walked two blocks before he saw the large building, set off from the main road. It was then that he remembered it was a psychiatric hospital.

At first, that thought frightened him, but then he remembered the words of Ms. Ledd. "There is nothing to fear, God is here." Those words gave him new courage. He walked through the gates and up the driveway. Inside was a receptionist at a small desk.

She smiled at him. "Yes, may I help you?"

"I want to see somebody. Uh, Junior is the only name I know. I don't even know his last name. But he's in room 314 and he asked me to come." He showed her the note as though it conferred special permission.

"Describe him to me," she said. For a moment, Chase thought about how little he actually knew of his friend. Almost nothing. He didn't even know why Junior was a patient here.

"He's black, tall, kind of thin, but strong looking. His hair is long and braided. He has a deep voice—"

"Oh! You must mean Jerome! He's a regular." As soon as she said those words, she covered her mouth self-consciously. "Sorry, I shouldn't have said—anyway, come this way. Yes, he is in room 314."

A regular? Chase realized exactly what she meant. No, that couldn't be true. Not Junior. But he followed her down a long hallway. She stopped at room 314, opened the door, and motioned for Chase to go inside.

Junior lay quietly in a bed. He wore a hospital gown. His eyes were closed. Although Chase felt somewhat angry at himself for not knowing more about his friend, he instantly forgot it. Junior looked so thin and frail he figured his problems were far greater.

Chase stared at him and wondered if he should say anything.

"Quiet as it is kept," Junior said and opened his eyes. "You are as sick as your deepest secret." He paused and it was obvious that he had difficulty speaking.

Chase took his hand, held it for a minute, and then sat down beside the bed. "I—I've missed you."

"I know." Junior stared at the boy for a long time before he said in a voice so weak and low Chase had to bend down to hear him clearly. "I have always wanted to get completely honest with you, but my dis-ease prevented me. I am human too, as you now can see."

Chase squeezed his hand. "That's okay Junior, you're still the best."

"Thanks, Chase, but I also know you must feel some disappointment in me. That is all right. I ask you to remember one of the notes I gave you. It said, 'People don't tell you how much they know until they know how much you care.' Do you remember that?"

"Of course I remember—"

"Well, your coming today is exactly what I needed. Thank you! I am obligated now, through the grace of God, to make amends to you and to share my story."

Junior pulled himself up and Chase placed several pillows behind his shoulders and head. His cheeks had shrunk and his face looked thin, as if he hadn't eaten in days.

"Forget how bad I look. I'm ready to tell you about myself. My name is Jerome—but I want you to continue to call me Junior. I am the son of a retired army veteran and school teacher. Someone here said that I had the personality of an abandoned child. I first fought the idea, but later found out that during my early childhood, I did not live with my parents—I lived with my aunt and uncle in a small town in North Carolina."

Junior looked up at Chase. "My parents were shocked that I did not recall that fact. Anyway, whatever the case, I apparently had blocked out those times for reasons that are still unknown to me. My therapists say that those times were painful for me and led me to be very independent so that people would not have to do things for me. As a child, I remember living with my parents for the first time on a military base in Florida. The memories are faint, but I do recall being in kindergarten and hearing that President John F. Kennedy had been shot and school being let out for the rest of the day. Believe it or not, that is pretty much all I remember before the age of five.

"My childhood after that was very pleasant. We moved quite a bit because of my father's army affiliation, but by then I had already developed a strong will and an independence that made adjusting to new surroundings and new people easy. I played a lot of sports just as you do, year round, and I was quite good at them all. I became submerged in sports as a child. I was a good student and always did my homework, but I never read much for pleasure. I do not read as well today as I should because of it, I think.

"We moved from Florida to Germany and from Germany to Texas. It was in Texas that my brother and I became very close. My father was away from home quite a bit. I remember his fighting in the Vietnam war for one-year stints on two separate occasions. I think he fought in the Korean war many years ago too. He sent cassette tapes in the mail with his voice on them from Vietnam. As we listened, we knew they had been sent weeks earlier, and we wondered if he was still alive.

"I remember how hard it was on my mother without a man in the house. My brother and I were fairly big and sometimes she struggled with us. We never disrespected her though. My brother became my father in many ways. He taught me how to do practically everything—how to throw a baseball, how to catch a football, how to shoot a basketball, how to be a young man. His love was basketball; he practiced every day from morning 'til night. He became so good that he won a basketball scholarship to the University of Texas. He was quite an achiever—he did all those things even after breaking his femur bone three times.

"While in Germany we discovered that the reason that his leg kept breaking was that he had a cyst growing on it—it made the bone weak. He had it fixed there and was left with a metal plate in his leg. Oh, he was quite a guy, and I surely miss him."

"What do you mean he was quite a guy?"

"He has already made his transition."

"You mean he's dead?"

"Yes. I will tell you about that, but let me first continue. When I was thirteen, we moved to Alabama. Times were good, and I was very happy. I went to junior high and high school there. I was voted the best all-around guy, was an honorable mention all-state basketball player and the first black to graduate with honors from my high school."

"Wow. When was that?"

"It was 1976—the bicentennial. I remember giving the salutatorian speech at my graduation. Several people in the audience complained—loud enough for me to hear—that it was a mistake for me to be the salutatorian. They had never seen anyone black open the ceremonies before."

"I'm sorry—"

"Anyway, after graduation I attended a small, predominantly black university in New Orleans. I had several outstanding teachers; I graduated with honors and was accepted to one of the most prestigious medical schools in the country. I went, had four wonderful years there, and did very well academically. After graduation I was selected to complete my surgery training there."

"You were a surgeon? Come on, Junior, I find some of this hard to believe. After all, you're sick and in a mental institution—"

For a while Junior said nothing. "I know it is hard for you to believe. I may not have told you all the truth, but I have never lied to you." He took in a deep breath and coughed as he let it out. "Medical school and residency were very stressful. It took everything I had to keep my life in order. In 1988, I received word that my brother had died. The details were not clear, but he passed suddenly after a bizarre accident involving his girlfriend."

Junior sat up straight in bed. Tears filled his eyes, and he pulled a tissue from a box beside his bed. He leaned close to Chase and shouted—weak as his voice was—"Since then, I have never been the same! Half of me seemed to leave with his transition. My concentration and decision-making ability suffered after that."

Junior leaned back against the pillows and closed his eyes. Chase sat quietly and wondered if his friend had fallen asleep.

"Sorry, it's still painful to face all of this," Junior finally began to speak again. "You see, I have been married and divorced. I have a son. He is about your age, but I have no idea where he is. It is something I feel terrible about—every day.

"Despite all my personal problems, however, I graduated from the surgery program and went to work. Yet I never accepted my brother's death. I had never appropriately grieved. His loss was never taken to heart by me. Instead, unknowingly, I turned to alcohol to take away the pain. Because of my independence and my strong will, I did not know how to ask for help. Over a period of time, I became addicted."

"You? Addicted? I mean, after all you've taught me and—?"

Junior held up his hand. "Hear this first. I could not function without a drink, just one drink. Then I needed two. Then more. I lost everything—my wife, my son, my job, even my life. I wanted to die, but I did not have the courage to kill myself. One day I walked into the bathroom and stared at myself in the mirror. It frightened me so much that I screamed, 'Oh God! I am just a shell, a body without a soul.'" Choked by his own emotion, Junior paused and breathed deeply.

Overwhelmed by Junior's tears, Chase reached for a tissue, held it out to him awkwardly.

"Then it got worse," Junior said. "Inside my head, I heard a voice that said, 'Every rock bottom has a trap door.' At the time I had no idea what that meant, but I have since understood. I had hit my personal bottom—rock bottom, the end, or so I thought. It was time for me to make a choice to change my ways."

"What did you do?"

"I made the choice to change, but it was too late. Now I am paying for it. You see, I have liver cirrhosis from alcohol abuse."

"Hey, man, I'm so sorry."

"I know, I know. Those meetings I attend are Alcoholics Anonymous meetings. Do you still have the coin I gave you?"

"Hey, of course I do," Chase said and he pulled it from his pocket.

"I received that coin at my very first meeting. The problem is I decided to take charge of my life too late. Although I do not drink today, the damage done over the years is irreversible. Now I lay here wondering how long I have to live, and if I am going to pull through this time."

"You'll make it, Junior! You have to!"

"Perhaps."

"So are you really a Dream Merchant?" Chase asked. "Please, I need to know. Or did you just make that up?"

"Again, I will tell you that I have never lied to you," Junior said. "I am a Dream Merchant in the flesh. It all happened during my last hospitalization, about a year and a half ago. My heart stopped several times, what they call a code blue. When that happened, I gave up. I decided to die. As I let go, I saw a bright light and a tunnel. I wanted to go down that tunnel so badly, to end it all, to get out of this life. But as I approached the end of the tunnel, I felt as if a hand was on my chest, pushing me backward. I kept going on anyway. That happened maybe three times, heading forward, being pushed back.

"Finally on my last attempt to enter the tunnel my brother appeared. He looked just as he did the last time I had seen him, except he was surrounded by a glowing field of energy—that is the only way I know how to express it. He reached out and his hand touched me. Immediately, the jolt from his hand gave me an enormous burst of pleasure, as if he had ignited me."

Junior reached out for Chase's hand. It was cool, but Chase could sense the energy under the skin.

"I knew it had been him pushing me back, that it wasn't my time to go. And in a rushing wave that I can only describe as divine energy infusing my soul, I was *told* I was to be a Dream Merchant, that my remaining life would be dedicated to helping someone make the transition to human *being*.

"And then I awakened in the intensive care unit."

Chase stared at his friend. "It's crazy. It doesn't make sense. It's against everything I've ever believed, but—"

"But what?"

"I believe you." Chase took his friend's hand and squeezed it. "I don't know why, but I believe every word."

Junior began to cough and it weakened him. He was in obvious pain. "Get a nurse," he whispered.

Chase ran down the hallway and found the nurse. She pushed ahead of the boy and went into the room. "Wait outside," she said.

He backed away from the door and, as he did so, he bumped into someone coming out of the room across the hall. Automatically, he turned around to apologize and was astonished to see his father. "Dad? *Dad*? What are you doing here?"

"I'm here because," he said and paused, "I'm here because I can't beat this on my own. How did you find me here?"

"Um, actually," Chase pointed to the room across the hall. "I'm visiting my friend."

"Your *friend*? What friend?"

Just then the nurse came out of Junior's room, smiled at Chase, and told him he could go back in. Chase turned to face his father. "Dad, come on." He took his hand and pulled him into the room. "This is Junior."

Chase's dad looked at the wasted man lying in the bed, his eyes closed, his braids a tangled mass across the white pillow. He didn't know how his son could possibly know someone like this. "Who is this guy?" Dad asked, almost a whisper. "I've never met him, have I?"

"I told you about him once. He's Junior, you know—the one I was having dreams about, the one everyone was looking for. The Dream Merchant."

"Dream Merchant!" He father swore and then pushed closer into the room. "You! *You*!" His voice was barely controlled. "Leave my son alone! Stay out of his life! You hear me? Stay out of his life!" Chase had come inside but his father grabbed him by the shoulders and turned him back toward the door. "Don't you ever listen to him. Your Mr. Dream Merchant is nothing but a sick, homeless drunk. He's crazy!"

Chase shook his father's hands off his shoulders. He walked over to Junior's bed, protectively, as if he had to choose sides. He saw a calmness settle on his friend's face.

"Sir, if the messenger is so dark," Junior said, "then why is the message so bright?"

"What kind of nonsense is that?" Dad asked. "I don't know what you're talking about—"

"Chase, please forgive your father. Anger is part of the process. It is his protectiveness in being your father. I hope your Double Vision had already told you that."

"Yes," Chase said, "and I understand."

"How dare you tell him to forgive me! What is this nonsense you are talking?" Chase's father stared at them both. Then he took a few steps closer and peered more intently at the man in the bed. In that moment Chase saw the anger drain out of him, whether through his compassion as a physician, or shear exhaustion, he couldn't say. Then in a calmer voice, his father asked, "Don't I know you from somewhere?"

"You do and then again, you do not."

"Please, don't play games with me," his voice was tired now.

Junior took a deep breath, smiled, and said in a quiet voice. "Your anger with me is merely projection. You do not hate me; you hate my ways, for in a way I am you. Although we are quite different physically, I am your mirror image."

"My what? What's that supposed to mean?"

"Come closer," Junior said. "My voice is weak, and I am extremely tired." He motioned for both of them to sit.

"When the Heavenly Father created this world in his own image," Junior said, "he created everyone in duplicate—duplicate in the heart and soul, I mean. You do not know this—at least you did not until now—but I am your mirror image. That means I think the same thoughts as you do. I have had almost identical life experiences as you have. I went to a similar college and medical school as you did. I had the same job as you. My wife was similar to yours in many ways and I have a son the same age as Chase. The major difference between you and me is that you have now asked for help and I did not. Out of my fear and ignorance, I chose to keep alcohol in my life, which made me commit a slow suicide. For reasons that you do not know, you have been given the opportunity to live your life to the fullest—the fullness that God intended for you."

"This sounds like strange, crazy talk to me," Dad said, but he didn't move.

"Yes, I know, but listen. We were supposed to meet today. As you stared at me lying here, it was intended to scare you. Observe my body closely. For I am you if you do not change!"

Dad started to get up and then he looked at Junior again. For several seconds, he couldn't turn away. He couldn't speak. Tears welled in his eyes.

Junior took up both their hands. "I want to share something with you." He began to pray: "To everything there is a season, and a time to every purpose under heaven. A time to be born, and a time to die; a time to plant and a time to pluck up that which is planted. A time to kill and a time to heal; a time to break down, and a time to build up. A time to weep and a time to laugh; a time to mourn, and a time to dance. A time to cast away stones, and a time to gather stones together; a time to embrace and a time to refrain from embracing. A time to get and a time to lose; a time to keep, and a time to cast away. A time to mend and a time to sew; a time to keep silence and a time to speak. A time to love and a time to hate; a time of war and a time of peace."

"Ecclesiastes 3:1-8," Dad said and brushed away his tears. "That's my favorite passage of the Bible."

"Yes, I know," Junior said. "It's also my favorite."

Just then, an announcement came over the intercom that visiting hours were now over. Everyone had to leave.

Junior nodded to Chase as if to say, "Yes, leave."

When Chase left the room, he paused to look back. The two men were still holding hands, sobbing. It was only the second time that Chase had ever seen his father cry.

fourteen

Meter Relay

CHASE LEFT THE TOUCHSTONES INSTITUTE and started toward home. Evening was coming on and a stillness had settled over everything. He understood that his friend was dying. No one had said the words aloud, but he knew with an utter certainty, and it hurt him to think about that.

Then he thought of his father and his tears. He didn't believe Junior the first time he had told Chase that he had much in common with his father. The two men couldn't have seemed like further opposites in Chase's mind. But now Chase and his father had seen what Junior called the "man in the mirror," realized that his dad had been given the opportunity to see, through Junior, a glimpse at his own fate, his own possible future. He somehow knew his father was going to be all right. That gave him peace.

A sharp voice broke the stillness. "Chase!"

He turned back and spotted an old blue Chevrolet moving slowly toward him along the curb. His heart rate picked up, and he automatically checked out the other side of the street. Then he recognized the driver. It was Brick.

"Brick! Hey, man, when did you get out?"

"Couple weeks ago," he said. "Need a lift?"

Chase hesitated, remembering the previous ride he had taken with Brick. "I don't know—"

"Not like the other time," Brick said, "I'm different now. I'm clean, man. For real."

"I don't know man. I mean, I'm close to getting off probation," Chase said. "I just don't want to mess up."

"I'm serious," Brick said. "There's no dope in here, okay?" He stuck out his arm to shake hands. As he learned forward, the sun's rays caught a huge, gold cross on Brick's chest. Its reflection caused Chase to blink. "Brick, what are you doing with that cross around your neck?"

"You got one," Brick said and pointed to the exposed chain under Chase's collar. "Why can't I?"

"How did you know—? Oh, yeah, you're Brick and you know everything."

"Yeah, something like that."

Chase's eyes seemed riveted to Brick's cross. Although he would never be able to explain it to anyone, he knew it was all right to get inside the car. Junior had spoken about the powers the cross held: "Pay attention to it. Its powers are insurmountable. It will, by its simple presence on your chest, screen the people who approach you. Those that live by the word of God will find you and feel drawn to you, even though they may not know why."

"Coming?" Brick asked and pushed open the car door.

Chase hopped in. "How was it up there?" he asked as soon as he closed the door.

"Tough, man, tough. But you know, it was just what I needed. I was tired of living the way that I was living. Know what I mean?"

"Yeah, I think so," answered Chase. "What're you going to do now?"

"Change man—-change!"

"That's good."

Brick stopped for a red light. Four of Brick's old friends were standing nearby, passing a bottle of Turkey Wine around.

"Hey! There's my boy!" yelled one of them and he raced toward the curb.

Brick didn't turn even when the others called him as well. Chase's attention shifted from watching them approach to observing Brick. His hands gripped the steering wheel and his jaw was tight, eyes focused on the traffic signal.

The light turned green and Brick tromped on the gas pedal.

"I guess you are serious," Chase said.

"Believe it. New playmates, new playgrounds, new playhouses. That's what they taught me."

"That's great, Brick. I'm really happy for you."

Brick smiled.

When he did, Chase thought he looked younger, softer, and had lost that hard, tough expression that had been a part of him.

Brick pulled into Chase's driveway and stopped. "Uh, there's, uh, something that you need to know, something I have to tell you."

"Hey, sure—"

"But I need your word that you won't reveal the source."

Chase felt himself tense as he said, "Okay, what is it?"

"This doesn't come from me. You got that?" Brick lowered his voice as if someone else might hear them. "Something is going down on that same street corner, you know?"

Chase sensed what Brick was trying to tell him. "You mean—"

"Yeah. Where your boy got shot."

"What's going down? When?"

Brick's hand went to the cross on his chest and he stroked it as gently as if it had been a pet. "Can't say that. Listen, just let that Judge friend of yours know. Let him handle it. Don't do nothing more. Just tell him that something's going down. Maybe if the cops just hang around there, it won't happen. I could get smoked just for telling you this."

"I wish you'd—all right," Chase said. "I'll tell him just that. Will he know what I mean?"

"He'll know."

Chase smiled. "Right. Brick knows—"

"Uh, one more thing," Brick interrupted him. "Don't call me Brick no more. My name is Gerald, but you can call me G for short."

"Okay, G!" They slapped each other's hands. In that moment, Chase knew without a doubt that a change had taken place. "Gerald—uh, G, hmm? That's cool. Like that."

"Don't forget the message, okay?" Gerald said and put the car in gear.

"All right—G," Chase watched the Chevy pull out onto the street. Gerald honked and waved as he continued down the street.

Down the street Chase saw a flashing red light, the unmistakable sign of an ambulance, coming in his direction. As it sped past him, for some reason Chase knew it was going to stop somewhere nearby. He took off running. "I need to be there," he said aloud to himself, surprised at his own words.

Two blocks away, he saw where the ambulance had stopped. Savannah's house. He blocked out his panic and surged forward. A swarm of people had gathered around, mostly out of curiosity. While still a hundred feet away, he spotted Savannah and her mother. They were clinging to each other and crying.

He saw two paramedics place a stretcher inside the ambulance. Chase only glimpsed the man's ashen face, but it was enough for him to recognize Savannah's father. Then the ambulance pulled away.

A neighbor put her arms around Savannah's mother and led her away.

"Savy! Savy!" Chase pushed through those who had not yet moved on.

She turned and Chase could see her face was swollen and tear-stained. She stood limply, arms hanging at her sides. Chase rushed up to her and held her tightly.

"What happened?" he asked.

"Daddy just passed out. He was sitting in front of the TV and talking to me. Then—all of a sudden—he grabbed his chest and began to complain of chest pain and—" A fresh wave of tears stopped her from talking. She laid her head on Chase's shoulders and wept. Her fingers tightened their grip around him and her body shook.

"It's all right," he said soothingly. Yet even as he spoke, he felt in her the unspeakable words she couldn't say, the fear that she was going to lose her father.

As he held her tight, her fear seemed to engulf him. He thought of his own fear of losing his father and losing Junior. He tasted vomit at the back of his mouth. He swallowed hard repeatedly and willed himself not to be sick. In those moments, he became aware of the cross pressing against his chest. It worked. The fear vanished.

More than vanished: a new confidence came to him, certainly one he had never experienced before. He stroked her shoulders and whispered, "Your dad is going to be all right." He knew he spoke the truth even though he didn't understand how that knowledge had come to him. "Trust me."

Before Savannah could reply, a neighbor backed out of his driveway to take Savannah's mother to the hospital.

Chase took Savy's hand and walked over to her mother. "Ma'am, I'd like to take Savy over to my house. My mom's home. She'll be fine there."

Savannah's mother nodded and allowed a woman to lead her to the car. She looked like she was in shock.

"Shouldn't I be at the hospital?" Savannah asked.

"Your mom has friends. She'll be fine," Chase said, again with a powerful sense of certainty about his words. "As soon as we get to my house, you can call the hospital and stay in touch. Okay?"

Savannah allowed Chase to lead her down the street to his house. They held hands but said nothing. At his house, he took her inside and explained to his mother about Savannah's father.

Mom called the hospital and left her number for Savannah's mother to call as soon as she knew anything.

"Mom, I—today—I saw Dad—"

"Tell me later—"

"No, I mean it was good. He's getting help and—"

"Tell me later."

The hardness in her eyes made Chase realized she didn't want Savannah to know about his father. "Mom, it's all right—"

"We'll discuss this later," she said sharply. "Do you understand me?"

"Okay," he said. He didn't tell her that Savannah already knew about his father. So did half the neighborhood, he had discovered. It was hard for Dad to hide his drunken behavior when the neighbors saw him coming and going the way he did.

His mother offered to get them something to eat, and Chase followed her out to the kitchen and told her briefly about seeing his father. "He's getting help, Mom, that's what you need to know."

Mom said nothing. She made them both a sandwich and then excused herself. "I—I, uh, I have a headache," she said.

She went upstairs and closed the door of the bedroom behind her.

Chase remembered the message Gerald had given him. He called Judge Dunn. He finished by saying, "This is all I know."

"You don't have any information about a time?"

"No, sir, I don't. Just soon. And I've got a feeling these guys are tied in with Ernie's death." Chase was ready to hang up and then he said, "Oh, I'm not sure, but I think the car is an older model Caddy. And something else. It has a hole in the muffler that makes a lot of noise. You can really hear it coming. Somehow my memory is better now, Judge. I think I just blanked all this out that night. I hope this helps."

The judge thanked him and said, "Ernie always looked up to you, you know, and was proud to be your friend."

"I know," Chase said. "Thanks."

They ate their grilled cheese sandwiches, and then Savannah called the hospital and talked to her mother.

"Dad's stable now. That's all she knows right now," she told Chase, "but she'll call here as soon as she learns anything more."

After he sat down beside her, Chase took her hand. He told her about his own trip to the hospital, about his father, and about Junior. He knew she tried to listen enthusiastically, but she was still so worried about her father it was difficult for her to concentrate on what he said.

To his amazement, Chase understood her response. Wow, he thought, I just never had much awareness before about how someone else felt, especially when I felt I had something important to say.

"Say, Savy, want to try something?" He asked as he stood up. Still holding her hand, he pulled her toward the stairs.

"What do you mean by try something?"

"Just something," he said and laughed. He started to lead her upstairs.

"Chase, I'm not sure—"

"Hey, it's cool. Come on."

He took her past his bedroom. At the end of the hallway was a flight of uncarpeted stairs. He went up first, opened the door, and snapped on a light. "Okay, come on."

"Chase, I—this doesn't feel right—"

"Hey, it's going to be fine. Promise. I've never taken anyone else up here. Even my parents don't come up here. This is what you might call my quiet place, but I call it the Sanctuary."

"Sanctuary?" she raised a skeptical eye.

"Just look."

Over the past year, he had fixed up the small attic room. Everything that Junior had given him he had put in there. He had a small desk where he wrote almost every night in a journal. On walls that he painted a pale blue, he had framed and hung pictures of Uncle Alexander and Ernie. On a table were other mementos that had belonged to his uncle—a pocket knife, a hair brush, and his favorite poem, Rudyard Kipling's "If," that was framed.

A worn carpet covered the floor, something he had retrieved when they had recarpeted the dining room. He had installed soft green lights that cast a peacefulness over the room.

"This is where I escape," he said. He lit a candle. Its waxy fragrance soon filled the room.

A variety of glass mobiles hung from the ceiling. Chase reached up and touched them and they revolved slowly, reflecting the light in different ways. "No moment is ever the same when you stare at them," he said. He opened a tiny window a fraction so that a soft breeze flowed through the room.

"It's beautiful," she said as she looked around.

"I come here when I need to find myself, y'know, when I need to be alone, to think, and not be distracted. You're the first person to ever come in here—"

"Like I said . . . thanks!" she said and kissed his cheek.

"I've wanted to bring you here for a long time. I just never had the nerve before."

Chase had placed large pillows on the floor. He pointed to them. "I lie there and look around. Then I think of being outdoors on an autumn night. Just me and the night and nothing else."

He closed the door and turned on the CD player, which filled the room with soft flutes, distant drumbeats and melodic chants.

He took her hand. They went to the corner of the room, and lay next to each on the pillows and stared at the slowly rotating mobiles. The soft aroma of the candle seemed even stronger. She stared at the pictures on the wall and when she asked about them, he told her about his guardian angels.

"Now I understand why you come here and why this is special," she said.

Chase leaned on his elbow and, in the semi-darkness stared at her face. "Don't worry about your dad," he said. "All things are possible to those who believe."

"What?"

"I was quoting, uh, y'know, from the Bible. Mark 9:23. I've been told it helps in times like these."

"You read the Bible?"

"Please, don't think I'm some kind of a—"

Savannah gently put her hand over his mouth. "Shh, and before you start to apologize, I want to tell you this is the nicest thing any boy has ever done for me. I think you're wonderful." She took her hand away.

"You do?" he asked.

"Yes, I do," she said and then they both relaxed and watched the flickering candlelight. Time seemed to stop and both felt a deep, quiet peace descend over them.

"Chase! Chase!" he faintly heard his mother's voice. He jumped up and opened the door. "Yes!"

"The hospital just called. It's good news!"

"We'll be right down."

Chase blew out the candle. For a moment they stood in the darkness. He felt her presence, and thought of how beautiful she was. His body began to tingle and he wanted to take her in his arms and crush her against his chest. It still shocked him that he could feel so strongly about a girl.

"You're a little afraid in here with me, aren't you?" she whispered.

The softness of her voice made the tingling increase. "No, of course not," he said. "Why should I be afraid. It's my place—"

Again, she placed her hand gently over his lips. "It's okay. You don't have to answer." She removed her hand. A second later she leaned against him and kissed him lightly on the lips. He wrapped his arms around her. After an embrace, she pulled away.

A second later, she started down the steps.

Savannah's mother had called to say that the heart attack had been minor and her father would be fine. Savannah called the hospital's cardiac care waiting room and spoke with her mother. When she put down the phone, her relief was obvious.

A few minutes later, Chase walked her home. Savannah's aunt Athena had come to spend the night with her so her mother could stay at the hospital.

At the door, Savannah thanked Chase, gave him a quick kiss, and opened the door.

"Goodnight," he said and started to walk away.

"You're a real piece of work, Chase. I've never ever met anyone quite like you."

"Thanks," he said, aware that he was blushing.

"Promise me one thing."

"Of course. Anything."

"Take me back to the sanctuary again."

"Sure. Anytime!"

Chase went to bed with a smile on his face. He had trouble

going to sleep. He thought of his dad, Junior and Brick, but mostly his thoughts kept turning toward Savannah. He kept remembering the kiss in the room, the softness of her skin. He liked the way her body felt against his. "More of Savy," he mumbled. "I want more."

....

"More of her, huh?"

In this dream, Junior is strong, healthier than Chase has ever seen him before.

"Hey, Junior, you look great—"

"More of Savannah, huh?" There is a sternness in Junior's voice that bothers Chase. "Just what do you mean by that?"

"Y'know, just to—to be with her, I guess."

"Do not lie to me, son. I was not born yesterday. Now get honest with me."

"Okay," Chase says and drops his eyes. "I was thinking about sex."

"You know nothing about the subject."

Chase doesn't answer. It has been embarrassing enough to admit his thoughts.

"Young man, you are going to get your little boat rocked."

"I don't know what you're you talking about."

"The ship. That is what I mean. The ship you sailed on in here."

"I'm not following you."

"Then listen up," Junior says.

His voice sounds different than it ever has before. Chase hears anger, but he also hears a man of the streets, a side Chase hasn't seen in Junior before.

"I mean the ship you sailed in here on tonight and talkin' that crap about the 's' word. So you don't get it yet, do you. Okay. It's the *relation*-ship you're getting ready to set sail on. Do you think you're ready for the trip? Or are you going to enter it like most of your little friends do, without a true commitment? Out to get what you can? Is that the kinda kid you are?"

Chase is hurt. "Who are you to say what I know and what I want?"

"I said to cut the crap. I know because I was once fifteen years old, just like you. So right now, I gotta ask you this: Have you prayed on this? Have you talked about this with your guardian angels, especially your uncle Alexander? Have you discussed this with your senior advisor? Have you sought word from your friendship council? Ah ha, you haven't."

"No," Chase whispers.

"I didn't hear you, kid. Speak up."

"Okay, No! No! No!"

Junior shakes his head. "Then you really don't know squat about this, do you?"

"I know things. Y'know, I read and—"

"Listen up, then. You remember the story of the two glasses— the wine and the water?"

"Of course I do."

"Then remember this too. The 's' word is the most powerful drug on this earth. People use it just like they use alcohol and illegal substances. It can destroy families and friendships just like wine. God intends for this act to be the ultimate expression of commitment, as a way of man and woman totally giving themselves to each other. Got that? It wasn't intended to be used to hide pain, grief, misery, insecurity and the likes."

Chase nods slowly. He doesn't like Junior talking to him this way, but he knows it is what he needs to hear.

"You must never forget what I'm telling you right now. When I was your age, we used to say, 'Boys need a place; girls need a reason.' See, so listen up, because I'm telling you to slow down. Oh, you can convince Savannah. She cares about you, and she's going through some of the same struggles you are, kid. So here's what I'm telling you, and you'd better listen good. Slow down. Before you can effectively enter a relationship with someone, first you must have a balanced relationship with yourself. Do you hear that? First, with yourself."

"I'm working on that—"

"I know, but you're still green. Healthy relationships need intimacy and intuition—and they need them in that order. The first intimacy must be that of loving and caring about yourself."

"I'm not sure what you mean."

"Think of Word Perfect again. Pronounce the word intimacy slowly."

Chase does. "Oh, I get it. Intimacy is in-to-me-see. I mean, I get it sort of—"

"It means to see into yourself first. You must first know yourself. After that—after you know yourself and care about yourself—then, and only then, can you give your best to someone else. We call that self-love. Got that? Self-love allows you to be into it, to be engrossed—to give it your all. This is the intuit part."

Chased nods in understanding.

"See, kid, you're fifty percent of every relationship you enter whether it's work or play. The better you are, the better the relationship."

"So you're saying that if I care about me and who I am—if I respect Chase—I'll respect and care about others?"

"You're catching on, kid," Junior says. "A guy I know said, 'Relationships are like bombs. The more delicate they are, the bigger they can blow.' You've already shown Savannah your soul—your spiritual side. That gives your union great potential. Don't enter into anything more without total commitment. Hear that?"

He nods. "Total commitment."

"Yeah, kid, and if you do enter in with less than total commitment, you'll let her down. And listen good to this. If you let her down, the damage will be irreparable. You'll have misrepresented yourself to her and to your Higher Power. The latter is most dangerous. That's why many of your friends will go on and have many unsuccessful attempts at relationships."

"Yeah, I know about some of the other kids."

"Of course, you do. And I'll tell you what happens. They develop battle scars that remain with them the rest of their lives—pains that'll interfere whenever they try to start new relationships. You don't have to get caught up in that."

"I won't. I mean, I don't want to."

"Good. Then first seek balance in your life. And I warn you, kid, balance ain't just walking the line between two extremes or two women. It sure ain't wearing a chip on each shoulder. Balance means order, and that's what you gotta have. To have order, you must order it."

He pauses and smiles at Chase.

The boy nods.

"Pray for self-love, good intuition, balance and order. They're the prerequisites for any relationship. To enter a relationship without them is self-sabotage."

As Junior speaks these words, he seems to change again. No longer is he a man off the streets, but once again he becomes the lecturer, the teacher that Chase had first met. His voice is strong and forceful. It rings with authority.

"Do you remember Newton's third law?" Junior asks.

"Sure, from my physics class."

"And—? Come on, son, what is it?"

"For every action there is an equal and opposite reaction."

"Excellent! That is true in the physical world and just as true in the metaphysical world. When you are dishonest or untrustworthy in a relationship, Newton's third law goes into effect. Or as I sometimes hear people say, 'What goes around, comes around.' Do you understand?"

Before Chase can answer, Junior says, "I know you do. Now it is the same law that teaches us the necessity of contrast."

"Now I don't understand again. The necessity of what?"

"Do blind people know darkness?"

"Only if they'd once seen the light."

"Yes, exactly. Without bad there can be no good. Without wrong there can be no right. Without down there can be no up. Without in there can be no out there. Without pain there can be no pleasure and without a crucifixion there can be no resurrection. That means that sometimes bad relationships can be good."

"I don't follow you."

"If people have intuition, they can become aware of the wrongs they have done and then they can correct them. Intuition is the key that opens the door of understanding. I like to think of it this way: Intuition is God talking to you; prayer is you talking to God. But as you well know, some people lack intuition. They are also unwilling to look at themselves. They stay trapped by a vicious cycle of self-abuse through their relationships. That is a cycle of guilt, shame and loss of self-esteem."

Chase concentrates on the words. He feels Junior is throwing a lot at him and he doesn't want to miss anything.

"Now, guilt—the great paralyzer—renders them actionless. Shame teaches them to hide. And the loss of self-esteem allows them to go out and pick another unsuitable mate. The spiral goes ever downward. They become wrapped up in themselves. And, my friend, when you are all wrapped up in yourself, you make a very poor present."

"Yeah, I'm with you."

"If you decide to engage in a fruitful relationship with Savannah, that is your choice. But if you do, move forward with great caution. Give her your best. Commit yourself fully and without holding back. Treat her as you would like to be treated. Respect her as you would your own mother or a sister if you had one. Be grateful for the gift she represents. Find the right attitude in gratitude. Be loving and kind. Remember this too: The first two syllables in the word relation are the most important: re and lay. Say them."

"Re-lay."

"My son, relationships are like a 400-meter relay in track and field. They are about the right team and the right timing. Pass your heart as you would pass the baton. Give your best from start to finish. Winning the race depends not only on you giving your best, but also on the people you pick to run with you. If you decide to enter the race, I hope you will run the race of your life, for I know what you have yet to find out."

"What's that?"

"If you keep your eyes on the prize, it will materialize."

fifteen

Momentum

A MONTH AFTER JUNIOR'S LAST appearance, Chase made the following entry in his journal:

It's been a while since my lengthy session about the "s" word with Junior. I've thought about him a lot.

Although he's dramatic at times, he always seems to make his point. I've learned a lot from him.

He's probably been out of the hospital for a couple of weeks now, but he hasn't contacted me. Dad's still at Touchstones. He committed himself for two months, so he still has a few weeks before they release him. Mom and I visit him twice a week at the institute. They're not just visits though. They include an hour of family therapy.

I didn't care much for the therapy part at first, but I feel pretty good about it now. I guess the main reason is that I've gotten to know my parents in a way that I wouldn't have otherwise known them.

We have a nice counselor and that helps. He really listens and he makes all of us listen too. Best of all, Mom and Dad both have opened up to each other, and to me as well. They're telling me things I had no idea about, and I'm able to see their strengths and weaknesses as individuals and as parents.

The therapy isn't much about me, I mean nobody asks me a lot of questions or makes me talk. I'm learning by just being there. I have a better understanding of myself by knowing my parents better. It's amazing to me what just sitting, talking, listening and being honest can do.

I'm really looking forward to Dad's coming home. Hopefully, we will all be a family again. I used to know something was wrong, but I couldn't figure out what it was. They wouldn't tell me anything, and I thought I'd done something wrong. Now I know better. Life is getting better all the time.

Then there's Savannah, I love that name. I could write about her all day long. We have grown much closer over the last few weeks. I've taken Junior's advice. Savannah and I have talked a lot about us, our feelings and the "getting physical" part of our relationship. We've both agreed to take it slow. This going-slow business tests my patience. It's not something I want to share with my friends.

Chase put down his journal and thought about what he had written. Then he added:

I know the only limitations I have are those I place on myself.

Chase walked faster than usual to the Center for Conscious Living. Concerned about Junior, he decided to pay him a visit. When he arrived at the Center, Ms. Ledd was ironing again. "He's still in session," she said. "It's private, but he said it'd be all right for you to go back there."

Chase walked past her and headed toward the rear of the house.

"Hey, boy!" she called out, and he turned. "Remember, we see things as we are, not as they really are. Interpretation is everything. It's an extension of character."

"I guess I've never really thought much about character before."

"Yes, you have."

"I have?"

"Yes, character is an inside job. It is who you are when no one else is around. You got that? You've got plenty."

He smiled and thanked her and went down the hallway to the far end. The door was ajar and he could see Junior and hear other men's voices. He peeked inside. A short, light-skinned black man called out, "Yo, come on in."

Chase looked away quickly as if he hadn't seen or heard him. He felt embarrassed to be caught peeking inside. When he looked again, the same man motioned for him to come inside.

He shook his head.

"'Scuse me, brothers," the man said and walked to the door. "We know about you, Chase. It's okay for you to come in."

Still he hesitated and peeked again. He saw nine men sitting in a circle. He felt like an intruder.

"Hey, boy, you need to come in here with us," the man said. "Here men learn to share with men about real life issues. We don't do no talking about the game, the score, the play or the babes. We just talk about living life on life's terms."

"I don't know...I mean—"

He took Chase's hand and pulled him inside. There was an empty chair behind the circle and Chase sat down. For the next twenty minutes, he heard the men speak about their pain and disappointments, about the mistakes they had made and the people they had hurt. More than one man cried. When he did, someone would pat his hand, hug him or say something so he didn't feel alone.

As Chase listened, he realized what a privilege it was to be allowed to be there. He saw men—real men—who weren't afraid to talk about life the way it really is, who spoke of self-doubts and fears, who could say, "I messed up, and I'm sorry." He found that many of them had childhoods similar to his own—relatives with alcohol abuse problems, or difficulties involving smoking, drugs, sex or violence. As he listened, he realized that the form their problems took didn't matter much. In many ways it seemed they were all the same.

"Now it is time for our closing prayer," Junior said. The men stood in the circle and one of them pulled Chase into the group. They joined hands and waited for Junior to pray.

"Heavenly Father, we ask that you allow us to stay in the process—the process of becoming. Let us develop. Let us be. Let us come. Remind us that we are not human beings having a spiritual experience, but spiritual beings having a human one. May we take this life one day at a time. Forever is today, for we only have this moment. Teach us to be men of action, for evil thrives when the good do nothing."

Junior stopped praying and fell to his knees. The others dropped hands and knelt as well. Chase followed their action.

For several minutes, only the distant sound of a barking dog interrupted the silence.

"My brothers, listen to the word," Junior said. "The past is history, the future is mystery. Today is a gift, that is why we call it the present. Amen."

"Amen," said the others.

The meeting ended and most of the men left the room.

Junior motioned for Chase to sit in his customary spot. The boy sat down.

"Now we will truly learn about the power of prayer and the phenomenon of momentum. Do you know what momentum is?"

Chase, remembering the definition from his physics class said, "It's the product of the mass and the velocity of a body."

"Correct. Now, loosely it can be described as the force built up by a moving body, a moving spiritual body. But to describe it in physical terms is simply an understatement." He stood up. "I think it would be better if we go for a walk."

Obediently, Chase followed the older man outside. They turned left and after they had walked two blocks, they entered an area of Atlanta he didn't know. Soon they came to a strip mall. Two of the buildings had "for rent" signs pasted to their windows.

"What is that?" Junior pointed to one of the "for rent" signs.

"An empty store."

"Why do you say it is empty?"

"Because there's nothing inside and no one's in there."

"Really?" He walked right up the plate-glass window, looked inside and said, "I see plenty in there."

Chase walked up close. Shielding his eyes with his hands he stared inside. "I don't see anything. It's empty."

"Sorry, but you are incorrect my friend. It is not an empty space. It is a space filled with opportunity. Someday, someone with the right idea will make this place happen. It all starts in your mind, son, all in your mind.

"Listen now. You see, there are three kinds of people. Those who make things happen, those who watch things happen and those who wonder what happened. To be the first kind—the one who makes things happen—you must have a dream. A dream will allow you to see such a physical space as this as a room filled with wishes in the making."

He led Chase to the next unrented space and stared inside. "It is interesting that to a pessimist, when a person has a vision, it is an hallucination. To a dreamer it is simply a vision. When more than one person has that vision, the pessimist thinks it is a miracle. To the dreamer, it is simply a vision in transition. Finally, in life, when all people have that same vision, the pessimist is forced to call it reality. To the dreamer, it has been that from the start. We dreamers realize that it is a process—a process that requires action.

..., and that means hard work. Another way to say this is that it takes a lifetime of hard work to become an overnight success. Make a note of that."

"All right," Chase said. He pulled out a pencil and his small journal and wrote down the words. He saw the familiar intensity in Junior's eye.

They walked back to the Center for Conscious Living and sat down in the room. "Momentum is what I want you to learn about today. Momentum is the force that pushes the following equation." On a small chalkboard he wrote:

Dreams + Action = Reality

Chase repeated the formula.

"Dreams are the driving force of infinite possibilities. It is ultimately the 100 percent belief in one's self that comes with the realization that your Higher Power is always in charge. You must turn over to Him whatever it is you want, and it is yours for the taking. That assumes, of course, that your wish list is proceeded by daily prayer and followed with action."

"How do I tap into that?"

"Good question," Junior said, "and the answer is the Sacred Seven."

Before he said anything more, Chase numbered a list to seven, ready to write them down.

"First you must have a dream. Second, transform that dream into a wish list by writing it on paper. Third, give it support by sharing it with another trustworthy human being—and I hope you heard me say trustworthy human being and not a mere human doing. Fourth, every night pray to your Higher Power for your life to be His will. After all, He knows what is best for you, so really, you are asking Him to give you what you need and not necessarily what you ask for." He paused and waited for Chase.

"Fifth, pray for goodwill for family and friends as well as those in need that you do not know personally. Sixth, work hard regardless of the circumstances. Remember, the darkest hour of the night always comes just before dawn. It is when you are hardest hit that you must not quit.

"Seven—use this only when you are at your wits' end—write a letter to God. Put a stamp on it, and mail it to whatever address you think He is at. Do not be surprised when it does not come back." He paused and asked, "Do you have all of the Sacred Seven points?"

Chase nodded and read them back to him.

"Correct. Now, if you work on these on a continuous basis, you will secure momentum and your dream will become a reality. Remember this: Gifts from God may sometimes come in ways unimagined, so be on the lookout. Oh, one more thing to warn you about: Step six is the most difficult to master."

"Work hard regardless of the circumstances," Chase read. "Why is that the hardest?"

"There is a saying, 'easy come, easy go.' Nothing in life worth having comes without hard work. What most human doings do not and perhaps cannot tell you is that nothing of real value in life comes without failures or mistakes in some form. As you have been told, mistakes are the bridges between inexperience and wisdom. And a failure—if you choose to call it that—is still a step in the right direction because you have tried. The sixth step tells you to persevere when everyone doubts you. Now read those Sacred Seven points to yourself three times."

Junior sat quietly until Chase finished.

From his back pocket, Junior pulled out a rubber slingshot, the kind that looked like a "Y" with thick rubber bands on the cross pieces and a leather pouch for a stone. He held it out to the boy.

Chase took it and examined it.

"Do you know how to use this?"

"All the kids around where I live know how. We used to play with them all the time."

They went outside and Chase picked a small stone from the ground. He placed it inside the leather pouch and stretched the rubber by pulling it as far back as the band would allow. Then he yelled "Outta here!" and let go. The stone traveled almost fifty feet and landed just where he had aimed. It struck the side of a trash can.

"Good shot!"

Chase smiled, and waited. He knew a new lesson was coming.

"Now, tell me what kept that rock going."

"Momentum?"

"Think about it. What had to happen first?"

"Well, I put the stone in and pulled the sling back as far as it would go."

"Yes, and what had to happen before you pulled the stone back in the sling?"

"Hmm, well, I saw myself pulling the rubber strings back, and letting it go, and it landing over there—at the garbage can." Chase smiled because he realized now what Junior was trying to show him.

"Yes, you do understand. Life works that way—like a slingshot. In order to go forward, sometimes life pulls you backward. If you view this as part of the process and not as a setback, it is easier to go with the flow and not abort. As with the rock in the slingshot, sometimes in life the greatest of difficulties—or being pulled back—are simply the fuel or the energy needed to give us the momentum to move forward. And believe it or not the more you are pulled back, the greater the distance you go forward. And where we land is where we originally envisioned landing in the first place. That is, if we have a vision or a dream. And also with life, if at first—"

"I know, if at first you don't succeed, try, try again." Chase smiled and said, "Mom says that a lot."

"You're coming along just fine, son. Never take your eyes off the prize. If you do—"

"I know, I know. If I take my eyes off, I won't hit it."

"That is it exactly. Aim for improvement. Shoot for success. You have heard the expression, the right angle is the try angle. Well, an old friend of mine used to say, 'If you want to experience the rainbow, you have got to put up with the rain.' Nothing sums up the sixth step better than that."

As they stood outside of the Center for Conscious Living, Chase sensed it was time to go, and a sadness filled his heart. They were spending so little time together anymore.

"Be at peace," Junior said as he put his arm around the boy's shoulders. "Recognize the word moment in momentum. You must be totally in the moment to have momentum! The word moment is there to remind you that this is all you have: this very moment. Junior removed his arm and placed his hands in his pockets. "There are two days you must forget and only one you must remember."

"Huh?" Chase asked.

"Forget yesterday because it is gone. Forget tomorrow because it never comes. Live in today. Enjoy this day because you have traded a day of your life for it."

He shook the boy's hand. As Chase stared at him, he felt as if they were like two men who had been on a dangerous mission together and had now almost finished with their task. Chase felt Junior's energy and presence. He felt more confident than ever before. He clasped both his hands around Junior's. "I'll never forget you, man! Never."

"I believe you. Now, one more thing before I go. I want to leave you with a final puzzle to solve. There are three other Word Perfect meanings in the word moment. I will leave them for you to find. Good luck," Junior winked at the boy. "You feel the energy between us, don't you?"

"Yeah, it's powerful—something I've never felt before."

"Good, you are making your transition quickly into a human

being. I can feel your energy as well. There are ways that I can tell. I just want you to know that I am proud of you, son—very proud of you."

Chase released Junior's hand. Inside he felt warm, energized, and powerful.

sixteen

Leftovers

THE PUNGENT AROMA OF RED BEANS and rice filled the kitchen and slowly spread throughout the house. As he recognized what his mother was cooking, Chase smiled. He wondered if it was a peace offering for Dad.

After two months of rehabilitation, Mom had agreed that he could come back into the house. Even though Dad insisted he was free from his disease, Chase had seen the questions in Mom's eyes and an uncertainty in her smile. Chase wondered if Dad's problem was really behind him. He wanted life to be the way it was when he was a little boy—fun and peaceful. "I just want my father back again," he thought.

Because he wanted to be the one to open the door when Dad came home, he sat in the living room with his homework in his lap. When the doorbell rang, he wanted to be the first to rush to his father. After Chase started reading his advanced biology textbook, he became so absorbed in it, the ringing of the doorbell startled him.

"Dad!" he dropped his book and sprang from his chair. He threw open the door and his dad stood before him, a single suitcase in his left hand. Chase grabbed the suitcase and brought it inside. Then he turned to look at his father. He couldn't remember ever seeing such a big smile on his face.

"Son, I—" Dad said and wrapped his arms around the boy. Twice he tried to speak, but the words choked in his throat as he held his son tightly against his chest.

Chase understood what words couldn't convey. He later explained to Savannah, "I felt an energy running through us. Something like I'd never felt with Dad before. He kept hugging me and wouldn't let go. It was different, powerful."

When Dad released his son, he looked up and saw Mom. For what seemed like another long time to Chase, they smiled at each other. They seemed to hesitate initially. Then Mom took a step forward and held out her arms.

Chase knew then that everything was all right.

Dad ran across the room and hugged her, raising her up as he did.

"I'm so happy. So happy," Mom said.

"I love you," Dad said as he kissed her on the cheek.

Chase knew his father didn't say those words easily and they sounded real.

Chase felt as if he were peeking into a private moment between his parents. He felt so pleased to see them hugging each other. It had been years since he had seen such a thing.

"Please forgive me," Dad said.

"Oh, you know I do," she said.

"I'm a different man. Can we try again?"

Mom kissed his cheek and stared into his eyes. "It already is a new beginning. For us, for all of us."

Tears ran down their cheeks. They didn't seem to notice. Their eyes focused on each other, as if they were really seeing each other for the first time and loving what they saw.

Chase couldn't hold back, so he joined them in a three-way hug. Most of the time, they stared into each other's eyes with a love Chase had never seen before.

"We're a family again," Mom said. "A real family."

"That's the way it's going to stay," Dad said.

"And that's all I want," Chase added. He smiled at them, but he realized that mixed feelings fought inside him. He loved having his dad back, but would it last, he wondered. Will he leave us again?

"My, my, I can't remember when red beans and rice tasted so good," Dad said three times during dinner. Mom beamed from the across the table.

"It feels like the good ole days," Dad said. He turned to Chase. "When we first married, your mother fixed them a lot."

She laughed. "What he means is that we were so poor and they were cheap, so we had them three or four times a week."

"But she cooked them with love," Dad said. He clasped her hand. "Just like she did today."

Chase liked the meal Mom fixed, but even more, he liked the conversation that went on around the table. Dad began to talk about his sickness because he wanted them to know everything was out in the open and they could talk about it.

"My drinking troubled me for years," he said. "I tried for a long time to run away from it."

"I wish I could have helped," Mom said.

"No, nothing you could do. I just hurt so much inside," he said, "I couldn't talk to anyone about it."

"You can talk to us now," Mom said softly.

"And that's why I'm going to be well from now on." Tears filled his eyes as he spoke.

was all new behavior for Dad. Chase didn't say much, but ,tantly marveled at the change he saw in his father.

íter Mom cleared the table and put the dirty dishes into the ˛ .washer, they sat down again. Dad opened a thick, blue-covered book. "This isn't the Bible, but for me—for right now—it's the most important book in my life. We call it the *Big Book of Alcoholics Anonymous.*"

For perhaps another hour they sat at the table. Dad spoke of the lessons he had learned at Touchstones Institute. Every few minutes, he paused and opened his book and read a short portion. Chase smiled as he saw the tiny strips of paper that marked favorite places. Dad had obviously been reading it a lot.

"See, son, this book saved my life. From this book and from the people I talked to, I've learned how to live my life one day at a time. A lot of pain is still there, but not as bad and I don't feel it like before. Before it was there every waking moment, but now it kind of comes and goes. Most of all, I don't need anything to dull the pain anymore."

While he spoke, Mom had become too choked up to say much. Mostly she touched his hand or smiled. Three times, she leaned over and kissed his cheek. Chase hadn't seen such warmth between his parents for a long time. This is how a family should be, he thought.

"This book and the people there have shown me how to get out of the rat race and into the human race." Dad said. He stopped and his face lit up with a big smile. "See, it's like one of the counselors said, 'Even if you win big in the rat race, you're still a rat.'"

Chase laughed and so did Mom, even though they both realized that the joke wasn't too original.

"Here, son, read this aloud, will you?" Dad handed Chase the blue-covered book and pointed to an underlined portion on page 449. "And, son, I hope—yeah, and I even pray—this will be the only time you ever have to read anything out of this book."

Chase picked up the book and read the marked passage:

"Acceptance is the answer to all my problems today. When I am disturbed, it is because I find some person, place, thing situation— some fact of my life—unacceptable to me, and I can find no serenity until I accept that person, place, thing, or situation as being exactly the way it is supposed to be at this moment. Nothing, absolutely nothing happens in God's world by mistake. Until I could accept my alcoholism, I could not stay sober; unless I accept life completely on life's terms, I cannot be happy. I need to concentrate not so much on what needs to be changed in the world as on what needs to be changed in me and my attitudes."

The words were simple, and yet powerful. The wisdom applied to everything in life, not just for people like Dad with a drinking problem.

He looked up at his dad's outstretched hand. Dad didn't have to say a word.

The words of the book were enough.

....

Chase is aware of the sound of water. With his eyes closed he imagines the quiet, rhythmic slap of waves against a shore, the taste of salt on his lips, the grains of warm sand under his body.

He sits up and looks around. The morning sun is warm but not yet strong enough to burn his skin. Junior is lying next to him, stretched out on a beach towel. He assumes his eyes are closed, but he is wearing dark sunglasses so Chase can't tell. His breathing is slow and even, so Chase thinks he might be sleeping. He is wearing faded jeans and a torn tee sheet.

Chase knows it is a dream, but he has no concept of time. He has the sense that they have been lying there for hours without a word between them. The tide has turned and the first waves lightly brush Junior's feet. He doesn't move. Waves gently roll in, reaching higher on the beach. They become increasingly larger and stronger.

Chase feels as if they are thinking about everything and yet nothing. A peaceful, quietness embraces both of them.

Junior sits up, and pulls back several feet from the incoming tide. His toes dig deep into the sand.

"This is my favorite place. It is my mirror," he says as if they have been talking all morning. "This is where I reflect. It is the place where I am best able to take a look at myself and see myself emotionally and spiritually."

"Why is that?"

For several minutes or so Junior says nothing. He clears his throat and says, "Look at the place closest to you where water meets the earth."

Chase has no idea what Junior means, so he stares into the water.

"What do you see?"

"I don't know. What you want me to see?"

"Keep looking."

"All I see is the tide as it comes closer and closer to your feet."

"Very interesting. Now, keep that thought."

Chase wants to ask what he means by that, but Junior starts to talk again.

"As you already know, water is a very powerful element. It can calm fire and it can move the earth—two other elements of this world. At the same time, it can be made angry by fire and be consumed by the earth. It is the chameleon of elements. At one moment it takes the shape of its surroundings; at another time, it disappears before the wind, only to fall from the sky to replenish itself. Where my feet have dug in is the place where water and earth meet. Every place where elements meet is sacred."

"Sacred? C'mon, what do you mean?"

"Try it this way. They are places where the spirit is free.

Whenever you find a place where two elements meet and are contained in a safe way you will find peace. Even more important, you will feel a compelling urge to review your life before God. That is why all oceans, seas, lakes, and ponds provide relief. That is why the smell of a burning campfire and the heat from its fire provide a feeling of tranquillity. That is where earth meets fire. Do you understand?"

"Yeah, I think so," Chase answers.

"A minute ago you mentioned the tide. Think again of Word Perfect. In the word tide you can find two words."

Chase shakes his head. "Two words?"

Junior laughs. "This is harder, so I am going to tell you. The first is id. According to Sigmund Freud, id is one's self-preserving tendency, or in other words, the true, unconscious self. The second word is edit—tide spelled backward—and it means to prepare a text in the form to be read or heard. The gift of the junction of elements is that it allows us to be with our true unconscious selves and also allows us to edit our pasts and our futures. That is one reason so many people come to places like oceans. Many human doings are truly unaware why they seek such places. Human beings, however, know the answers are in such places, and they search for them."

Chase doesn't fully grasp everything Junior says to him, but he has long since stopped worrying about that. He has come to realize that even if he doesn't get it all when Junior tells him, he will understand when the right time comes. For now, he must listen and learn what he can.

"Walk with me," Junior says.

They stroll down the long, deserted beach. A cool breeze softens the effects of the sun's penetrating rays.

"You see, at this place where elements meet, time as we know it disappears. Hours become minutes and minutes become seconds. That place is the zone between the conscious and the subconscious. It is where the spirit worlds exist in harmony. *Time* becomes *emit*—a word that means to give out or to give off. We human beings decide to give ourselves to the spirit in the zone. We know that we have been there when we are suddenly zapped back into reality by a loud noise or another's touch. Then we realize we were gone, yet we were here, and time as we know it, has passed."

Junior stops walking. He turns around and points to the footsteps in the sand. "What strikes you as peculiar about your path?"

At first Chase shrugs as if he doesn't see anything peculiar. "Well, it does seem odd that the further back I look, the less I can see of each footprint in the sand."

"Excellent! Life is very much like that. The further we move away from the past, the more we change and distort it. The less we see it as it really was, and the more our minds remold it to fit our present circumstance. As you have noticed, my footprints have changed too. This symbolizes that the phenomenon is true for everyone's recollection of the past."

Chase nods in understanding and wonders why this lesson is important.

"You wonder why I want you to grasp this? I shall tell you. You must find a way to keep the past as true and as accurate as possible to avoid distortions. Now listen carefully. You must keep a written log of your life, call it a journal or a diary. In it, you will record events as soon as possible after they happen. You do that so you don't distort the truth of your life and miss the wisdom in it."

"I already keep a journal."

"Yes, I know, and you must continue to write in it faithfully. When you look back over what you have written you will have a true appreciation of the past so that you can best engage the future. Such knowledge ensures success in life. Success is not winning or losing, it is the recognition of the spiritual progress we have made on the journey. Success is learning to love the game of life beyond the prize. Stay with your journal. Do not neglect writing in it: It is vital for your growth. Record all that you read, see, and hear and keep your journal in a special place."

"Do you keep a journal?" Chase asks.

"Most definitely." Junior kneels on the beach. His large fingers trace the mark of a butterfly in the sand. "Yes, I keep a journal. I call it my leftovers."

"That sounds like a strange thing to call it."

"Perhaps, but I think of it as food—for thought. I have passed many of them over to you. Naturally, you heard the short version. They are my life in summary. My leftovers are like your mom's two-day-old red beans and rice. They taste better with time. To you, my leftovers are like a feast. To me, they are merely things I have gone through. Your life is also full of wisdom, and you can use it to enrich others. To do so, you need to remember and record everything as the truth because it is true. It was Jesus who said that if we know the truth it will set us free. That statement is a leftover from someone else's experience, but it has enriched my life, and I hope it will yours as well."

"I get it. Your leftovers have already enriched me."

Junior smiles at the boy. "Yes, I know. Truth is important, because in truth, there is knowledge. When we share that knowledge it becomes wisdom. Therefore truth is wisdom. Further, in truth lie lessons from God, and those lessons may come in many forms. Sometimes they manifest themselves in disguise, even as evil."

"As evil? Now, that doesn't make sense to me," Chase says.

"Then listen as I say it this way. Evil exists in this world for one reason—to evoke a greater good from human beings. We must learn to look for the truth in all that occurs on this earth, whether it is good or bad."

Junior lays his arm on Chase's shoulder and they begin to walk back the way they have come. After a few feet, he stops and points to the ground ahead. "What are those?" he asks and kneels down again and plays with the loose sand.

"More footprints. At least that's what I see. And they're not just yours and mine. Those others belong to somebody small, a kid maybe. And those—" Chase points to others nearby, "I think they were made by two men with really big feet."

"Yes, that is correct. Now, the lesson. The lesson here is that someone has walked this path before us. Such is life. Do not be fooled into thinking that your experiences, trials and problems are unique. They are not only yours because lessons in life from God are for everyone. And wherever you are, God is."

"You're getting heavy on me again, but I follow you."

"Excellent." Junior pauses and stares at the sun as it hovers over the horizon. "Remember, son, what I just said: Wherever you are God is."

They begin to walk again in silence.

Soft yellow, blue and violet rays stretch across the horizon and reflect on the water. Each phase of the sunset produces startling new colors. "We really lost track of time," Chase says.

"I prefer to think that we have been in the zone—the place where time becomes irrelevant," Junior says. "We must part soon, but before we do, I want you to know that I am proud of you. You will soon make your transition into a human being. I must be honest with you, though. I may not be here when you make that transition."

"Why not? I want you here and I couldn't make it unless—"

"Shhh," Junior says softly and puts his finger to his lips. "Just trust the process, son, trust the process."

Chase nods, despite his many questions.

They face the ocean and enjoy its beauty. The coolness of the waves wash against Chase's feet as he thinks of earth meeting with water. He feels a deep peace cover him like a soft blanket. Yes, he thinks, we are truly in the zone.

As he thinks about the word *zone*, he smiles because it contains the word *one*.

It makes sense. "In the zone, I am one with the universe."

Junior smiles. "Yes, you have learned the lesson."

seventeen

Awakening

CHASE HAD FORGOTTEN TO SET HIS ALARM. He was grateful for whatever it was that had awakened him; it was 8:07 a.m. and he had overslept half an hour. The TV set was still on and the morning news was on the screen. He turned it up.

"Last night, with the help of an anonymous tip, an undercover police task force interrupted a drive-by shooting attempt in Southwest Atlanta," said the anchorwoman.

Chase sat up in bed.

"Three youths have been caught and are being held without bail pending further investigation. Although shots were fired, no one was injured. The authorities feel there may be a link to three other incidents of drive-by shootings in the city of Atlanta."

"Yes!" Chase yelled. "G was right!"

He jumped out of bed and took the fastest shower in his life. He dressed while his body still glistened with moisture. After picking up his books, he stopped in the kitchen long enough to grab a fistful of cold cereal, and then he ran from the house.

Just as he approached the last block before school, he saw Savannah. She walked slowly as if she dreaded going to school. That was definitely not normal for her. He caught up with her before she reached the next corner.

"Hey, Savy, what's up? I've missed you—"

"Hi, Chase," she said and took his hand. They walked together in silence.

Chase and Savy hadn't hung out together in more than three weeks. He had waved to her at school and called five times. Always she said, "I'm real busy—some family things I can't talk about." She would ask him to be patient with her and then end the conversation.

In some ways, he hadn't minded not talking to her. His dad had come home; he was enjoying spending his evenings with him. Several nights passed without even turning on the TV. It still amazed him to see his father sitting in his stuffed chair reading from the Big Book and then the Bible. Most nights he read a paragraph or two aloud to Chase.

Finally she asked, "How's your dad?"

"Fine, but what about you?"

"I'm sorry for being scarce of late. I'll try to be around more in the future. We're having a few tough times at home. You know how it goes."

"If you want to talk about it, I'm here. I mean, I just want you to know that I am willing to listen."

"I know, Chase."

Even though they said nothing more, Chase felt the warmth of her hand in his. He felt lucky just to be walking down the same street with her. She was beautiful and smart and good and it felt good to know that she was his lady.

Just as they reached the school steps, the first bell interrupted their silence. She stood on her tiptoes, gave him a quick kiss, and said, "See you later."

While Chase sat in his first class, he had a sense that something, somewhere, was wrong. In English Lit. the week before he had learned the word "foreboding," which meant to sense something bad was going to happen. That's how I feel, he thought. It's like waiting for a bad sound you know you're going to hear. Chase tried to push away the feeling. His life was the best it had ever been. As he tuned out all the noises around him, he listened to voices within. He wondered if he really heard Ernie say, "It'll be okay. It'll be okay."

After a few minutes, he still had no idea what the foreboding was about, but he felt calmer. He had the sense that whatever it was, he would be strong enough to face it.

As soon as he walked inside the door of his physics class, Chase knew something was wrong. A heavy vibe hung over the room, although no one said a word. When he looked at Mr. Seymour's desk, he saw a middle-aged white woman he didn't know.

"Where's Mr. Seymour?" Chase asked.

She held up her hand for him to wait until the others were seated and the bell rang. "My name is Mrs. Fields, and I'm substituting for Mr. Seymour, who is ill."

"What's wrong? When will he be back?" Chase asked.

"How serious is it?" asked another student.

"I'm sorry, but I don't know. The principal has asked me to teach for the rest of the year, so we can assume it's serious. I can tell you that he has retired for medical reasons. I went by his home last night to pick up his lesson plans and books. He asked me to tell you that he has enjoyed teaching you and wishes he were able to continue. But," she said and took a deep sigh, "his doctor will not let him. Now, let's start class. According to Mr. Seymour, you are on page 233. Today . . ."

Her voice drifted on, but Chase heard nothing. Somehow he made it through his classes that day, but grief and a sense of deep loss stayed with him. It didn't seem right for Mr. Seymour just to drop out of his life like that. It just wasn't fair.

When he went to his last class and faced Mrs. Fields again, his grief had intensified. Biology was his favorite class and his best subject. But today, no matter how hard he tried, Chase couldn't concentrate on the lesson. He wanted to get out of there, maybe to go be alone, or do something to take away his anxiety.

Finally the bell rang and the students hurried from the class.

"Chase, please wait a minute," said Mrs. Fields.

He walked up to the desk. "I wasn't at my best today, and I'm sorry. Nothing personal against you, Mrs. Fields, but Mr. Seymour, well, y'know, he was my favorite teacher—"

"I know," she said. From her desk, she took out an envelope and handed it to him. Even before he took it, Chase recognized the strong, bold handwriting of his teacher. In the upper left-hand corner, he had written his address. "This contains a special assignment from Mr. Seymour. He didn't tell me what it was, only that I shouldn't give it to you in front of the other students."

"Thanks." Chase took the letter and placed it in his backpack. He ran out of the classroom and down the hallway toward the school parking lot. Once he was away from everyone else, he sat down under an oak tree and opened the sealed envelope.

Tears filled his eyes but he easily read the two lines of writing:

"Greatness lies not in trying to be, but in trying to help. I would appreciate a visit."

Chase laughed. Giving him a message like that was just like something Junior would do.

He felt better already.

Chase stopped at home to tell his mother about Mr. Seymour, but he didn't see her. It was Wednesday, the day she did the grocery shopping, so he wrote a note and left it for her on the front door.

Fifteen minutes later Chase arrived at Mr. Seymour's house. At the front door of a wooden, ranch-style house, he rang the bell. An elderly nurse in a white uniform opened the door. "He's waiting for you," she said and pointed down the hallway. "Second door on the left."

Chase paused at the open door and stared at a hospital-type bed in the corner. Mr. Seymour lay on the bed with oxygen tubing up his nose and IVs stuck in both arms. The image shocked him, and he leaned against the door jamb.

"Chase, come close," the teacher said and lifted his hand a few inches. "I've been waiting for you."

Chase came forward and stood on the opposite side of the bed. He stood very quietly. The late afternoon sun sliced through the curtain, leaving a shard of light across the old man's body. His dry, scaly hand reached out for his.

"Chase, it's okay, sit." Mr. Seymour closed his eyes. "I have just two things to say to you." His voice was so weak Chase had to lean forward to hear. "The first is that you have been my best student in thirty years of teaching, and I wish you nothing but the best in your life. The second is that I wanted you to meet my son."

"Your son?" A confused look passed over Chase's face.

"I've asked for all my children to be here. Chase, I consider you, too, like a son to me. But—my son—I wanted you to meet him." He closed his eyes, as though he were picturing his son in his mind.

"When he was a child, he had a mind like yours—sharp, quick, and witty," the old man said. "He was intelligent and I was proud of him. Now he's grown and has done great things with his life. Although he doesn't think so, I'm still proud of everything he has done." The old man coughed several times. When he stopped, he breathed deeply as the oxygen flowed. "I love him very much. Very much."

Chase could hear voices from the front of the house; the nurse was opening and closing the heavy front door. And then the sound of footsteps coming down the hall.

Chase was not prepared to see Junior enter the room. He stared at him, astonished and dumbfounded.

Junior's braided head was bowed either from grief or the trials of his own personal disease. A woman was holding onto his arm, her face obscured by coat and hair. Chase assumed it was a nurse or an aide from the Touchstones Institute. They sat in chairs side by side, next to the bed. Junior reached both his hands out to his father's hand; Chase could see his face was streaked with tears. He could not remember ever having seen Junior's peaceful face etched with so much pain.

"Chase—my son hasn't been inside this house in over twenty years. He has made mistakes—many in fact. But no matter the mistake, he has always been my son. My relationship with him has consisted of his sending me letters from around the country with no return address. Almost a year ago I knew he had returned to Atlanta because of the postmark, but still no return address. He was too ashamed. He couldn't accept that my love was greater than his shame."

Junior's sobbing filled the room. Chase felt his pain but could not look at him. He kept trying to think of something to say to comfort his friend, but he realized there were no words for the kind of pain Junior was experiencing.

"In a letter several months ago, he told me of a special friendship he had developed with a young man." The old man's voice grew if he were standing at the chalkboard in physics class. "He described the young man in terms of great admiration and respect. His description was so vivid I knew it was you. Don't ask me how; I simply knew." A twinkle filled his eyes as he said, "The students don't call me See-More for nothing."

"You know about Junior and about—?" Chase asked.

"Yes, I know everything that has happened. Jerome has told me, but mostly, I knew it because of the change going on within you." He paused and his eyes moved from one face to the other. "I am acutely aware of the teaching that has been going on through my son. Like Jerome, you have a brilliant mind, but I was afraid that you'd begun to feel superior. Actually, at the beginning of the year, I think you did—"

"Superior? I didn't feel—"

"You wouldn't have used that word perhaps. But you had no compassion for the weak or the troubled. You thought only of yourself."

Chase nodded. "Yeah, that's true."

"And you changed. You changed almost from day to day. I've watched you grow. You have become thoughtful, kind and sensitive. You care about people, especially those who are hurting and alone. Now your fine mind will mean even more to you and the world."

"Father, don't talk so much," Junior said.

"I have to say these things," the old man answered and smiled. He made an obvious effort to squeeze his son's hand tighter. "I said I was proud of you, Jerome, and I am. You have given this boy a gift—the greatest gift you could ever give anyone. You gave of yourself. For that, I am proud of you and eternally grateful to God for the miracle he has allowed me to see."

Junior leaned over toward his father. Chase could clearly see the resemblance of father and son—he wondered why he had never seen it before. Perhaps because he never really thought of Junior as a real person, a person with family. In some ways he felt Junior had sprung fully formed from his own dreams; he remembered how he wanted to keep Junior all to himself. He remembered the day he was hurt because Junior had driven off without him, how he seemed to have another life that didn't include Chase.

Behind Junior was the sunlit window, and the off-white stucco

wall of Mr. Seymour's bedroom. The woman beside Junior was crying softly, holding a white handkerchief in her long fingers. Chase
hadn't been paying much attention to her. But now, as he looked,
he saw Junior's head come up, as if in slow motion, and the sun
give life to his cocoa-brown skin, his honey-colored eyes, as he
turned to face—

It was Courtney Ewing. In a moment that lasted forever, a
moment that bounced between dream and reality, Chase watched
Junior turn to speak to the mayor's wife, just as he had tried to do
that first night at Gloria's, so many dreams ago.

"You're—you're the mayor's wife," Chase said awkwardly.

"Yes, I am, Chase. I'm Courtney," and she extended her hand to
him, and spoke with kindness, sadness. "I guess I know more about
you than you know about me. Junior's told me—"

"About *me*? He told you about me?"

She turned to Junior. "You should tell him."

"There is no easy way to say this Chase. Courtney is my sister."
Junior paused to stare at his father and then bent down and kissed
his forehead.

The old man blinked and smiled.

"*What?*"

"Yes."

Chase's mind replayed the entire movie of his friendship with
Junior, back to the very first night he had met Junior in his dream.
"I saw you that night, in my dream. You saved her."

"I wasn't there to save her, Chase. That was an accident." He
smiled sadly at the unintended irony. "No, I was there to *find* her."

Junior leaned back in his chair with some effort. His body
seemed to be in pain—Chase could now clearly see the emotional
toll that had been etched in Junior's face.

"The story itself is not important. It is the end of the story that
matters. Courtney is the only child of a woman with whom my
father was once deeply in love. Her name was Matilda; she was not

my mother. He met her many many years ago while he was stationed in Germany. Her father objected strongly to any relationship between them—you see, my father was an American, and he was black. Matilda's father put a lot of effort into keeping them apart, but it was already too late. She was pregnant.

"Then my father got his orders to leave Frankfurt; he was now to be stationed in North Carolina. He never saw Matilda again, never received answers to the many letters he sent her. She never got them—her father saw to that. She, in turn, thought she had been abandoned. When a beautiful baby girl was born, she was put up for adoption."

"That baby girl was Courtney?"

"Yes. Do you remember the day I told you about my life—my childhood and my family? I mentioned then that for the first years of my life I lived with my aunt and uncle in a small town in North Carolina. My mother had sent me there to live. A darkness had descended upon her and father. I was born while my father was stationed in Germany. But he returned to us confused, lost, devastated by his love for Matilda. Of course, he told my mother. He struggled. My father faced the same fork in the road as I faced and as your father faced." He smiled sadly. "The disease of alcoholism runs deep, you see. There was a three-year period of time that he walked the streets as I do today."

"But you told me about how your childhood was so pleasant, about your brother and sports—"

"Yes, Chase. My father eventually pulled it all together and our family survived. But there was always the painful knowledge in his heart of the child he left behind. Much later, after my mother died, he spent months trying to locate his lost child. And he eventually found her—in Atlanta."

Mr. Seymour's eyes were closed. His breathing was becoming much more labored, and Junior turned toward him, still holding his hand.

"Let me tell the rest," Courtney said. "Father could not bring himself to intrude upon my life. He had no idea what I knew about my birth parents, and he knew he had no right to bring that information to light. When Junior's wanderings also eventually led him to Atlanta, father wrote him a note, told him how much he still loved him, had always loved him, and told him about me."

Courtney stopped and wiped tears from her eyes.

"That night at Gloria's he saved my life, twice, and he said he had a message for me. But I wouldn't listen. You know, that night I thought he was some crazy street person. And then later, when we tried hard to track him down, and offered rewards—well he just couldn't come forward, not to that much attention. It is not his way."

Chase remembered the one day he had come upon Junior in the street. He was on the pavement, helpless and bleeding . . . and then the policeman suddenly realized that Junior was the "elusive one"—what was it Junior had said? *All I want is to be left alone. Is that too much to ask?*

"When Junior knew father was dying, he felt he *had* to reach me. So in the end, he did come forward, but we agreed not to annouce it, not to make it public. Junior has asked us instead to donate the reward money to the Center for Conscious Living, which we are happy to do."

There was a long moment of silence.

"This is unbelievable!" Chase whispered.

"I know," said Courtney. "I'm still trying to digest it myself."

In the silence Chase became aware of Junior's intense vigil over Mr. Seymour. The old man's eyes fluttered several times.

"Is, is he—" Courtney whispered to Junior.

"Yes. He is near the end," Junior said, and bent over and wrapped his arm around his father's shoulders. "Father, I love you."

"I love you too, son." His voice was barely audible. His dark eyes stared into those of his son and he said in a low voice, "I'm ready. I'm ready to move on."

Suddenly panic broke in Chase's chest like a bird trying to beat its way out. "You can't go, Mr. Seymour," Chase cried out. "You can't! I'll tell the nurse. I'll call 911 and they'll help—"

"Shhhh," Junior said. "Do not try to stop him. He is ready. This is his right. Let him go in peace." Junior barely said the last words as he tried to choke back the tears.

"But he can't go like this. I *need* him."

"Sit down," Junior said in a surprisingly soft voice. "We must honor his last wishes. He wanted Courtney and me at his side. And he also wanted you to be here. Honor this last request. Take his hand, hold it and feel his spirit leave his body. It is a special honor to be here as he makes his transition."

On his side of the bed, Chase took Mr. Seymour's right hand in his. On the other side, Junior and Courtney both gripped his left hand.

"Peace," Courtney whispered. "I love you."

The old man never opened his eyes again.

Junior, Courtney and Chase gently laid Mr. Seymour's hands across his chest and took up each other's.

"Let us pray," Junior said. They all bowed their heads. "To transcend is to grow. And to grow is why we are here. Let us see what has taken place today as an extension of life. For Father's spirit is free . . . free to roam with you, dear Lord. And there is no better place to be. It is in your name that we pray. Amen."

As they released hands, Chase thought he felt a soft wave of air drift upward, and the room became still once again.

eighteen

Goodbye

THE NURSE CALLED THE EMERGENCY medical team. When they arrived, they made Chase, Junior, and Courtney leave the room while they put Mr. Seymour on a stretcher. Slowly, the three of them followed the medics out to the ambulance. A crowd of neighbors had gathered. No one cried; no one spoke. It was if they, too, had experienced the moment of deep peace.

The ambulance drove away. As Chase turned to go home, he saw Savannah in the crowd. He walked over to her. "What are you doing here?"

"I knew where Mr. Seymour lived, and I knew you'd be here." She smiled and put her arms around him.

Chase nodded. He saw the ambulance a block away trying to make a left turn.

"Everything is going to be okay," she said. "I know it."

"Yes, I believe you," he said. "But it's sad to think I won't ever see him again."

Savannah kissed him lightly and from her jeans pocket she pulled out a greeting card and placed it inside his jacket pocket. "Read it later," she whispered.

"But what is it?"

She placed two fingers over his lips. "Later."

Chase looked around for Junior and Courtney so they could meet Savannah, but they were gone. He knew they hadn't gone back into the house or he would have seen them. "Let's go," he said to Savy.

They walked hand in hand to her house. Neither of them spoke. When they reached her house, she brushed Chase's cheek with her hand and turned to walk up the steps. There were no final words, no hug.

As he watched, he had a strange feeling about her leaving. Her pace, slow and deliberate, made him think of a prisoner in an old movie. Her walk had the same kind of finality about it as if she were walking toward the electric chair.

A terrible sadness came over him and he stood for a long time staring at the closed door. Instead of going directly home, he walked a dozen blocks out of the way. For now, he didn't want to think or feel. He just wanted to be alone.

Street lights had come on by the time Chase reached home. He stared at his own front door, and a shock ran through him. The note he had left his mother was still taped there.

He unlocked the door and went inside. "Mom! Dad!" he called, already aware that no one was there. He flipped on the lights as he went through the house. No notes anywhere. He checked the refrigerator and saw that she hadn't replenished the milk.

Dad wasn't home either. For the past few weeks, he had always been home by dark. He checked the answering machine, but there were no messages.

Confused, he slumped onto the sofa and waited. "Something's

really, really wrong," he said, and then wondered if he had just let his imagination run away with him. Visions of car accidents and muggings filled his mind, but he tried to push them away.

Then he remembered the card from Savannah. He reached into his pocket. It was a beautiful card with a picture of a man and woman on the front. It looked as if they had been holding hands and had now pulled apart. He was waving and she was blowing him a kiss.

He opened the card and read the printed message:

"You are traveling through the rest of your life, so choose your destination carefully. You'll arrive soon enough, so you don't have to hurry. As you go, don't stick to the well-traveled roads. Discover the back roads, forgotten paths and endless trails. Hear new voices, and see strange sights. Embrace ideas that are different from yours.

"You'll realize the value of your travel isn't where you find yourself at the end of the journey. The true value lies in realizing who you have become somewhere along the way."

He then read a handwritten note from Savannah:

I couldn't tell you this in person because it hurts too much. Our family is moving to Chicago. To think that I may never see you again hurt too deeply to tell you in person. Even if we never meet again, Chase, I want you to know that my feelings for you are everlasting. Wherever you are in life, just remember that a piece of me is with you—heart and soul. I'm sorry to bring this news to you at such a difficult time. But then, there is never a good time for such news, is there? I love you.

She signed her name at the bottom.

Utterly devastated, Chase sat quietly in the living room. It was a moment when he wished he could cry, but no tears came. His pain was too deep, he had turned numb. In a single day he had lost two important people in his life—one by death and the other by distance—moving a thousand miles away.

She would never go back to his special room, to look up at the stars again with him. He'd never kiss her soft lips again or close his eyes and inhale her perfume.

For a long time, Chase sat staring at nothing, feeling empty and alone. Suddenly aware that it was almost eight o'clock and he hadn't eaten, he got up and walked into the kitchen. Tears slid down his face and he wiped them away. More tears came and he began to weep uncontrollably. A wave of anger came over him and then the pain of his loss hit him like a heavy punch into his chest.

He sat at the table and pounded the heavy oak with his fists. He stomped his feet, but for a long time, he could find no relief.

As the tears slowly subsided, he remembered Junior's words about hitting rock bottom. "So where's my trap door?" he asked and he began to cry again.

Finally, Chase got up and made himself a peanut butter-and-jelly sandwich. He took a few bites, but he had no appetite. He got up to throw the partially eaten sandwich in the garbage, and a sliver of light flashed off a piece of glass. He bent down to pick it up, and opened the garbage can to throw it away. Inside he saw a broken bottle of Jack Daniels. "Oh, no," he moaned. He picked up the large shard of glass and stared at it before he saw the smear of blood along the jagged edge.

"Oh, no, God, no." He ran toward the door. Then he saw it.

Taped to the back of the door—where he hadn't bothered to look when he came in—was an envelope from his mother. With his hands shaking, he opened it. She said that Dad had started to drink again and was back in the hospital. She was going to stay with him until visiting hours were over.

Chase fell to this knees and tears poured from his eyes. "How much more, God, how much am I going to have to put up with today?" Filled with fear, anger, and diminishing faith, words began to pour from his mouth. "Lord, I don't want to just hear about you anymore. And I don't want anymore teachings about you. I'm tired of having my feelings stirred up. The messages frustrate and confuse me, because they only remind me of how far away you are. From now on, please, don't send me anymore messengers because I need *you*. I want you to give me a sign! Do you hear me? Are you up there?"

nineteen

Transitions

IT HAD BEEN SIX WEEKS since his father's fall. Chase had closed himself off. He went to school, came home, spent most of his time in his private sanctuary. Chase had no sense of time passing, only of pain searing his heart. He hadn't seen Junior since Mr. Seymour's death. The dreams were gone, Savy was gone, his father was gone, his mother was tired and withdrawn—everything and everyone had left him, and Chase had descended into a deep pit of loneliness.

He looked at the pictures of Ernie and Uncle Alexander staring down at him from the wall—his guardian angels. He could still hear the words of Junior's teaching:

"Your guardian angel is more accessible than God. During diffi-cult times, human doings tend to abandon the spiritual principles they have learned. They will often be aware of the existence of a Higher Power, but lack faith in Him. Human doings begin to doubt the process. They ask questions—you know the kind—'God, where are

you when I need you?' 'God, if you are really there, won't you come to me?' 'God, why me?'

He was painfully aware of being a human *doing*—a human doing nothing.

The doorbell brought him back to the present. He made the long descent to the front door quickly.

"Hello, Chase, remember me?" It was the same man who had come, what seemed like a long time ago, to tell him that Junior was hospitalized.

Before Chase could answer, the man handed him a sheet of paper and said, "I'm sorry to be telling you this, but your good friend is back in the hospital."

"Junior?"

The man turned and left.

With fingers trembling and his heart beating rapidly, Chase opened the folded sheet of paper. "Is this another of his riddles? At a time like this?"

Then he read the whole thing aloud:

Why do we park in driveways, drive on parkways, live on byways and pay for freeways? Answer: Because life does not always make sense. God is here to add comfort. He may not always come when we call, but He always arrives on time. Until then, when life gives you lemons, add a little sugar, and make lemonade.

When we do what we can, God does what we can't. Be strong, have faith, and always remember Philippians 4:9.

Finally, my little friend, we do not have all day. Get your tail to the hospital.

Chase started to run out of the house, but he remembered the Bible verse, so he picked up the Bible his father had been reading for the past two months. He didn't know where Philippians was, and he had to waste several seconds until he found it.

To his surprise, his dad had highlighted that very verse: *"Whatever you have learned or received or heard from me, or seen in me—put it into practice. And the God of peace will be with you."*

Chase read the verse three times, wanting to be certain he understood the message Junior intended for him. Yes, he thought, as much as I want to see my friend, I know what I have to do first.

Something about Junior's message scared Chase, but he went anyway to the Touchstones Institute. "I'm going on faith alone," he whispered to himself, "because I know it's what I'm supposed to do." As he heard the words in his own ears, he realized his fear had vanished.

He poked his head inside the visitors room, where he knew he'd find his mother. She sat in a corner, her head bowed, and she didn't look up until he called, "Mom."

She came forward, embraced her son, and said, "He'll want to see you."

"What happened to him?"

"You ask him," she said. She took his arm and walked him to his father's room. "He's in there. I'm going back to the waiting room."

Chase pushed opened the door and his father looked up. Their eyes met and held for only a second before his father dropped his gaze. He turned toward the wall and started to cry softly.

For only a fraction of a second Chase watched and then he walked over to his father. No words had yet passed between them, but the boy understood that his father was ill, not just doing something bad. His father had a sickness, a terrible disease that millions of people also have.

"Dad, I'm glad you're here," Chase said. "I'm glad you knew you needed help."

Then the boy and the father hugged each other. Instead of letting go, Chase held his dad. "I wish I could take away your pain," the boy said, "And I wish I could make you better, but I can't. You have to do it alone, Dad, but I'm here to help you."

"I'm sorry, so sorry—"

"I know, Dad. Here's something I bought for you last week," Chase said. "I've been saving it until I felt it was the right thing. Guess that's now."

Chase handed him a card and it contained a poem called, "After A While," and was taken from the works of Veronica Shoffstall:

"Will you read it to me?" his dad asked. "Please?"

"Sure," he said and took the card.

After a while you learn the subtle difference
between holding a hand and chaining a soul
And you learn that love doesn't mean leaning
and company doesn't always mean security.
And you begin to learn that kisses aren't contracts
and presents aren't promises
And you begin to accept your defeats
with your head up and your eyes ahead
with the grace of a woman, not the grief of a child.
And you learn to build all your roads on today
because tomorrow's ground is too uncertain for plans
and futures have a way of falling down in mid-flight.
After a while you learn that even sunshine burns
if you get too much.
So you plant your own garden and decorate your own soul
instead of waiting for someone to bring you flowers.
And you learn that you really can endure
that you really are strong
and you really do have worth,
And you learn and you learn
with every goodbye you learn...

When Chase finished, he handed the card to his father who read it silently. A tear dripped down his face and onto the card. "Thanks," was all he was able to say through his trembling lips.

"Something else," Chase said. From around his neck he took the gold cross and laid it in his father's hand. "This is what Junior calls my shield or my coat of arms."

"That's—that's—that belonged to Alexander—"

"Mom gave it to me. She said Uncle Alexander wanted me to have it. Now I want you to have it."

Dad began to shake and he could no longer hold back the tears. He sobbed, his wailing filled the room. Chase took the card from his father's hand and laid it on top of the stand next to his bed. He clasped the cross around his neck.

"I'm no good, son. I don't deserve—"

Chase gently placed two fingers over his father's lips the way Savy had done to him. "I understand, Dad, I really do, and I love you. No need for you to say anything." He put his hand inside his father's and held tight.

After several minutes, Dad's convulsive crying lessened. "So ashamed—"

"Shh," Chase said. "Say, Dad is it okay if I tell you a story?"

His dad nodded.

"Once there was a little boy who was playing outside. He came upon a tree and saw something wonderful, more amazing than anything in his life. A tiny butterfly fought desperately to free itself from its cocoon. The boy felt sorry for the poor thing, so you know what he did?"

Before his dad could speak, Chase answered his own question. "Why, he freed the butterfly. It was a dumb thing to do, but he didn't know that.

"Once free, though, the butterfly couldn't fly. You see, Dad, the butterfly needed that struggle to get the necessary strength in its wings to fly. Anyway, he thanked the little boy for helping him, and joined a pack of caterpillars. As they crawled across the fields, the butterfly crawled along with them. For many weeks, he traveled with them. They accepted him as one of their own. The day came when they made him king of the caterpillars because they respected his beauty.

"One day the now-old, grounded butterfly looked up and saw a magnificent creature flying above him in the cloudless sky. It had wings much like his own, but they were more beautiful and more powerful. The creature glided gracefully in the soft majestic winds with a simple execution of its colorful wings.

"The old butterfly stared in awe. 'Who's that?' he asked the caterpillars. 'That's the butterfly, the creature we all dream of becoming—the master of the wind. He belongs up there. We belong down here. That's why we're caterpillars, remember?' The old butterfly continued to stare into the sky.

"The others crawled off together and left him.

"Dad, the poor butterfly lived and died a caterpillar, because that's all he thought he was. And it happened because he had been denied his necessary struggle to live and be what God had planned.

"Dad, I hope your struggle adds life."

He squeezed his son's hand.

They sat and stared into each other's eyes for several minutes.

"You're such a fine young man, a special gift to my life," Dad said before he drifted off to sleep.

Once his father slept soundly, Chase went down the hall and told his mother. "Junior's here, too, and I need to see him."

He stopped at the nurses' station and found out Junior was back in room 314. He walked through the open door and stared at the man in the bed. At first, the man didn't look like Junior, and he started to turn away. Chase could see that his arms and legs were like sticks, but his stomach ballooned out, like a pregnant woman's, beneath the thin white hospital sheet. His face had also swelled up, like soft bread dough left to rise, and his ears seemed to be curling back into his head. He was breathing in short gasps, as if he had to fight for every intake of breath.

"Chase." Even with the IV in his hand, he motioned for Chase to come inside with a graceful sweep of his thin arm. Chase was brought back to the first time he had seen that gesture: in the very first dream, Junior sitting on the white-washed wall, gesturing Chase toward him. In that sweeping motion, Chase traveled the distance between then and now—could not accept that a year had gone by and had led them both here. Then Junior smiled and, when he did, he looked more like the friend the boy had known for so many months.

"I got your message and I came to—"

"My young friend," Junior spoke in a whisper. "I congratulate you on your transition to a human being. Yes, you've made it. What you did just now for your father was to give him understanding, acceptance, and hope. It was beautiful. And I felt proud of you."

"You saw—?"

"Ah, Chase. God's ways are strange ways," Junior said. "Now sit, please."

As the boy took the chair, in some way he would never be able to explain, he knew this was the last time he would ever see Junior. Once again, he felt a sense of grief, and yet he had a sense of peace as well. Chase stared into the face of his friend. He could see the pain clearly—Junior seemed unable to speak anymore, so they sat in silence. Junior's breathing became more labored.

Chase got up to call a nurse, but Junior, his eyes still closed, shook his head. "Okay," Chase said. "I'll honor your wish."

Then Junior's eyes suddenly flashed open. "Is Chilly still around?"

"Yeah, I think so." Chase hadn't seen him for awhile, but knew he came and went.

"Good. Do something for me. Keep an eye on him, okay?"

"Okay."

"Chase?" Junior's eyes were closed again. Chase could hear a small gurgle as he labored to breath.

"Yeah?"

"Stay with me, okay? There is one more lesson for you to learn."

Chase pulled his chair closer and took Junior's large thin hand in his own. Junior was completely quiet and still, but Chase could see his chest rise and fall with each breath. After a while, he thought Junior must be sleeping. Still holding his hand, he laid his head upon Junior's chest and closed his own eyes—he was exhausted. He would rest, and be there when Junior awoke.

....

The sun warms them both. Chase opens his eyes and realizes he is back on the beach; Junior is beside him, his feet half buried in the sand.

"I have something to tell you," Junior says, "but first you must promise me never to tell either of your parents."

Junior has a gleam in his eye, and his request for secrecy seems so boyish that for a moment Chase remembers Ernie, remembers all the boyhood pacts of secrecy between them.

"I promise."

"Okay, listen. Your father will recover. In fact, he will go on to do great things with his life. The wisdom and love you have just shown him has laid the foundation for his courage to fight his awful disease."

"But how do you know that? I mean, that's in the future and—"

Junior lifts his hand to stop the boy. He smiles. "He will succeed because I am his mirror image. In earthly terms, I have not succeeded. Being mirror images, we know about each other. I know everything about him, including his past and his future. He and I have a special, vital connection and I can tell you because I know what will happen to him."

Chase feels his eyes moisten, but he only nods. Finally he says, "Thank you. I promise I won't worry about him anymore."

"That is why I have told you. Now, I have something else to say. Like you, I, too, will make my transition tonight. Without you I would not have had the chance to redeem myself in my own heart. With my passing, your father will be freed of the energy bond that exists between mirror images."

"What? You've lost me—"

"Trust me on that, Chase, even if you do not understand what I am saying. Your father will feel light, insightful, happy, joyous and free. Guided by the inspiration of family and friends, he will live a spiritual life. He will regain his practice and win the respect of other physicians and patients. He will now build a solid and loving relationship with your mother, and he will be a better father to you—someone you can talk to the way you have learned to talk to me. Your dad will be successful at living life on life's terms. He will learn to do it one day at a time, but you will need to be there for him."

"Of course, I'll be there whenever he needs me."

"But more than that," Junior says. "You must caution him when he tries to go faster than one day at a time. You two will share an incredible bond through a common experience—the uncanny ability to dream and to make your dreams a reality."

Junior pauses, looks up at the sky, at the seagulls wheeling and squawking above them.

"Your father will start an organization that will touch young-sters like you. The organization will help them dream and teach them the wisdom of his life. I cannot discuss the details of his mis-sion with you. But I can say this much: If he were to touch the life of only one teen—and I assure you there will be many—he will have found the necessary redemption in his heart to make his own transition when God calls him one day.

"I wanted you to know that, and it must be our secret."

Junior turns to face him and takes Chase's hand in his own. "You have a special gift, son—the gift of spirituality. For you to continue on to your next transition from human being to spiritual being, you must do one thing—study the *ritual* in *spiritual*.

"Learn the history of your African, African-American and American ancestors. Study their pain and study their successes. That way you will learn of your true spirit and who you really are. You will learn your people's ways to tap into the spirit world of powerful, unlimited resources."

"Okay, I will."

"Your life will not be easy. The things you need most to learn, you will not—you cannot—learn in school. You must seek them yourself. Resist the flow around you. If you 'go with the flow,' you will often get soaked." He pauses and chuckles at his little joke. "It will also dilute your spiritual consciousness. It will prevent you from tapping into what you already know but will often need to be reminded of—the God in you. Unfortunately, the world you live in is not fair. There is evil—especially one particular vicious evil called racism. It is cunning, baffling, and powerful. Such evil disguises itself and speaks out in many ways through newspapers, television and even language.

"Listen carefully to language. It says more than we are often aware. Take the word *black* for example. In our eyes, black is a beautiful color. To many, however, it is a word they use negatively. Think about the linking of black with other words such as the black plague, blackmail, blackball, black magic, blackout and the one I despise the most, black sheep of the family—all negative. Be conscious of abundant injustices surrounding you. I have given you only one example. Now you must watch for others because injustices exist everywhere. They are most dangerous when they roam on the subconscious level within you.

"Always remember your teachings. It was a black cat that led you to me. Black is part, but not all, of who you are. Never let anyone speak to the contrary. Never deny your blood, for it is rich. A fellow Dream Merchant once electrified the world with his words on this subject of racism. On August 28, 1963, at the Lincoln Memorial Dr. Martin Luther King, Jr. gave his 'I Have A Dream' speech. It set a tone for the search of racial justice in this country. Through his godly voice, he captured the hearts and ears of America."

Junior shifts his hip and digs his hand down into the pocket of his faded jeans. He brings out a piece of paper folded several times. As he gently unfolds it, Chase sees that several passages are highlighted in yellow ink. Junior hands the paper to Chase.

"Read the highlighted words aloud."

The boy begins to read:

"I have a dream that one day on the red hills of Georgia, sons of former slaves and sons of former slave-owners will be able to sit down together at the table of brotherhood.

"I have a dream that one day, even the state of Mississippi, a state sweltering with the heat of injustice, sweltering with the heat of oppression, will be transformed into an oasis of freedom and justice.

"I have a dream my four little children will one day live in a nation where they will not be judged by the color of their skin but by content of their character. I have a dream today!

"I have a dream that one day, down in Alabama, with its vicious racists, with its governor having his lips dripping with the words of interposition and nullification, that one day, right there in Alabama, little black boys and black girls will be able to join hands with little white boys and white girls as sisters and brothers. I have a dream today!

"I have a dream that one day every valley shall be exalted, every

hill and mountain shall be made low, the rough places shall be made plain, and the crooked places shall be made straight and the glory of the Lord will be revealed and all flesh shall see it together."

Tears glisten on Junior's face. "Chase, that piece you have read from is the most powerful statement I know of for people of color in this country. So listen well, son. Know your history. Have a dream!"

"I will," Chase says. He looks at Junior's face, his moist eyes radiant, his gaze on something on the distant horizon, something only Junior can see. Chase knows this is the Junior he will always remember. Somewhere outside the dream, Junior is dying, but here, in the zone, the sun approaches the horizon. The sky will stay crimson and orange and violet for just as long as they want it to last—there is no time here.

"Chase, one more thing I need to give you." Junior hands him a small piece of paper. "Here. Read it."

"I Believe In You," Chase reads. He looks up at Junior. "It's a poem."

"Go ahead," Junior says.

There is faith in your eyes,
Love in your touch, and hope in your attitude.
I thrill with you at life's joys,
Run with you through tall grasses
And bow with you in worship

You are the fragile dreams of yesterday
Life's radiant reality today
And the vibrant stuff of tomorrow
I believe in you.

Chase looks up, wipes the tears from his own eyes. "That was for me, wasn't it? Thanks."

Junior smiles. "Everything has been for you."

....

He awoke, his face wet, his head still on Junior's chest, Junior's frail hand still in his own. Chase hugged him close, closed his eyes, and prayed softly for Junior's transition to go smoothly.

He listened to the sound of Junior's faint, irregular heartbeats. Although he tried to tighten his eyes against it, again the beating heart took him back to the street corner and Ernie's death. This time, he was an observer and a participant. He saw himself holding Ernie tightly as perspiration poured down his face. As before, bullets blazed overhead while he begged Ernie to hold on. "Don't die Ernie, don't die!"

"Look up!" Ernie whispered.

And then Junior's heart stopped.

twenty

Living Large

JUNIOR HAD MADE HIS TRANSITION. Chase began to cry. He took Junior's hand and placed it on his cheek. He held it there for a long time. He was brought back to the present by a loud thump at the window. He looked up. It was Chilly.

Chase walked to the window and opened it. He pushed up the screen just enough for Chilly to squeeze through. The cat purred as Chase held him tightly to his chest and sat on the end of Junior's bed. For a few seconds they sat quietly together, but soon Chilly wiggled himself free from Chase's embrace. Slowly and deliberately the cat crawled up Junior's body until he reached his head. Just then Chase saw a note in Chilly's collar. He removed it. It read: *"There always comes a time when the pupil becomes the teacher. Good luck on your journey."*

Chase stared into Junior's face and saw a peacefulness that hadn't been there before. Chilly turned to face Chase, and just like when they first met, their eyes locked on one another. Chilly's blue-green eyes could not hide the sorrow. It was almost as if for one moment Chilly had the capacity to feel things like a human being. A peacefulness then came over Chilly, too, and he dropped his gaze. He turned to Junior and rubbed his face along Junior's cheek. Chase knew he, too, was saying farewell to his friend.

A tap at the door interrupted the moment. "I'm sorry, you'll have to leave now," the nurse said. "The doctor will be here in a minute." Chase wasn't sure if she knew that Junior was gone.

Chase turned back to the bed. Chilly was gone.

He walked away from Junior's room, and for a moment, in the hallway, he had forgotten where he was. He wasn't sure of what to do, or where to go. He went back to his dad's room and stood in the doorway, wondering if he should go inside. His father's face looked peaceful and he breathed slowly and evenly, so Chase assumed he was asleep. Yet he stayed and watched.

His dad's eyes opened. He looked up at his son and said, "Junior has moved on, hasn't he?"

Later, after Chase was ready for bed, he went up to the sanctuary. He lit six candles. "One for Mr. Seymour," he said as he lit the first, "one for Junior, one for Dad, one for my uncle Alexander, one for Ernie, and one for me."

After he got on his knees, he opened a box and took out a single sheet of paper. It was one of the many pieces of writing that Junior had given to him. The candlelight provided just enough light for him to see the handwritten poem. It was another one by Edgar Guest called "Lord, Make a Regular Man Out of Me."

This I would like to be—braver and bolder
Just a bit wiser because I am older
Just a bit kinder to those I may meet
Just a bit manlier taking defeat

This is for the New Year, my wish and plea
Lord, make a regular man out of me.

This I would like to be—just a bit finer
More of a smiler and less of a whiner
Just a bit quicker to stretch out my hand
Helping another who's struggling to stand
This is my prayer for the New Year to be
Lord, make a regular man out of me.

This I would like to be—just a bit fairer
Just a bit better, and just a bit squarer
Not quite so ready to censure and blame
Quicker to help every man in the game
Not quite so eager men's failings to see
Lord, make a regular man out of me.

This I would like to be—just a bit truer
Less of the wisher and more of a doer
Broader and bigger, more willing to give
Living and helping any neighbor to live
This is for the New Year, my prayer and my plea
Lord, make a regular man out of me."

....

Chase finishes reading the poem aloud. A breeze gently rustles the paper as he holds it in his hands, a breeze that is warm and moist. Chase looks up and smiles. He is in the zone.

He can feel the sand between his toes and taste the damp saltiness on his lips. In the distance he can see two sets of footprints in the sand; this is where he and Junior have walked.

"Son, there is something I must pass on to you." Chase turns around and it is his father, not Junior, he sees. He too is sitting on the sand, his legs hugged close to his chest. "Two more things Junior told me, and he said I must pass them on to you. First, he said that life is a daring adventure or it's nothing. I wasn't supposed to let you go without saying that."

Tears begin to flow down Chase's cheeks.

"Son, here's the other thing he said. It's a big world out there, and you must live large in it. Live large. That's the secret. He said to tell you to remember that triumph without risk is to win without glory. Work hard in life because there's an interesting principle that is universal: Those who work the hardest seem to have the most luck."

Through his tears, Chase smiles. "Sounds like something Junior would say."

"Remember that triumph and disaster are one and the same. They are just different sides of the same coin, or different ends of the same process. They stand back-to-back, looking in opposite directions. Confront disaster head-on and hold your head high. Know that it's not how far you fall in life that counts, but it's how high you bounce back."

A whitecap of water pours over Chase's feet. The water ebbs away, and peace washes over him. As each surge of water touches Chase, touches the earth, it washes away a bit of Chase's pain, loss, fear and confusion.

"Dad—" Chase asks a bit timidly. "Why are *you* here?"

"Son, I'm always going to be here for you."

....

On Saturday afternoon Chase and his father drove out of Atlanta together. Inside his dad's Buick, they rode for hours before they reached the Georgia coast. They followed I-95 until they had gotten past Savannah. Each time they needed to make a turn, Chase knew instinctively which way to go.

"We're almost there," Chase said and toid his father to make a right turn. They drove slowly down a narrow, winding beach road.

For about ten minutes, Chase stared at the beach from the road. They were close.

"There it is! That's the place," Chase said. "Stop. That's where I walked with Junior."

Dad stopped the car. The boy grabbed the urn of ashes and ran to the beach. He felt the wind against his face and the sea oats part as he trudged over a sand dune. He heard the gushing waves of the ocean. Salt pressed against his lips and the moist air made his hair feel damp and sticky.

"I'm with you, Junior," he called out. "Your spirit is free—free with the wind on the shore, free with the waters of the ocean, free with the sun and the clouds in the sky. It's here where I'll leave your ashes, scattered across your favorite place—the place where elements meet, where the zone exists, where we're one with the universe, the place where we feel one with God."

Chase tossed the ashes into the wind. They swirled around him and seemed to go upward, upward, upward.

Chase and his father talked about Junior for the entire drive back from the Georgia Coast. When they arrived home, a late dinner awaited them. They ate together and Chase excused himself and went up to his attic retreat.

In the sanctuary he stared at the pictures of Ernie, the mementos of Uncle Alexander, the white coin and the many notes that Junior had given him. He paused and took in a deep breath, and closed his eyes. He imagined them all. One deep breath followed another, and he fell asleep.

....

Chase screams.

He is in the nightmare again. He has come full circle.

"Ernie—*Ernie-e-e!*" Bullets blaze overhead as he holds his friend tightly. "Don't die on me, Ernie, don't die!" he says.

"Look up!" Ernie says. Seconds later he is dead.

In this dream, Chase finally has the courage to ignore the terror of the bullets that fly over him. He looks up to the sky and holds Ernie's limp body in his arms. A brilliant light breaks through the clouds and fills the sky. It is more beautiful than anything he has ever seen. As the light streaks upward, he hears Ernie whisper, "I'm okay, my friend. I'll be watching over you."

twelve lessons on life from

Mr. Dream Merchant

1. THE GIFT IS IN THE STRUGGLE. Pain is a necessary part of life; misery is optional. The struggle is just the beginning of something better to come. Stay focused and keep your eyes on the prize.

2. PREPARATION CONQUERS INTIMIDATION. Memorize the words of Ben Franklin: "When you fail to plan, you plan to fail." With preparation comes the belief in yourself, and with this comes the awareness that your Higher Power is only one prayer away.

3. SEE WITH DOUBLE VISION. Learn the principle of Double Vision. There is a previous experience behind everyone's actions and words. Listen not only with your ears, but also with your eyes, heart, and intuition. By using this gift, you will never betray yourself.

4. THINK WORD PERFECT. Your words are an extension of your physical and spiritual being. Think before you speak. Your words may be forgiven, but they are not forgotten. Strive to respond, not to react.

5. PRACTICE THE FIVE PRINCIPLES of Presence, Positivity, Patience, Perseverance, and Powerlessness. With their mastery comes the ability to live life on life's terms one day at a time.

6. THE FRINGE BENEFITS OF LIFE are available to everyone. The Fringe Benefits include friends, opportunity, success, and satisfaction. It requires of you only the desire to change. Change is one of a few constants in this world. If you embrace change, it opens your life to infinite possibilities.

7. JUST SAY YES. To just say no to drugs isn't enough. You must also say yes to all of the Fringe Benefits that God has in store for you. Stay positive. Say yes to life itself.

8. RELY ON YOUR DREAM TEAM. Develop your dream spiritual team consisting of a Higher Power, a Guardian Angel, a Senior Advisor, a Friendship Council, and a coat of arms. With these helpers, you will always have the home court advantage!

9. BUILD ON RELATIONSHIPS. Remember, the first two syllables in the word relationship are the most important. Relationships are like relays in track and field. To win at them you must carefully select your teammates, work hard, and have perfect timing.

10. ACQUIRE MOMENTUM one moment at a time. Practice the Sacred Seven and transform your dreams into reality. Remember, Momentum is the force that pushes the equation

Dreams + Action = Reality

11. KEEP TRACK OF THE LEFTOVERS. Keep a journal of your life. What may simply be old memories or leftovers to you, can

become new insights for others. Your life is important, for the hands that write history (His story), also write your story.

12. BE AWARE, be alert. Awakenings in your life, however painful, are new beginnings. Turn to a power greater that yourself for guidance. Obstacles are simply God's direction in life. They exist to promote change. Your awareness of this fact is the essence of the transformation from a human doing to a human being.

Credits

Page 8: "Father Facts," gleaned from an article entitled "Disappearing Act," *Creative Loafing Magazine*, June 14, 1997, Volume 26, #4, Atlanta, GA.

Pages 13, 59, 91, 168: Youth Awareness Class Facts, taken from *Substance Abuse in Adolescents*, Pediatric Clinics of North America, Volume 42, #2, April, 1995.

Pages 41-2 and 74: Excerpts from hymns "Amazing Grace," and "His Eye is on the Sparrow," taken from the *Hymnal of the Christian Methodist Episcopal Church*, CME Publishing House, Memphis, TN, rev. 1986.

Pages 108 and 262-3: Excerpts from speeches of Dr. Martin Luther King, Jr.: "I've Seen the Promised Land," April 3, 1968, Memphis, TN, and "I Have A Dream," August 28, 1963, Washington, D.C. License to reprint granted by Intellectual Properties Management, Atlanta, Georgia, as manager for the King estate.

Page 128: Poem "I Can't" by Doris Beason from the book *Inspiring Devotions for Church Groups,* by Amy Bolding (Grand Rapids, MI: Baller Book House, 1960, 1976, 1985).

Pages 129 and 266-7: Poems "Lord Make a Regular Man Out of Me," and "The Looking Glass," both by Edgar Guest, reprinted by kind permission.

Pages 162-4: Poem "The Two Glasses," by Ella Wilcox, from the book *The Best Loved Poems of American People,* by Hazel Felleman (Doubleday, 1936).

Page 229: The excerpt from Alcoholics Anonymous is reprinted with the permission of Alcoholics Anonymous World Services, Inc. Permission to reprint the excerpt does not mean that A.A. has reviewed or approved the contents of this publication, nor that A.A. agrees with the views expressed herein. A.A. is a program of recovery from alcoholism *only*—use of the excerpt in connection with programs and activities which are patterned after A.A., but which address other problems, or in any other non-A.A. context, does not imply otherwise.

Page 255: Poem "After A While," by Veronica Shoffstall. Used by kind permission of the author.